PICTURES OF REDEMPTION

PICTURES OF REDEMPTION

Flynn's Crossing Romantic Suspense Series
Book 1

Yvonne Kohano

K
E

Nanokas Press

A Division of Kochanowski Enterprises

Copyright © 2012

PICTURES OF REDEMPTION
FLYNN'S CROSSING ROMANTIC SUSPENSE SERIES BOOK 1

Nanokas Press/KE Press books may be ordered through booksellers or by contacting:

Kochanowski Enterprises/Nanokas Press
PO Box 1274
Clackamas, OR 97015-9594
www.yvonnekohano.com
yvonne@yvonnekohano.com

Pictures of Redemption is a work of fiction. People, places, events, and situations are the product of the author's imagination. Any resemblance to actual persons, living or dead, or historical events, is purely coincidental.

This book contains an excerpt from the forthcoming book *Flashes of Fire* by Yvonne Kohano. This excerpt may not reflect the final content of the forthcoming edition.

Any people depicted in stock imagery provided by Thinkstock are models, and such images are being used for illustrative purposes only.

Certain stock imagery ©Thinkstock
Cover design: John Kochanowski

ISBN: 978-1-940738-31-4 (sc)
ISBN: 978-0-9893-3058-9 (e)

Original Publication: 10/15/2012
Nanokas Press re-release date: 6/15/2015

Also by Yvonne Kohano

FLYNN'S CROSSING ROMANTIC SUSPENSE SERIES

Pictures of Redemption, Book 1
(Serena & Dane)

Flashes of Fire, Book 2
(DK & Vince)

Naked Intolerances, Book 3
(Gabby & Rick)

Tastes and Consequences, Book 4
(Mac & Roxy)

Blooms on the Bones, Book 5
(Tess & Powers)

Wine Into Water, Book 6
(Marguerite & Deke)

Love and the Christmas Tree Nymph, A Flynn's
Crossing Seasonal Novella

Love's Touch of Justice, Book 7
(Jake & Marlee)

This Proposal Between Us, A Flynn's Crossing
Seasonal Novella

Measure Twice, Love Once, Book 8
(Geno and Agnes)

And more to come!
Learn about upcoming releases at
www.YvonneKohano.com.

Subscribe to Yvonne Kohano's enewsletter to be among the first to learn about new releases and special offers. Visit www.yvonnekohano.com for more information.

Follow Yvonne at www.yvonnekohano.com, on Facebook as Yvonne Kohano, and on Twitter @yvonnekohano to learn what tickles her about being a writer, and at www.GooseYourMuse.com for creativity tips.

PICTURES OF REDEMPTION

Prologue – Two Years Ago

The explosion was sudden, and in that second it seemed time stopped and everything – truck parts and flying debris, voices, even light – disappeared for a few long breaths. When it all came screaming back, there was pain so profound that he wondered if he could survive it. He could hear sobbing, realizing with shock that it was his own.

He never cried.

To his right, two soldiers who he had come to regard as friends were gone, vanished, leaving behind a haze of red and fragments no longer resembling anything human. Where the truck had been mere seconds before, there was a twisted wreck of unidentifiable metal and burning tires.

Dane attempted to stand, to run for cover or maybe into the fire, he wasn't sure which. His legs were slow to respond and rifle fire pinned him in a crouch against the stucco wall. Heat added sweat to the blood dripping in his eyes. Confusion left him relying on years of experience and well-honed self-preservation to survive.

Around him, the others were also trying to make sense of it. This quiet sector had been peaceful for months. Then three days ago, it exploded. Friendly locals could no longer be trusted. Fighting continued day and night, and resources were slow to reach them. They were on their own for the time being.

And now an IED and a bloodbath.

And carnage.

Blood seeped into Dane's boots from his legs, though at least they were still attached and he could feel his toes. His buddy Anderson to the left was seriously damaged, and it sounded like he was screaming for someone to shoot him. The good guys or the bad guys – maybe both? His legs were gone, a hell of a way to consider living.

None of this should have happened. This was supposed to be a safe area. Two years in Afghanistan and while he had seen plenty of bloodshed, Dane hadn't seen anything like this agony. How many were dead, how many missing limbs, how many otherwise scarred for life, sometimes in ways that weren't obvious? More of the injured were now crying out as they became aware of the extent of their wounds.

Slowly, Dane crawled under fire to an open doorway and welcoming darkness, clutching the gear that had instinctively stayed in his hands as the truck rolled from the explosion. The men in the best shape were dragging any wounded they could reach into hiding. The radioman was screaming their position back to headquarters and the static reply sounded like '…at least two hours'.

Two hours until help arrived?

Dane felt his vision fade and fought not to pass out, though that would have been a blessing. The combination of pain, disbelief, and noise made him feel disconnected from the scene. Time passed, he wasn't sure how long. His bleeding seemed to slow, and someone passed him field dressings to cover the worst of his wounds. He wasn't sure if he was one of the lucky ones or if it was just a matter of time.

Out in the street, three soldiers remained, two either dead or unconscious, and the one legless guy, Anderson, still screaming for someone to shoot him. Enemy blasts kept anyone from venturing out too far, and his squad was returning fire and trying to protect him. His voice rose and fell, and right now, he was yelling at the top of his lungs. "Just shoot me!"

Dane saw it all in slow motion. He wiped the wet from his eyes and readjusted his helmet. He crept to an opening blasted in the exterior wall. His hands, slick from his own blood, fumbled for a minute. He didn't ask himself what he was doing, going on instinct and training. He lifted his gear, sighted, adjusted for the distance, and squinted into the light.

And he shot him.

Chapter 1

"I honestly don't know how I'll keep the programs open since the county and the state are cutting funding again. It was bad enough last time, and all of our usual donors are tapped dry. This economy isn't helping. More people need us and fewer people can lend a hand. Recovery isn't coming fast enough to relieve the strain for organizations like ours."

Serena Williamson paced the width of the shop, back and forth until the flowers looked like they were waving in a light breeze. Tess Willowspring continued her arranging, the third of twelve centerpieces for a wedding this weekend. Buds and Blooms in the foothills town of Flynn's Crossing was the recommended events florist for many of the major resorts and restaurants in the area, and this was going to be another busy weekend. But Serena knew that Tess could multitask with nothing coming out worse for the distraction, and she needed her best friend as a sounding board right now.

"What do you plan to do?"

"I don't know. The art therapy program for grieving kids still has enough grant money to last through another year. Some of my therapists and counselors are willing to keep working pro bono if they have paying clients in their own practices. Thank god the rent is low or we'd be in the street, just like some of the people we help."

Serena didn't stop pacing, causing Tess to tsk-tsk in sympathy as her friend continued. "Balance has been able to help so many with their crisis issues, their personal tragedies or chronic mental health. We've had a lot of success in keeping members of our community out of institutions here in Flynn's Crossing and across the county since we opened six years ago. But economic times were better then. Now the people we used to ask for donations are the ones on our doorstep, crushed over the loss of a home or a job or even their families."

Serena stopped at the broad front window of the old Victorian that served as both shop and home for Tess. Situated at the end of Main Street where the town's original old residences rose at the beginning of the hills, the place had a unique view of the bell tower, the courthouse, and the old brick buildings that had been saved from probable ruin only a decade ago. After years of decay, the locals decided to make themselves a destination stop for visitors on the way to Lake Tahoe and the many other enjoyments of the region. Now scores of people each day took the convenient exit off the state highway to putter in the unique shops, eat at the restaurants, visit the nearby wineries, and stay at the bed and breakfasts.

Serena was always grateful to live in such a peaceful and friendly place where almost everyone was accepting and accepted. People had each other's backs and did the best they could to maintain the small town supportive atmosphere, despite the big city of Sacramento an hour away. Flynn's Crossing was unique, and Balance was one of the reasons it could take care of its own.

"Almost every nonprofit in the region is suffering financially, and those that aren't are the ones lucky enough to have a big grant or two left to cover their operations. Our situation isn't any different, but that doesn't make it easier to handle." Turning abruptly, Serena's pacing resumed, hard to do in the small space between the many displays that lined the walls and crossed the floor of what had once been a genteel parlor.

Serena took in the colorful displays, inhaling the scents of dozens of different kinds of flowers. She usually felt a lift when she came into the shop. Native American flute music played softly in the background. The flowers made it a happy place, positive and uplifting and beautiful.

Today it wasn't lifting her spirits though, and it had nothing to do with the place but everything to do with the tough decisions she was going to have to make.

She took another deep breath. "The board met last night, an emergency meeting. If we can't find a major donor within the next month, we'll have to cut some programs. The ones that we operate under grants are protected for now. But the state and county mental health departments covered a sizable chunk of our veterans' services, and what the feds give us doesn't add up to enough to keep those open."

Tess looked up sharply. Their little community and the whole region had sent countless of their own to serve in the military. The types of ambush fighting common in the last two international battlegrounds of Afghanistan and Iraq and the nature of the injuries so many had survived meant that there was a substantial need for the counseling services Serena's agency provided. Losing that would mean that many of their retired military and active duty neighbors would fight their battles all over again, except they'd be fighting them without support, alone and unable to move past the worst horrors anyone could imagine.

"Maybe it's time to visit the county board of supervisors, or maybe the governor. Surely someone realizes what it means to cut these programs," Tess suggested.

"I think everyone knows what it means, but if they have to cut basic health care and education and services to the disabled, where do we fall in that mix? Our supporters have been very vocal to their elected officials. I've written letters, visited the capitol and talked to the legislators from our district. I even talked to an aide to the governor. They all have the same thing to say, that they understand how important these programs are, but the funding line gets drawn someplace, and unfortunately for our clients, it was drawn right through their support."

Both fell silent. Penelope, the golden tabby who ruled the shop, rubbed against Serena's leg and she absently bent down to scratch her. Tigger, the new addition who thought he was king of the hill, raced over, knocking a plant stand onto one leg in his hurry for his share. With a practiced hand, Tess, grabbed the stand and set it back on all four feet as she gave the kitten a stern look.

"How long will it be until you grow up and learn how to behave like a gentleman?" she scolded. Tigger stared back from his place under Serena's other hand and purred and he didn't look the least bit sorry.

"What I need is a donor, a new donor, a major new donor, a benefactor," said Serena, a faraway calculating look in her eye. She was running the numbers in her head, looking for some place else in the budget to cut, thinking about angles and options.

"I thought you said all of the usual donors are dry."

"I know I did, but I'm thinking I need to head down into the city and see if I can raise some new money there. The people in these mountains have been terrific, but with all of the other needs around here, we're competing with fundraisers for firefighting and school programs and emergency medical care. Many of our neighbors moved up here to escape city woes, but some of the neediest end up back down in the valley. I'm sure that someone would be willing to help us out, neighbor to neighbor."

Tess looked at her friend doubtfully. "Your optimism is refreshing and inspiring, but don't get your hopes up on this. Everyone's hurting, and unless someone has a good reason to help, they'll probably keep the money in their own backyard, if you know what I mean." She set the centerpiece aside and turned back to Serena. "Besides, who do you know that isn't already being asked by every nonprofit in the area?"

"Not sure yet, but there has to be someone in Sacramento. Look at all of the new development, a lot of it coming from new money and new blood. Maybe they haven't been asked yet, at least not enough to be tired of giving."

Serena turned on her heel so fast that the cats scattered and Tess nearly dropped the vase she was holding. "Time for some computer research. There has to be someone I can appeal to in Sac to donate enough to keep us going." With her hand on the door, she turned and gave Tess a big bright smile. "It's Balance's turn now!"

Tess sighed. Serena was always so upbeat, but she was also sometimes unrealistic about the good intentions of the rest of the world. Tess shook her head and picked up a stem of lilies. "I hope your Aunt Serena doesn't find a huge disappointment out there," she said to the cats.

Serena giggled. "You're talking to your cats, you know!"

Tess turned back to Serena and gave a wave to move her out the door. "I know, but sometimes they make more sense than the humans of the world. Go on, sweetie. I hope you find that magical donor with deep pockets to save the day."

Chapter 2

Dane sat at the edge of the canyon's rim, his legs mere inches from the steep drop-off. The buzzards were riding the updrafts in lazy circles, sudden dives marking a scent of rot that they needed to investigate. He wondered if that was how someone might find him someday, from the sick odor of flesh long dead or the circle of hungry birds above.

It did him little good to think about the future. There wasn't any future for a man like him. What he'd done marked him forever as outside of polite society. His family didn't want to think so, but it was true.

His family, yet again, wouldn't leave him alone. His brother Powers had ridden into the city on his proverbial white horse, ready to save Dane from himself. The signs were already there. But Dane wanted to be left alone.

Why couldn't Powers see that he wasn't brooding? This wasn't some phase of the moon and Dane would come to his senses once he'd been alone for a little while. In fact, he deserved to be alone. He was a pariah, an exile, not a recluse by choice. It was better that he keep his secrets and his past to himself. No one needed to know anything about him around here.

The canyon was vast, the ridges separating the forks of the river that roared down into the Sacramento valley obvious in the late afternoon light. In July, the foothills were hot, dusty, and golden, with shots of blue from the unfailing sunny skies and the sparkling ribbons of the rivers running through it. At this hour, the breeze was a constant blessing, fighting off the heat of the afternoon.

Dane thought of his brother, probably standing right now in the window on the top floor of some posh office building in Sacramento, looking out over the construction empire he would undoubtedly conquer in the coming months and years. Or maybe he was in the sleek living room of his high-rise condo, examining his prospects in the valley. Was he thinking about family then, or about control and conquests?

It didn't matter to Dane, as long as Powers left him alone. Somehow, he doubted that would happen. His older brother always felt compelled to fix things, even things that couldn't be changed. He didn't realize that Dane was much better off this way, building his fortress to block out the rest of the world.

Chapter 3

The web searches were taking longer than Serena liked. She had almost exhausted every database, trying to find someone, a foundation or a person, who hadn't been asked for a donation by nearly every nonprofit organization in the region. That list was getting shorter by the minute. And her treasured morning cup of specialty brewed coffee was almost gone too.

She considered taking a break to walk up the street to the Brew Bank Bakery for a second large cup of high octane. She had started her day like every other day, stopping in at the local coffee haven for her morning caffeine fix and a side of local gossip. Stuart and Sarge, the owners and life partners, always had their fingers on the pulse of everything going on. Sarge was the gabby one, and he could go on for hours about events in the county. He could fill you in on the latest stories about who was opening a new shop or restaurant on Main, or who had to close down and the reasons why. Stuart, quieter in so many ways, knew more about the people, and his insights, while not shared as readily, helped you learn more about the rest of the personal story.

Balance's office, set in a block of similar health and social services organizations a short walk from Brew Bank, held large and small conference rooms, cubicles for counselors and other staff to use when they weren't in sessions, and communal break and public areas. The space itself was nondescript, housing the files and forms that were required in any counseling practice. What made it unique, though, were the committed people who worked there.

Serena considered herself lucky in finding a community that could benefit from her mental health

Yvonne Kohano

counseling organization, one that included the dedicated people to help make it happen. Between them, they'd served the needs of hundreds since the doors opened in 2005. Her worry was that soon, too soon, Balance wouldn't have any resources available to continue the care their clients required.

The ringing phone on her desk diverted her, and she picked it up even as she checked the caller id. Adult Protective Services.

"This is Serena."

"Hi Serena, it's Nancy at APS. Seems the full moon must be out forever right now." The word forever came out as so many drawn out syllables. Nancy's chocolaty voice was a sharp contrast to the personality she showed the world. She was brusque and abrupt most of the time, unlikely to show the soft heart she hid inside. But when her smile cracked wide, her teeth were white in that dark face of hers and her eyes sparked with mischief and good will. Today, though, no evidence of a smile came through the phone.

"What's up, Nancy?"

Nancy sighed. "We got this call from yet another source that there is a guy living in a cabin up near Emigrant Valley and they think he's a problem. They say his cabin is a shack, he's a weirdo, and the land looks like white trash lives there, if you know what I mean. He's chasing off anyone and everyone. Why just the other day, he screamed at a little girl trying to raise money for the school band program. Now who would do a mean thing like that?" She huffed in outrage.

Now it was Serena's turn to sigh. Most people lived in these foothill and mountain towns because they wanted space and the rural lifestyle. They appreciated the close proximity of Sacramento and its jobs and city pleasures. But what they really loved were the wide vistas and protective canyons, the pine trees and rocky crags and outdoor activities, the agriculture and wineries and eateries, and even the ebb and flow of tourism that brought much-needed revenue to the foothills.

There were others, though, who were here because they could fly under the radar. They didn't take kindly to anyone sticking a nose in their business. A few were running from the law. Some were running from bad memories or bad choices. And some were trying to run away from the darkness inside their own hearts and heads. They wanted to be left alone.

"Who would let a girl wander around to these remote houses anyway?"

"Well it wasn't to the cabin, exactly. The girl and her friends were at the grocery store and when he walked up, they asked him. And he yelled at them! The mom recognized him – seems he walks up the road pretty often. He lives at the end of the gravel near the store, about a mile beyond the family. The mom says he's scary, and this caller said the same thing. And they both said they hear screams at night coming from his place. Mostly, though, they think he's strange."

Sometimes the narrow-mindedness of people surprised her, and other times, not so much. But this was one of the times when she could easily lose patience. A few folks simply fell on hard times and others thought poorly of them as a result.

Nancy continued, "The neighbors say that he keeps to himself, and he wears desert fatigues when he walks to the store. I've heard about him before – comes into town occasionally. Never raises a fuss but makes everyone uncomfortable. Kind of like he has a reputation, if you know what I mean. Just stares at 'em and they say his eyes are dark, like there's no emotion behind 'em." Serena could almost hear Nancy shudder on the other end of the line, despite everything the woman had seen in all of her public service years.

"Is he dangerous?"

"We don't think so, but we'd like you to check on him. If he's a vet, maybe you can get him some help."

Serena sucked in a deep breath, thinking about the numbers of vets who were going to be lacking any services shortly if she couldn't find more financial support.

"Will do. Just send me the referral." She paused before making her pitch. "You know our funding is probably going to get cut, right? If you could point out cases like this when we go to the Board of Sups..."

"Y'know I can't talk about specific cases, Serena. But you help us out all the time and I'll do what I can. By the way, how's your search for some new donors coming?"

Serena cringed. The blessing and the curse of living in a small community – everybody seemed to know everything about your business.

"Not so well. I'm checking the databases, but it's hard to find anyone who hasn't committed their limited available funds already. I'm looking for someone – something – new."

Serena could hear Nancy's door closing over the phone line. Then she dropped her voice to almost a whisper. "There's a new foundation – Vision Quest – that came to Sac. I hear they're looking for nonprofits that help vets and active duty military. Whoever started the foundation wants to remain anonymous, but they seem to be legit. I heard about them from a friend of mine in the city. Maybe they could help, and since they're new, not everyone has rushed at them yet." Nancy's voice returned to its usual level. "Thanks for helping us out, Serena. I'm sure this guy just needs someone to talk to."

Serena grinned. "I'm sure that with the proper new support – emphasis on the new – we'll be able to get him whatever he needs!"

Chapter 4

The dust, the heat, the blood, the shame. That's what he remembered.

Each day, every day, he followed his ritual. He cleaned his gear. The routine calmed him, made him feel he was in control. Heat made the pounding in his head worse, but after a while, it was all a continuous daze in his mind. Everything carefully ready for service, he put it away in a case he kept hidden under the bed and cleaned up the evidence. He wasn't promising any new causes that he would fight for them, but he also wasn't going to get sloppy just because those battles weren't for him anymore.

It was a store day. He hated it, but he needed supplies. The boots pinched now, but he still wore them. They were part of the ritual, like the shirt, no matter the weather. The camis helped his control. He could blend into the landscape, the golden brown of the foothills in early July.

Dane hoisted a backpack to his shoulder and headed out. The gravel would crunch underfoot, so he kept to the edge of road, stealth in the rural quiet. The steady cadence of his boots on the ground reminded him of things he would rather not remember, but that too was part of the ritual. He would follow the plan and get his necessities, and then he'd retreat to the safety of his cliff-side perch. Retreat could be honorable in some situations.

The dry heat might feel like he was in-country, but the scents were all wrong. That kept him centered and in the present. The smell of spice and sage underfoot could be intoxicating if you let it. The flowers were blue, a unique kind of glowing purple blue that he remembered his brother saying reminded him of their mother's eyes, a likeness he shared but he'd rather not remember. The flowers' oil stayed on his boots and lasted for hours, and sometimes when he slept the smell got confused with his memories of his mom and her eyes, before the horrors his own eyes had seen obliterated all good dreams.

Distance passed easily – that was another thing he had learned. It you followed the cadence and emptied your mind, the miles could go by blindly. But you wouldn't know what you're seeing, and that was hard for him. He needed to see what was happening, no way around it. It made him feel safe, and it was what he did, what he'd always done, what he was trained to do.

Dane's mom had said that about him early and often – he always seemed to be watching things carefully to see what was happening. He'd angle his head and analyze the situation, forever observant. His eyes mirrored hers. Hers had laughed, and so had his, though he wasn't aware of it at the time. He giggled, and so did she. When her light went out, he felt lost, and that made him all the more watchful of the world around him.

The miles passed quickly when he was deep inside himself, as he was most days. Soon he no longer noticed the crush of the sage under his boots and the way the heat baked the ground on the hot afternoon. The swell of breeze coming up the canyon was lost on him. There was traffic, and some might have slowed at the sight of him, but he tried not to notice, blending into the forest and meadows as best he could.

Roxy's loomed in front of Dane. The gourmet grocery store was a local landmark. It didn't matter what hour you were there – if they were open, they were busy. He'd tried coming early in the morning, but then the long distance commuters where competing for their house roasted coffee and freshly baked pastries, provisions for the start of their long days. Later the parents coming to and from school drop-offs were cramming the registers. Then the locals were going in for groceries. Lunch usually meant construction crews and agricultural workers and neighbors seeking a gourmet treat. And the folks coming from dinner at Roxy's restaurant next door checked in for some version of the chef's specials to take home in the evening.

But he had found that the early afternoons, before the kids-home-from-school rush started, it was a little bit quieter. Of course, it was also the hottest part of the day. Earlier in the year he could smell the sap rising in the pine trees. Right now, it smelled like spicy herbs and dust and heat. And that brought him full circle.

As always, he braced himself as he entered the brightly lit store. It was cheerful, with fresh vegetables and fruit stacked to mimic a farm stand display and long aisles filled with organic products in every category. You could find grass fed beef and wild salmon at the custom meats counter in the back. The staff was a cross between aging hippies and young grungers who all seemed to get along with their perpetual smiles greeting every customer.

Except him. He'd seen their smiles falter when he came in. He knew he looked different. It had been months since he'd bothered to trim his hair or beard, and his clothes were getting threadbare. The little shack he was living in didn't exactly have a lot of conveniences, so he made do or did without. And his voice was rusty from lack of use. There weren't many reasons for him to talk.

"Afternoon sir! Getting hot again out there! Anything I can help you find?" The young clerk with red hair and a sea of freckles pasted the smile back on his face and looked at Dane hesitantly.

"I'm, ah, I'm fine. I know where everything is." Dane's voice felt raspy and his throat was raw. It pained him to talk to people.

"We have some new items just in. Can I tell you about them?"

"I'm FINE!" Dane realized his voice was loud and rude but he only wanted to get his stuff and get out.

Before the claustrophobia of being inside crushed him.

Before the panic set in and he did something stupid.

"Okay man, okay. Just let us know if we can help."

Dane grimaced to himself. He didn't like being rude, didn't like who he had become, what the war had made him into. The kid was only trying to do his job. He tried to summon up a smile, though he thought it probably looked more like mean slash across his face. Or a maniacal twist – he'd seen that himself once or twice when he looked in an unexpected window's reflection.

"Sorry man, it's the heat, you know?" Dane tried again.

The young man looked at him a bit uncertainly but pulled out his best customer service training. "No problem. Cold bottled water's on Aisle 3 if you want some."

Dane hurried past and headed for the back. It was wild salmon season up north, and whenever he came to the store, he bought some fresh. It reminded him of his childhood home, of Portland and the grill going in the backyard, his dad starting a plank and adding half a fish even after his mom had died. The ritual had helped heal the family to the degree that anything could.

They were all about rituals, he mused.

"And how can I help you today, sir?" Today's perky butcher was all of five feet tall and about as wide, a brawny old guy that looked like he'd been around since fish first swam in the oceans. From the bright Roxy's nameplate on his bib apron, Dane had learned that his name was Peter, though the staff and regulars called him Salty Dog. At one time, he'd have been curious about the nickname and its origins, and he'd have found a story in the background and built something from that.

But not anymore. The stories were all dried up.

"Wild salmon, about a pound." Dane heard his voice croak and sound bitter, even to him. "Please," he remembered to add.

Salty Dog eyed him up and down. In the past, he'd given Dane the price per pound. Maybe he thought that someone who dressed in worn out fatigues and Army boots, even in the middle of summer, didn't have the cash to pay for it. But he'd wrapped brown paper around a cut or two for Dane often enough now that the butcher knew he wouldn't try to shove it into the backpack without paying.

It was depressing for Dane to consider what people assumed they knew about him.

Mumbling his thanks at the proffered package, Dane rounded a corner to select random vegetables, a few pieces of fruit and some yogurt, and headed for the front of the store. Business was starting to pick up. It made him anxious, all of these people wandering around. They were too close, and they were eying him with suspicion and disgust.

He saw the woman who owned the place, the famous Roxy herself, talking with another woman dressed in the ironed business casual that passed for executive attire in the foothills. They were standing between him and freedom. Ms. Executive had her back to him, but Roxy looked past her shoulder and said something, nodding his way. Ms. Executive turned, and her eyes caught his.

There was a flash, a jolt of recognition that stopped Dane for an instant. Sound ceased and time stood still. The woman opened her mouth in an 'oh' of surprise and seemed to be turning to step towards him. As the noises around him came pouring back in, Dane ducked behind a display of melons. The image of her lingered in his mind's eye, and he filed it away for later contemplation. Still, he had to get out of there.

Nearly sideswiping a mom with a toddler on her hip, he took another route to the checkout counter. The red haired kid was still there. Dane's nervousness must have communicated itself because he made fast work of scanning and bagging the purchases with no idle friendly chatter.

The feeling that he had to get out of there, outside where he could escape the confines of these walls, grew inside him. His heart was thumping more quickly in his chest and his breathing amped up to soft pants. Dane had his cash out before the last item hit plastic and made for the door like a man possessed, leaving the kid trying to hand his change in coins to empty air. He shoved the paper bag of purchases into his backpack while he trotted for the door.

A loud bang sounded from a nearby aisle. The sharp metallic ricochet cracked like a bullet inside the store. A couple of people shrieked and someone called out in shocked surprise.

Just that fast, he was back in the dust and the heat and the blood. And just that fast he hit the floor, crabbing backwards until the display of charcoal was at his back. He crept sideways, checking around corners for a clear line of sight. The door was fifteen feet away, then ten, then five.

And just that fast, he bolted and ran for his life. The demons were back and they were after him.

*****

"He's here a couple of times a week," Roxy LaFollette said. While she might spend most of her time in her restaurant next door, she knew everything that was going on in her store too. What she didn't see for herself, her staff felt free to tell her about. They liked working here, having a boss who appreciated them and a community that loved the goods they carried. As the only organic store in the area, it filled a special place in many local lives. It was the area's meeting place and social center too.

Roxy made a success of everything she touched. Serena was always appreciative of this stellar member of their girl tribe. Yes, she herself could boil water or fry an egg or grill a steak, but her food was never as stunning and inventive as Roxy could prepare. Those delights were the kind that people ate and raved about, then ate more of until they were groaning in bliss. Flynn's Crossing moved up a considerable number of notches as a foodie destination when Roxy came to town.

"Shawn said he came in a little while ago. He probably hasn't had time to get what he needs yet. Pete says he buys meat or fish regularly, expensive stuff, and he always seems to have the cash to pay for it. Bank bills in twenties, the clean kind you get from an ATM. Otherwise I'd be thinking he's raising a cash crop out there!"

Serena had to smile. Her friend Roxy was a tad bit irreverent with a sometimes-rough exterior, except when it came to her passions – pleasing people with food through her store and her restaurant. She could butcher a deer or toss a delicately dressed salad of microgreens with aplomb and authority. Ask her about the delivery schedule for products in the store and she knew it all to the minute. She was all business and knew what things cost down to the penny.

Still, her heart of gold was a soft touch when it came to people she cared about. Her membership in the girl tribe blew a refreshing wind of reality checks and balances into their discussions, and she was always ready to support her friends, whatever they needed.

"Let's hope it's just bank money and legitimate gains at that!" Serena responded. "Nancy at APS said that he's spooking the neighbors and yelled at some little girls in front of the store here. She thinks he's a vet and she wants me to check on him. I know where he lives, but I was hoping to kind of bump into him some place public to make it less, I don't know, formal. Less like I was spying on him and more casual, I guess."

"I heard about the cuts in funding. You can always put jars on the checkout counters, you know. And I'd be happy to cater a fundraiser for you if you want. How's the search for donors coming?"

"Nothing yet, but I have some feelers out. You know how it goes with any business in times like this – it's two steps forward and one step back. I just seem to be linking all of those single steps together into some kind of hideous dance right now."

Roxy rubbed her arm in sympathy. "I know what you mean! But you'll find a way. What you do is so important. And speaking of that, let's go find your next client. Wait, here's your chance. There he is by the melons. He's kind of hard to miss." Roxy nodded past Serena's shoulder and Serena turned, taking in a blur of dark hair and camouflage clothes.

The descriptions of him had been accurate. His black hair was long and pulled into a ponytail, and his thick beard was shot through with gray. The fatigues were loose but clean. His agitation was obvious.

But it was his eyes that surprised her most. They were a vivid dark blue, wide and shocked on hers. His expression was a mixture of grief and surprise, and then almost as quickly, he shuttered the look and all expression vanished. A window into his soul slammed shut so quickly that Serena gasped in a fast breath and turned to follow to ask him what had happened. He was out of sight before she could take her first step.

She inhaled and exhaled deeply to get a handle on her suddenly jangling nerves.

"It's almost like he saw us and knew we were talking about him!" She didn't turn back to Roxy to see if she was watching the exchange. A shiver moved over her skin.

"Shawn said he's skittish like that, doesn't like any attention, doesn't even like to be greeted at the door. He moves fast, says little, and he's gone before you know it."

A mother and toddler came around the corner. Mother had a weary expression on her face and set the little girl on her less than sturdy feet. The toddler, being a toddler, was toddling at the end of a tether in great tooth-free delight down the canned goods aisle. Giving mom a big smile, she grabbed the nearest can and threw it to the floor with a loud crack.

Mom looked at Roxy in horror, but Roxy laughed and headed over to pick up the can of peas, assuring her that no harm was done.

And Serena turned once again to look in the direction of the mystery man. At the front of the store she caught sight of a blur near the floor, moving sideways quickly to the open entrance, Shawn standing at the register with his hand out in confusion. She was missing her random opportunity to meet the man. Even as she raced out the door, she knew she was too late to catch Mr. Mystery Vet. Before she had time to dig the keys out of her pocket, he was gone.

Chapter 5

He wanted – no, needed – to have his peace and silence back. Everywhere Dane turned, someone seemed to be pointing him out, seeking him out, trying to find him. His ten acres might not be big enough to keep them all away. Much as he hated it, they kept trying to reach him. And everywhere, there were reminders of his past.

He turned on the cell phone about every other day, though since he never planned to return any of the messages, he wasn't sure why he still did it. He thought back to the voicemail he received a week ago. His nephew Chris, a vet student at UC Davis, wanted to beat the torrid heat of the valley for a day and come up for a visit to his Uncle Dane.

Dane hadn't called back, expecting that the lack of an invitation would be enough to dissuade any visitor. True, directions to find him were sketchy. There was an address, but neither GPS nor online mapping software could pinpoint it.

Besides, the road that served as a driveway was bumpy, old gravel with lots of potholes and almost hidden by the trees and shrubs on either side. There was no sign, not even a street number. Just a lot of No Trespassing notices and a barbed wire fence marked the roadside and perimeter through the thick woods. Only people with a strong sense of adventure would want to know what was at the other end of the path.

A crunch of gravel startled him, and Dane took cover in the trees to see who had bothered to make the forbidding journey. A small truck appeared after a slow drive of a few minutes. Trees had been downed to create a space of about half an acre, and the driver stopped at the edge of it.

He looked around at the small rundown shack, taking in the tent next to the shack. There wasn't anything else in view, and Dane hoped that the guy would realize he had the wrong place and leave after a minute or two. There was no one here he could be looking for.

Instead, the tall youth stepped out of the cab and spun around, a big grin on his face. He walked over to the cabin and knocked on the door, and when there was no response, he turned to look around the clearing until he was facing Dane's direction.

Great, just great, Dane grimaced. Here was Chris, with the optimism of youth and as determined as his father, pulling in less than a week after his cell phone message had resulted in no response. He should have known better, as the boy was clearly not going to take no response as an acceptable answer.

The young man sat down on a log near the fire pit and continued to scan the area, obviously delighted with his surroundings. There was no point in hiding, because he knew Chris would only outwait him. He was his father's son, after all, in both appearance and determination.

Dane stepped out of the trees to the right of the clearing. He wasn't dressed for company, not that he ever was in his Army desert fatigues and boots. He kept his long hair pulled back in a loose ponytail. His beard hung down a few inches. He grimaced again, almost sorry that Chris would see him like this.

But it was his eyes, he knew, the eyes that looked dead, that were truly scary. Large and dark, the kind that looked through most people. That's what looked right back at him in the mirror too.

Chris spotted him and the boy's smile faltered. Then he raised a tentative hand in a wave as he stood up.

"Hey man, I'm looking for Dane Ashland. Someone at the corner store said that this is the address. I hope I have the right place anyway. Do you know where I can find him?"

Dane stared at Chris. He hoped the silence was getting spooky, and that Chris would jump back in the truck and race the hell down the gravel drive, potholed or not. But he didn't seem to scare off easily. Dane could almost appreciate that, the similarity to Powers striking again.

"Who wants to know?" Dane heard his own voice come out in a gravelly tone that cut as deeply as the rocks in his driveway.

Chris's smile faltered again, probably thinking that he was on a crazy man's land, and moved forward with a grin that was now more forced and a hand outstretched for a shake. "I'm Chris, his nephew. I wanted to visit before school got too busy. Do you know where I can find him?" he asked again.

Dane stared at Chris and the outstretched hand. He wasn't sure what to do with it. Acknowledge it, or deny any knowledge? Neither option was particularly appealing, but for vastly different reasons.

Slowly, he raised his own hand to take Chris's in a firm grip. "The last time I saw you, you were just finishing high school. It was before I left. Before the war and everything." Dane paused as the boy let out a huff of relief and the smile became more genuine. He hesitated, then added, "I hope that your dad isn't right behind you."

Chris stepped forward as if he was going for a hug, but Dane moved aside and turned towards the canyon view. He sensed Chris's disappointment and renewed hesitation.

"Uncle Dane, man, you've made it hard for people to visit! Is that really an address Dad got when you bought this place or the instructions to finding a lost treasure? I had to ask at the store. They told me how to find you, but they sure weren't friendly about it."

Dane grunted. No, they probably warned Chris off, told him to leave the crazy old man alone. "I'm not much for visitors," Dane warned again, hoping the boy got the message.

He turned to see Chris watching him with a mixture of sadness and curiosity. Evidently Dane's lack of enthusiasm for a family visit wasn't enough to send him on his way. The boy looked a little hurt too.

"Come on, Uncle Dane! Don't you want to know what I'm doing these days, what I'm up to?" Confusion chased the hurt on his face.

Dane knew why. He and Chris had always gotten along great. Couldn't be helped though. He wasn't the same anymore, and the sooner the boy realized it, the better.

He tried a different tactic. Pointing at the shack and the tent, Dane said. "This is my home now, not much room for visitors. I like my peace and quiet. That's about it." He clammed up then and stared at Chris.

The boy wasn't taking the hint. Walking around the clearing, Chris launched into a monologue that didn't require Dane to respond. He talked about vet school, his hope for a job when he graduated next summer, a girl that he had been seeing. Dane said nothing, no comments, no encouragement, not even anything that would pass for vague interest.

Chatter expended, Chris stopped and looked around again, then back at Dane. Continuing to stare at the boy, Dane felt a little uncomfortable himself, sorry he had to push the kid away. Chris started to fidget under the scrutiny, and swiveled his eyes around the clearing again as if trying to find something to connect them.

In the silence, he finally got the message. He moved forward, intent on a goodbye man hug. Dane left his arms at his sides making it one-sided, probably like hugging a sturdy tree. Chris jumped back in his truck.

"I'll tell Dad I found you in your slice of paradise," he forced a grin at his uncle, clearly hoping to get an answering smile.

Dane's mouth become more compressed, more like a contortion than any sign of joy.

"Don't tell him you found me, okay? I just want to be left alone."

Chris tried to hide his frown and covered his concern with a wave and a final promise to visit more often. Turning his pick-up near the old shack, he headed down the drive, meeting Dane's eyes in the rear view mirror one last time as he stood isolated in his little clearing.

*****

He had a lot of time to think about his nephew's visit. He was sure that the boy would report to his father right away. And that account would undoubtedly result in a visit from Powers, trying once again to fix things as he always did.

While Dane had never been a party animal and had always kept himself aloof after their mother died, he knew his brother would recognize that he had never before turned away his own flesh and blood without a full recap of everything going on in their lives. He hadn't been prone to the kind of dark and forbidding brooding that Chris would describe.

And he never was one to let himself go, always preferring neatly trimmed long hair, no beard, and classy threads. Now, his clothes were worn, though he made sure to keep them clean, just as he made sure his hair and beard didn't harbor any strange vermin. He looked odd, he knew, certainly not dressed in the kind of clothes that identified him as a man who made a good living.

Maybe that was it, Dane thought. He didn't have a living anymore, or at least not a job he was willing to return to. After his stint in Afghanistan and his injuries, he had 'retired' so to speak, choosing to settle in the mountains of California rather than returning to their Oregon hometown. He didn't write, didn't call, and didn't ask for help. Isolation, that's what he needed and all that he deserved.

He was afraid he wasn't going to enjoy it for much longer. One little tidbit that Chris had shared was that his father's current presence in Sacramento was going to be long-term, maybe even permanent. Powers had moved a branch of Ashland Construction, their family's firm, to the valley location. There were plenty of construction opportunities in the older parts of the city, in-fill projects turning vacant lots into new businesses and homes. This was one of the few types of construction that had not suffered in the recent economic downturn.

According to Chris, Powers was doing what he did best, finding projects with a high probability of success and making Ashland a name in the current recovery uptick. And spreading his money around, of which, Dane had no doubt, there was plenty. Powers had always been frugal and careful, never one to let on how much he had and never one to give it away, period.

That was one characteristic they shared, the desire to be careful with their money, though over the years, Powers had given Dane grief over what he labeled his bleeding heart desire to help everyone who asked with his unique skills. Not that Dane had many places to spend his money when he had been overseas. He'd worked instead of played because that's where his interests lay.

Being frugal got him this land, not the big windfall that some congratulated him on and others cursed him for. It was his outright, and no one could take away that or the peace it usually offered him. This place was his to stew over, his to hide on, his to build into the fortress he needed to keep himself away from connections he no longer deserved.

Powers still didn't understand why, didn't grasp the reason for what he termed Dane's isolationism. He thought it was the incident, as he liked to put it. What he didn't realize was that Dane had been like this for a much longer time. Their mother had been the linchpin that held the family together. Her warmth and spirit had made them all laugh and set their cares aside. When she died, they each tried to keep the family together, but one by one they failed. For Dane, it was the beginning of his cautious isolation.

And now, Powers was taking it upon himself to pull the siblings back closer together, or so he indicated to Dane when he'd visited during rehab. Dane let him know in no uncertain terms what he thought of that idea. Powers stormed out with only a couple of overtures to reunite in the past year. Dane ignored him.

But Chris's visit would undoubtedly change that, Dane knew. He couldn't make them understand why he kept to himself now.

This was all he deserved.

Chapter 6

The jingle of bells notifying staff of entering customers wasn't necessary at this time of day, since the bakery cases were all but blocked from view by the people in line ahead. Serena thought about leaving, but the aromas alone took her to her own personal happy place, and the hum of customer chatter coupled with the appealing surroundings and occasional big booming laugh made her smile and decide to wait her turn.

She ran over what little she had learned about Vision Quest in the past few days. It hadn't been much. Still no contacts, still no way to apply for funding, and still no other ideas about foundations to approach either. Time was ticking off the clock and the lack of results was discouraging. Even more reason to wait for something savory to temporarily hold off the blues.

At the head of the line, a tall man with black hair cut short examined the bakery cases with great interest. When he thought he wasn't being observed, he was sizing up the two men filling and ringing up orders behind the counter too. From her vantage point at the end of the line, Serena settled in for some classic people-watching, one of her favorite hobbies.

Behind the counter, Stuart still wore his full head of salt and pepper hair in a military buzz. He and Sarge both sported tattoos on arms exposed below the short sleeves of bakery-logoed t-shirts, mementoes of their military time. The barely disguised interest of the stranger made Serena curious, since he wasn't familiar and didn't appear to be a local.

"What can I get for you?" Sarge stood looking at the man expectantly, wax paper and tongs in hand ready to dive for the customer's selection in the case. Blinking again at the choices, the stranger pointed at a huge bear's claw covered in nuts and icing.

"One of those and a large coffee please." Pulling out his wallet, he looked behind him and realized there was a line of expectant traffic.

"Great place you guys have here! It surprised me to see that none of the chains have parked themselves in town. Every place deserves an old-style bakery like this. I bet you run out of everything all the time." The man dug around in his pocket, pulling out a handful of coins.

Sarge responded with a huge grin. "Yes sir, this has been a great place to run a business, that's for sure. The folks around here are real supportive, and we keep real busy filling all sorts of baking orders. We do cakes for celebrations and savory stuff for dinners, and of course, all of this!" With that, he waved his arms at the cases holding everything from croissants to tarts.

As he moved down to the register, the man continued his conversation with Stuart. "I couldn't help but notice the ink you both have. Ex-military?"

Serena knew their back-story, the years of hardship both men had endured when they came home to their foothills community. Clearly, the man was a stranger in town, because almost everyone else knew that history too.

Punching the man's choices into the register and pouring his coffee, Stuart replied, "Yes indeed. I did twenty years in the Navy, and my partner here did his time in the Army. We both came back to some family when we got out and met up at the vets program. Got this great idea for a bakery when the previous owners went belly-up in the last recession, and we've been busy ever since. We didn't even have to convert the old bank into a kitchen – that had already been done." His smile of proprietorship was infectious.

"Vets program, huh?" Still fumbling through what looked like large bills, the man perked up at the news. "I have a brother who's living around here. He had a hard time after a bomb blew up the convoy he was in – in Afghanistan. He can't seem to adjust or get back into things. Is there some kind of network around here he might be able to join, you know, to realize he's not alone?"

"We've got a lot of vets around here and active duty too. We take care of our own, and we've got a terrific local program to help with counseling and such. Balance, the nonprofit. They could give him some help, no doubt about it. Of course, he'd need to want to get some help. But we both say that if we didn't find Balance, who knows if we'd still be alive today."

Stuart looked past the man to see Serena standing at the end of the line and started to wave her forward, turning to the man to begin an introduction, but as he did, the man picked up his pastry and coffee and backed away rapidly.

"Balance, that was the name? Thanks so much! Between your great food and this news, you've put a whole new spin on my day!" And with that, he headed out the door so fast that the jingling bells crashed.

"Well that was strange," Sarge said, and shrugged his shoulders at Serena as if to say, who can tell these days?

Serena sighed. Another potential vet client, and still no guarantee that Balance would have the funding to keep those programs open. A big donor was becoming more of a necessity with each passing minute.

*****

The distinctive thwack of metal against wood sounded like progress to Dane. Other than that, the quiet was broken only by the caress of wind in the pines and oaks. It was this quiet and the view that drew him to his land in the first place.

He'd seen the ad for it online, and he had come to explore it one rainy day late last spring. It was still hard then to limp across great distances, and his cane tangled up in the weeds matted on the ground, the space neglected and never cleared the previous summer. Still, something pulled Dane to explore it, and he ignored the pain and hardship to poke around the old cabin set in the small clearing, full of furry critters who were the current tenants.

Curiosity won out again when he noticed the vague path at the corner of the clearing. It was worn by many footfalls over time, wide enough to indicate that the people who had lived there had traveled it often. There was supposed to be a view some place, and Dane was thinking that perhaps this would lead to it.

A few dozen yards from the old shack, the trees opened up to a view, and man, what a view. The land dropped away to a series of ridges set between valleys below. A taller mountain and a low range marked the horizon. Dane had stood, stunned at the spread of land below him, dazzling despite the rain. And then he knew he'd found the place he could hide, the place where he could escape his past and try to avoid his nonexistent future. His aerie on top of a mountain.

Allowing himself a small smile at the memory, Dane straightened and consulted his blueprints. The afternoon breeze blew with more force out here, offsetting the heat of the unrelenting summer sun. A large area mowed clean of June's dried grasses set back from the edge of the drop off was marked with paint in the dirt. It was the place he planned on spending the rest of his years on the planet, alone and as content as he would ever be.

"I would have knocked, but I can't seem to find the door."

The voice startled him almost as fast as he recognized it. Dane stayed in his crouch and turned slowly towards the entrance to the path a few yards away. Powers stood with his feet apart, emphasizing his tall and well-muscled body. He set his hands on his hips and smiled down at his younger brother.

Alert despite his recognition, Dane squelched the instinct to run for cover that any surprise brought to him these days. He hadn't heard a vehicle, but then he'd been making a significant amount of noise on his own with the stakes. Running would accomplish nothing. Maybe it was time to stop retreating and take a stand.

Finally, he rested back on his heels and straightened. He settled his face into what could pass for a smile, and his tall stance was a mirror image of his brother's. "It's been a while, Powers."

"Chris told me about the overwhelming warm welcome he experienced on his last visit, and I had to come up and see you for myself." Dane heard the sarcasm creep into his brother's voice. It seemed that no matter what, he and Powers set off negative sparks whenever they go together.

"He caught me by surprise on a very bad day. Most days, I'm not fit for company, but then you could probably figure that out yourself."

Dane didn't close any distance between them, and Powers finally shrugged and took a few steps forward, looking around more closely at the surrounding dirt.

"This looks like you've laid out some sort of plan here, Dane. What's this going to be?"

Dane took his own slow appraisal of the painted outline and a little bit of peace settled into his heart. This time when he smiled, it was more real. "A house, of course."

"You're building here?"

"The land is good, the neighbors aren't too close, and I have to find someplace. I've come to like this view and I'm getting kind of tired of that little cabin and the tent. The foundation will be dug and poured this week."

Powers relaxed his posture now, a big relieved grin cracking across his face. "So things are better, huh? It was ugly, but it's over now, in the past. I'm so glad you're setting what happened behind you, and…"

He stopped in abrupt surprise as Dane shoved past him roughly, moving quickly back towards the clearing and the relative safety of the shack.

Dane knew that Powers couldn't close the distance even as his brother turned to follow him. Years of distance running had given Dane the edge of speed despite his injuries, and surprise hindered his brother further. He was sure Powers was trying to figure out what he'd said wrong too.

"Hey man, I thought this was a good step, a step in the right direction! You've cut yourself off from everything and everyone for too long." Powers huffed behind him.

"Who says it's too long, you? You weren't there! You don't live it over and over again every night, waking up sweating with your throat raw, wondering if you screamed out loud or if it was just part of the nightmare! Yeah, I'm building something, something with soundproof walls, someplace where I can be alone, which is all I can be." Dane bit out the last words as he slammed the shack's door in his brother's face.

In the silence, Dane heard the footsteps stop outside the door, and he hoped his brother would respect the fact that it was closed. The click of the lock as he turned it helped make him feel more secure.

He heard Powers pant and pace on the other side. "Dane, I'm sorry. You're right, I don't know what it's like, but I thought maybe time was making things better. You shouldn't isolate yourself, bro. You need to get out, meet people, see that the world is not the terrible messed up place you think it is." He broke off and waited.

Dane wasn't opening the door and wasn't going to respond, not even to tell him to go to hell.

"Can we talk? About this, or about the house, or anything? Tell me about the house. I've moved to Sac for some projects, so maybe I could help." Powers left the thin panel of wood between them. It was probably amazing that he respected the barrier, since he usually didn't let anything stand in his way.

Dane let the silence stretch.

He heard Powers pace again and he knew his brother would be thinking about how to help him. He had told him often enough, in voicemails or letters, or on rare occasions like this in person, that he wanted to help. He had been full of advice, like it had been over a year, and while his physical wounds had healed, Dane obviously still had deep emotional scars from what happened in Afghanistan. Letting things fester any longer would only make it worse, and maybe make it harder for him to recover. And lots of words to that effect.

Tapping lightly on the door, Powers was trying again, his voice softer this time. "Let's go out, get something to eat, maybe a beer or two, and catch up. I'd like to know what's going on, see what I can do. Come on, Dane, maybe I can fix things."

Yeah, sure, Dane thought, just like he always tried to fix things.

When their mother died, Dane had been devastated. His thirteen-year-old world had come crashing down around him. Their father was never a demonstrative man and always too busy growing the construction business to be around much for his family. Other than the ritual of those weekend evenings of grilling, he became even more withdrawn and reclusive. Their sister got wild and uncontrollable, finally taking off for parts unknown as soon as she graduated from high school.

And Powers had taken it upon himself at the ripe old age of eighteen to fill in as a pseudo-parent. When Dane was hurt, Powers told him to stand up and get back in the fight. When Dane cried, Powers chastened him to grow up. When Dane fought with him, Powers fought back, and they fought often.

The distance between them grew as the years passed. It helped when Powers was in college, too busy between that and his job at the construction company to bother with Dane much. And by then, Dane had become quiet and watchful, learning how to parlay his skill taking in what he saw into living on the fringes. The years of living apart, often on different sides of the planet, did nothing to bring them closer together.

It hadn't gotten better after the incident in Afghanistan, though Powers had tried to be more supportive and less prescriptive. When Dane hadn't responded, he reverted to his usual dominating big brother persona, and that made things worse. Still, they were brothers and Dane knew Powers truly believed he had his best interests at heart.

This was one situation he couldn't fix.

As he waited in the silence, Dane picked out the songs of various birds, the rustle of wind in the surrounding towering pines, the breeze itself whistling through the cracks between the old logs of the cabin. It should have been peaceful. Right now, it felt tense, radiating from Powers into the shack through its tightly shut door.

Powers raised his voice in frustration from a greater distance, and Dane thought he must have paced over to the tent.

"Okay, I understand I don't know what you're still going through. Maybe somebody else, somebody objective and neutral, can help. Have you thought about counseling? Why don't you come down to Sac with me? There's plenty of room in my condo, and we can find you some professional help."

"Don't need any help, don't need any counselors, just need to be left alone," Dane yelled through the closed door. "Head out, Powers, and call before you come visiting again! Or better yet, wait for an invitation!"

With that, all was silent again. And Dane didn't plan to say anymore, even if Powers stood there until sunset.

Powers was silent for a time, and then huffed in what Dane knew to be frustration. "Okay, I get it. You're fine." Anger started creeping into his voice. "I'm leaving my cell phone number, in case you've forgotten it, and my new address under this rock by the tent. Let me know when we can get together. Let me know when hell freezes over!"

His footsteps crunched on rocks across the clearing. The truck door slammed with more force than necessary. Gunning engine and spinning wheels indicated that he had taken off down the driveway with gravel flying.

Quiet returned to the clearing again. Peace took longer. It was quite a while before the door to the cabin slowly creaked open.

Chapter 7

"I'm sorry, I'm sorry – I know I'm late, but I had to process some really weird news." Serena rounded the corner of Tess's house slowly, her forehead furled in thought and her voice quiet. She bit her lip uncertainly and she felt a bit lost. Maybe her friends could help her figure out if this was in fact good news or bad news.

The summer sun was still hot, but the greenery wrapping around the covered patio in the flower shop's backyard made it feel significantly cooler. Tess was gazing out over the flowers, fruit trees and vegetables. Dragonflies flitted over the small pond, and hummingbirds dive-bombed each other between forays into the fuchsias.

"How do you let your spice rack get so empty?" Roxy surged out of the kitchen door and stared at Tess, aghast. "Really, how do you cook like this?" Holding an empty container that was supposed to contain sweet curry powder, the outrage on Roxy's face made Tess burst out laughing. Distracted from her own musings for the moment, Serena smiled.

"First, I don't cook for myself in the summer – it's too hot. I eat a lot of salads and raw vegetables from the garden. Or I get you to cook for me!" Tess gave a cheeky smile, but got up to come over and take the offending shaker out of her friend's hand and give her a hug. "Really, you don't have to go through all this work for a girls' night. We can just relax, make something simple, and talk until we're all talked out."

"I am fixing something simple, a simple little curried potato salad using your potatoes, some cold poached salmon from the restaurant, and a wonderful arugula and tomato salad again from your garden. At least, that was the original plan until I realized that you are not fit to manage your own spice rack." But Roxy relented and smiled too, the usual kind of teasing they engaged in any time they were together.

"I'll come up with something, no worries. I'll raid the herb garden while we wait for Serena," she continued in a muttered dialogue about food options based on the limitless supplies in Tess's garden.

Serena stayed in the shade of the twisted old wisteria vine and watched her friends bicker. The give and take was so familiar, so comforting. She knew they would be eager to hear her news, but she hesitated. What if it really was bad, as bad as the intuitive feeling she had that this would change everything? They would be honest with her and tell her, but she wasn't sure she wanted to hear it. She wanted this to be good, or even better than good. But she couldn't shake the feeling that big changes, major upheavals, were around the corner.

"Where is Serena, anyway? She's usually the first one to show up, and at the rate she's going, she'll even be later than Gabby, who's always late." This came from their artist friend DK McGiven, lounging on a chaise opposite the chair that Tess had vacated, wine glass in hand and legs stretched out right down to her toes decorated with bright red nail polish. Tonight she had traded in her welder's coveralls for cutoffs and a tank top.

"She probably got wrapped up in a conversation with a client. You know how diligent she gets when she thinks that someone's close to a break through. She just turns right into serene Serena and pretty soon the client's turned the corner and are back on the road to a fulfilled and happy life!" DK chuckled and shook her head and Tess smiled in agreement as she dropped back into her wicker chair.

"Sorry I'm late – what did I miss? I was talking with Jeremy's sitter who's having boy trouble and I lost track of time. She's such a romantic. I couldn't tear myself away." A breathless Gabriella Cooley-Burke came through the shop's back door and braked when she saw only Tess and DK, wine glasses raised in a toast.

"Congratulations, you're not the last one this time Gabby. It seems that Serena must have lost track of time too. What could be keeping that girl?"

She was never late, Serena thought. That alone was going to make everyone curious when she spoke up again, loud enough for them to hear her. It was unheard of for her to be the last one to show up.

Gabby was frowning, which in her case scrunched her face up in a look that could pass for concentration in others. For her, though, it meant she was thinking about angles and what stories might be involved. She couldn't help herself, storyteller that she was. Her county job didn't give her many outlets for her active imagination.

"Is the gang all here now?" Roxy asked, back from her foray into the garden with a basket full of herbs, heirloom tomatoes and some baby zucchini with the flowers still attached. Looking from woman to woman, she frowned. "Where's Serena?"

"That's a good question. I'll call her and see what's holding her up. Good thing I had some extra wine chilling since it's her turn to pour tonight."

Stepping out of the deep shadow, Serena tried out another smile and announced herself. "Hey, I'm here! I just wanted to see how you talk about me when you don't know I'm around."

The group laughed at that, since they always had each other's backs. If they couldn't say the truth face to face, what was the point of the sacred girl tribe anyway?

"You look, I don't know, strange, Serena. Are you okay?" Tess zeroed in on her discomfort right way.

Serena blinked. She could do a great job hiding her concerns and her doubts in public, but the girl tribe was family. Trust Tess to be the first to call her on what her face was giving away. Soon, though, the other three women were shaking their heads in agreement.

"Sorry, but I needed to think about some news I got today. It's kind of, well, scary," and her smile faltered.

All of the women swiveled to look at her in surprise. DK recovered first. "Ah-oh, this doesn't sound good. Let's get you a glass of wine and you can tell us all about it. It's about money for the center, right? The state cut you off, or the county?" She rose and crossed to the galvanized pail that served as an ice bucket on nights like this. Turning back, she put the wineglass of cold golden liquid in Serena's hand, while Tess pulled Serena onto a chaise next to Gabby.

"Tell us all about it," said Roxy, as she put down a plate of olives, peppers and cheese on the side table and came over to join the group.

Serena tried to shake off the sense of foreboding and looked around at her best friends. Maybe they could make sense of this, because she wasn't so sure this whole deal was legit. If it was, it could save all of the center's programs. If it was illegal or even unethical, it could destroy the place. And what if she couldn't succeed?

"Tell us," Tess urged softly.

"It's the strangest thing," Serena started, taking a fortifying swallow of wine. "A donor has agreed to provide us with funding, even more funding than I need to keep the vets program, enough to keep everything open for the coming year and even put some money in the bank. It's amazing!"

Serena fell silent and her friends exchanged glances at the worried look on her face.

"But that's great, right?" Gabby asked.

"Who's the donor," DK chimed in. "A knight in shining armor? On a white horse? With pieces of gold falling out of silk saddlebags?" She grinned, attempting to lighten the mood.

Really, this should be good news.

"It's a new nonprofit, an organization called Vision Quest. All I can find out about them is that they were formed earlier this year, and they appear to have a lot of cash. On their website, they say that their mission is helping lost souls find their way to a better quality of life. It sounds kind of cheesy, but they seem to be a legitimate foundation." Falling quiet again, Serena idly toed the flagstones underfoot and took another sip of wine.

She avoided everyone's eyes. "I looked them up, before I mean, because someone suggested them. But I couldn't learn anything about them. There's no easy way to contact them and no funding application process that I could find. But then out of the blue, poof, they want to give Balance money."

"So what's the problem? This sounds like great news, exactly what Balance needs to stay on its own feet! It should be a time to celebrate!" Roxy pulled the wine bottle free and began to pour around in everyone's glasses, passing the appetizers with her other hand in practiced ease.

"I guess it is good news. It's just that it feels strange. The commitment for funding came in the form of a letter sent by a Sacramento attorney for the organization. I called, and he can't or won't tell me anything more about the foundation. It's weird not to know something about its founders, why they're interested in funding Balance, and where their money came from." She paused, twirling the stem of her glass and examining each of her friend's faces. "I'm worried that it could be illegal somehow."

Tess furrowed her brow. "Don't you have an attorney on your own board too? What does she say about this?"

"She reviewed the letter and checked out the foundation. It is incorporated and they do seem to have money. But she couldn't learn anything more about them either." Serena nibbled on some cheese, gazing out at the garden without registering plants or colors.

DK stared at her for a moment, then asked, "What makes you so uncomfortable about this? You are uncomfortable, that's clear. What's wrong?"

Serena tried to figure out where the weird sense was coming from. "I never applied for a grant from them. I had heard about them, but I was still trying to check them out. They didn't have a funding application link on their webpage and I was trying to script a request. Then boom – out of the blue, here comes this letter. It sounds, well, too good to be true. And you know what they say about that."

She closed her eyes, thinking about all of the hard work that would continue to help her clients if this offer was as good as it looked on paper. It would take the pressure off for quite a while, long enough for the economy to turn around and the government funding to resume. Blinking, Serena realized she was close to tears.

"Well it still sounds good to me," Gabby stated. "Rox, let me help you get dinner on the table. We really do need to celebrate this!"

"No, let me help," Serena stood suddenly. "I need to move around – I'm too keyed up. You sit – I'll help Roxy serve."

*****

Roxy tossed the baby zucchini and their flowers in seasoned rice flour and dropped them into hot oil. Seasoning the cooked fingerling potatoes with the fresh herbs she'd minced, she looked over to see what kind of progress Serena was making slicing the tomatoes.

The knife was in hand, the tomato on the board, but Serena was a million miles away.

"Okay, so spill. It sounds like this is a great deal, almost too good to be true. Is that it? You don't believe it's true?"

Serena played idly with the basil on the cutting board. She picked up the tomato and turned it over in her hand a few times. Finally she turned to Roxy.

"There are, ah, terms that go with the money."

"Terms, what kind of terms?" This had Roxy's attention. Scooping the last zucchini out of the oil, she came over to the cutting board, replaced the knife in Serena's hand with a wine glass, and took over slicing. It was a safer – and faster – alternative.

"There is a condition, one big condition, to getting the money. I have to help – Balance has to help – a person, help him get over whatever his problem is. Get him back to 'participating in society' the letter said. That's the condition."

"And who is the person? Anyone, or someone specific?" Roxy sliced fresh mozzarella, added it to the tomatoes on the platter, and began tearing basil over the top. Reaching for the olive oil, she turned to glance at the still silent Serena.

"Someone specific," Roxy said slowly, answering her own question. Serena nodded. "Who is it?"

"I can't tell you – can't divulge potential client information, you know? Let's just call him Bob. Suffice to say I think it's going to be a big challenge based on what I know about the guy already. I don't think he wants anyone's help."

Chapter 8

"So fill me in. What do we know about this mysterious guy?"

Eduardo del Campo, head counselor for the vets program at Balance and right hand in the operations of the organization, questioned Serena as they drove through the countryside. The hills were very brown, truly burnt to a crisp after the hot summer, and it was only approaching the end of July. They still had the dog days of August to face, a time when the heat brought out the crazies in everyone. Wildfire danger rose with each passing day. The cooler and shorter days of September couldn't come soon enough.

"He seems to be gun-shy and skittish. He wears worn Army desert fatigues. The one time I saw him, he had turned the pants into long baggy cutoffs and had taken the sleeves off the shirt too. He wears his hair long and has a beard. From the way he dresses and from something that was alluded to in the letter, I'm assuming he's a vet who served in Afghanistan or Iraq, and relatively recently. He yelled at a little girl in front of the grocery store a couple of weeks ago, and he seems to set the neighbors on edge because he's so odd. His name is Dane, but I don't know a last name."

"And I'm along because...?" Eduardo glanced over at Serena. "Moral support, or in my official capacity as a counselor?"

"Kind of like back-up at this point. I'm getting curious about Mr. Mystery Vet Dane. For a foundation to make him the reason they are donating, there must be something particularly special about him. I want to know what it is. And I want to help him. So yeah, counselor too. Maybe you can get him to join one of your vets groups."

"Sounds like it would be a good place for him to air his issues, if you're right. But not everyone came back from in-country screwed up. Some just want to be left alone."

Eduardo would know. He went back to school after his discharge from a career in the Army and earned degrees in mental health counseling. Perhaps it was to help others, or perhaps to find some answers for himself. He had never been very clear on that. Vets believed in him because he shared their story, had walked the talk. He had been with Balance from the beginning, and he was one of the few people, outside of the girl tribe, who knew what drove Serena to make the center work.

"Turn right at Roxy's. I know, but something just seems, I don't know, different about him. Something pulls me. Left, then next left – it's hard to spot."

"This isn't about you trying to save someone again, is it? Because we've talked about this and you know that nothing you do today can change what happened in your past." Eduardo twisted the wheel hard to avoid the larger potholes.

"It isn't about me. It's about helping a fellow human being. If he wants help that is."

Serena leaned forward a bit as they came into a clearing. It was large, and set in the middle at its back was a small shack, probably an old homesteader's place. Next to it stood a small tent in those ever-popular military fatigue colors. Trees ringed the clearing, manzanita and scrub oaks filling the understory and huge pines and blue oaks up above. A gentle breeze coaxed movement in the highest branches. A hawk flew high in the sky, taking advantage of breezes before plunging back down to hunt. Serena thought it seemed to be a very peaceful spot.

"How do you want to play this?" Eduardo asked as he turned off the car. "I can take the lead, or you can."

"Let me try first." Opening her door, Serena got ready to step out. "Stay in the truck for now. I'm a girl, so maybe I'm harmless," she said with a small laugh.

Stepping out into the heat, Serena heard a hawk's cry, along with the dance of the wind in the trees. And there was another sound, a sharp shot of a sound that came from beyond the clearing.

Leaning back in, she said, "If I'm not back in five minutes, follow me." Not waiting for an agreement, she shut the door and listened again for the direction of the sound.

There seemed to be a narrow path worn between the trees across the clearing, and another shot sounded from there. Serena squared her shoulders. Was he shooting something? Practice shots for hunting season? Just practice? Who would be shooting in a late afternoon at this time of year?

*****

Dane had earplugs shoved deep in his ears. The noise hurt and made him jumpy, but he needed the nail gun to make faster work of the framing for the house's floor. He didn't want this to take forever, and it would be nice to have a roof, a big solid roof, over his head before the winter's rains and occasional snows set in. He was intent on his work, and he jumped when he turned for the next piece of lumber and caught sight of someone standing at the edge of the trees.

A woman, a few years younger and half a foot shorter than him, blocked the path back to his cabin. Chestnut hair with casual waves past her shoulders lit with red highlights, almost like a halo. He registered curves in casual business attire and an athletic figure set aglow by the late afternoon sun.

But it was her face that drew him in. It was round and full featured, gentle expressive lines already drawn in place, laughter and a few frowns suggested but still calm and serene. It would be a face that ages well, as interesting and attractive in another couple of dozen years as it was now. He had a sudden ache to be able to capture this current vision to look back on at some future date.

He met her eyes, and he had that same scary sensation he'd had at the store. Time stopped. Sound ceased. He wasn't even sure if he was breathing.

Rising to his feet, he could see her lips moving. Not hearing the words, he shook his head. Then realizing why, he pulled the plugs from his ears.

She regarded him questioningly. She was in his space. He wasn't sure if he liked that or hated it. Cautiously, he moved forward.

"I said, hello, I'm Serena. I saw you at the store the other day, and I admit it, I followed you. I just thought I'd come and introduce myself." She advanced a distance into the cleared area, not breaking his gaze.

Dane said nothing. He was struck dumb. This Serena wasn't beautiful, but attractive in an earthy kind of way, natural and peaceful. And she stood staring at him with those continuing questions in her eyes. After a time, open curiosity replaced the questions.

"Have I come at a bad time? I heard what sounded like shots and I was curious. I can come back later. It looks like you're building something. I thought maybe you were getting ready for hunting season with some target practice!" Serena's laugh was unsettled after this. She was doing a lot of talking, more than he'd had to listen to from one person, other than his brother, in quite a while.

He had a sudden urge to step forward, take her hand, and hold it for a long time. Clearing his throat, Dane attempted polite conversation, something that he hadn't had to practice at all in months. "Not a bad time. Just busy working. Don't get many visitors." The croak in his voice from lack of use made him grimace.

Advancing a few feet closer, he could see that her eyes were hazel, a great match for those rich highlights in her hair. They were large eyes, set deep in her face, laughing eyes. Or maybe they were just laughing at him. He'd still like to capture that face, but that wasn't for him anymore.

She stared back. She hadn't backed up across the clearing, but there was cautious tension in her stance. Flat footed and ready to run. Dane kicked himself mentally – he really did have some social skills left, right?

And maybe Powers had been on target about one thing. He was a little better, and things were better. No reason to cut himself off completely.

She intrigued him.

Clearing his throat again, he started over slowly. "Sorry. Like I said, I don't get many – or any – visitors here. I, ah, I noticed you at the store too. I had to, ah, leave quickly." He smiled – or at least he hoped that's how it looked. In addition to being rusty from his self-imposed isolation, he never had worn his emotions on his face in the best of times, unless he needed to pull out his legendary charm to get what he wanted.

He stopped two paces away from the woman. His words seemed to hang in the air for quite a while before she responded, long enough for the wind to start its song in the pines again.

With a lift of her shoulders, she laughed with greater ease this time, a sound that covered an octave of notes in a scale. Walking forward, she stuck out her hand and waited for Dane to lift his. "I'm sorry, I didn't catch your full name."

Dane stared at the extended hand. He knew what society expected him to do with it – put out his own hand and grasp the one in front of him. He was sure it would be warm, soft. He wanted to take the welcome and enjoy the human contact. But something held him back.

He didn't deserve to be welcomed anywhere.

"Did I say something wrong?" She looked a bit confused, watchful and wary all of a sudden. Maybe she picked up on his aura, the negative energy that followed him everywhere he went these days. Her hand slowly settled back at her side.

Silently they stared at each other, watchful hazel eyes meeting his, questions, concerns, and again, that shadow of pity racing across her face. She seemed to be waiting for him to speak, but he didn't have anything to say. Social skills be damned, he'd never felt like he had to fill the quiet with empty words. Time stretched on, and the wind returned, making the clearing feel even more isolated, closed in and private.

"It's Dane, my name I mean." He stopped, embarrassed that this seemed to be the best he could do.

The woman waited for him to continue, and when he didn't, she shrugged, a small movement. "Since you don't get a lot of visitors, Dane," she said slowly, "would you mind if I dropped in to visit every once in a while?" She stood patiently, waiting for some indication of his agreement or refusal.

An occasional visitor, Dane thought. One that looks like her. He rolled her name, Serena, around in his mind. At another earlier point in his life, he would have welcomed her interest, and he would have been able to grasp her hand, show her the developing house, and point out the view.

But he didn't deserve that anymore, and while she didn't know it, it still made him angry that she was suggesting something – friendship – that he could no longer enjoy.

The seconds continued to tick by, and slowly her expression fell into sadder lines. She shifted and glanced around, her gaze lingering on the framing before coming back to his.

"Okay then, it's been good to meet you, Dane. I hope we see each other again." And with that, she took a couple of steps back, turned, and disappeared down the path.

Dane stared after her. See each other again? Why? He didn't seek her out, and there was certainly no reason for her to want to return. He flashed on that sense of recognition, and then just as quickly set it out of his mind. No, he was better off this way, on his own and out of the world's way.

Absently he rubbed his chest, trying to ease the empty feeling around his heart. With a sigh he was barely aware of, he headed back to the construction to add a few more boards. No, that beauty definitely wasn't for the likes of him anymore.

Chapter 9

"So what's he like?" Tess was intent on the roses in her hands, weaving them between delicate selections of perennial flowers to create a towering display. The hospital was having a fundraiser for the expansion project, and this centerpiece would grace the main table at the buffet. Luckily, the cooler temperatures of the past couple of weeks had encouraged the roses to bloom like crazy again, and she had plenty in her garden to share.

Serena inhaled deeply, the fragrances intense and spicy. Still silent in the wake of Tess's question, she stared unseeing into the middle distance. She wanted to participate in this conversation with Tess, but she was too distracted to think clearly.

"Uh, hello?" Waving her arms, Tess smiled hugely when Serena finally looked up at her. "Serena! Welcome back!"

With a visible jump, Serena swung her big eyes to Tess, a stricken look on her face. "What?!?"

Tess's grin got even bigger. Oh yeah, Serena knew she was going to provide fodder for a big story here.

"I said, what's he like? You know, the guy you have to save to get the donation to save the agency?" Turning away from the flowers and picking up her glass of lemonade, Tess settled into a comfy loveseat and waited with her eyes on Serena's face.

Serena fussed with things on the covered porch – a planter, some vines, the pillows on the deeply cushioned wicker furniture. Penelope the cat jumped up on the loveseat and wound herself into a ball, staring at the fussing along with Tess. The sun had just set and the air was starting to cool, and it felt particularly good on her hot cheeks.

"Oh, well you know I can't discuss his situation, even if he isn't a client yet. And we didn't talk for long – or rather I talked a lot and he talked very little. He's, ah, he's…" Her voice trailed away and with it, the stillness returned.

"You're not giving me anything to go on here. Come on, I sense a story, and you know that I love nothing better than a good tale – it feeds my Native American blood! I don't think this has anything to do with his client-or-not status. What does he look like?"

Pacing the length of the veranda, Serena idly picked up a short-stemmed rose from the table and lifted it for an appreciative sniff. Tess sat in silence, rubbing at the condensation on her glass as she watched her friend. Up to a point, she'd be patient about finding out what was going on. Serena was sure that Tess just hoped it happened before the first snows fell this winter.

With a deep sigh, Serena flopped into a chair and finally looked at Tess. "I don't know what's wrong with me. Seeing – let's call him Bob – was unsettling. He's very intense, you can tell that right away. It's in his stare, in his stance. He doesn't seem to be very friendly, and he didn't exactly welcome my visit or invite me back. He was too polite to tell me I was intruding on something, but I don't know what I was intruding on, exactly."

"So what does he look like?"

"Vivid dark blue eyes, bordering on iridescence. They seemed to glow, which really does seem silly, except when something dark and forbidding comes into his stare and then his eyes seem – I don't know, dead? Like there's no color at all. His hair is black with some silver starting to show. It's on the longish side. And he has a beard." Serena's voice dropped off again and focused in that middle distance of nowhere, remembering each detail so vividly in her mind that it surprised her.

"Is he attractive?" Tess prodded, having returned to placing roses strategically on the tower before her. Serena had dated a few men since she moved to the area, but they were usually very proper, button-down types. Dull too, in everyone's opinion, as they'd told Serena on a number of occasions.

Serena couldn't get involved with a client of the agency, but that didn't mean she couldn't look, right? Shaking herself again, she fussed with the rose in her hand and thought back over the impression Dane made on her. "He has a slender build, like a runner, but with lots of muscles too. He's not a stranger to hard work, but his hands are almost delicate, like he's a musician or an artist. He's building something on that property, did I mention that? It looks like it's the beginning of a house."

Quick to rise out of the chair, Serena tried to shake the image of him out of her mind and return to business. It wasn't what he looks like or what he's building that should concern her – or rather Balance. What's important was getting him whatever services this donor seems to think he needs.

Maybe, though, all he needed was someone to talk to.

Chapter 10

The wood dust smelled good, freshly cut and clean. Dane had worked nonstop for the past two days, hoping that the physical challenges and concentration on the structure would distract him from the visit that seemed to be in the front of his mind, like it or not. There was something about Serena that kept pulling at him. Maybe it was just that he hadn't talked with a woman – other than a clerk at a store – in a long time. No matter what the reason, though, he couldn't get the picture of her face out of his mind over the past two weeks.

In Afghanistan, plenty of the men carried pictures of their girlfriends and wives, kids if they had any. The women he'd worked with in the various squads were always happy to share their own shots – husbands, families, parents, whomever they had at home waiting for them. He hadn't had anything to share, and he took a good amount of ribbing for being footloose and free. While no one said it outright, he thought that in some ways, people felt sorry for him.

It wasn't a surprise, really. He hadn't picked his career - it had picked him. And it allowed him to keep everyone at a distance, a few steps away and with constant barriers between him and the reality of their world. He was happy with that, since the distance meant he carried the pain in his own heart and it didn't taint anyone else's.

Turning to the woodpile, Dane selected another board and hoisted it to his shoulder for the trip up the ladder. Things would be going faster if he hired some help to work on the construction. And maybe have someone deliver the loads of wood rather than make all of those trips to the lumberyard in his big pick-up. But that would mean that people would come here to his refuge, and he hated that. They'd ask what he's building, and then they'd want to know how long he'd had the property, and they'd want to know where he came from before Flynn's Crossing. And then they'd want to know what he did for a living to be able to afford to build a house in this economy.

They'd want to know about his past. No, that didn't work for him.

There was something about Serena, though. He wouldn't mind talking with her more. She seemed to be friendly in a good way, and she wasn't too nosy. She didn't ask him a lot of questions about what he was building, though it would have been logical based on the nail gun and saws and wood around the clearing. She seemed interested, but willing to let him take the lead in discussing whatever came to mind. Willing to let him talk as much or as little as he wanted.

He knew he wasn't talking much, but maybe he could change that.

Dane didn't want to talk about his past or his present, but then again, Serena's face drifted to the front of his mind and he put down the hammer he was using to set the current board on the wall. Rubbing his eyes, he saw, as he often had, the picture framed in his mind. This is how some of the best work often started, a picture in his mind and a desire to tell the story behind it. He felt the vague stir of excitement that always came with the pictures, the good ones.

But that was the past. That life wasn't for him anymore. He had pushed it, pushed the envelope, and it had cost him. He'd supported causes, and that had almost cost him too. And it had cost others.

Pushing down the pulse of guilty energy in his gut, he tried once again to set aside the vision of Serena as she glanced back at him before she walked into the path out of the clearing. Not for him. He wasn't worthy anymore.

Chapter 11

"So what do we do about your Mystery Vet now?" Eduardo was leaning against the door jam in Serena's cramped office, a coffee cup in one hand and a sheaf of papers in the other.

It had been two weeks since their visit to Dane's. Eduardo had returned to the property twice to try to engage Dane in conversation, but he'd been turned away – politely. Dane clearly didn't want any help from him. Serena had hoped that a man might build a better rapport.

She finally lifted her gaze to Eduardo. Her laptop screen had held her silent interest for quite a while. She hadn't even blinked. Now she shook her head to clear it and focus on her head vet counselor.

"Through their attorney, our mysterious donor Vision Quest wants an update on how we're doing with Dane. That was the condition of their donation, that we make progress with him, get him engaged in society again. I tried to explain that it's the client's choice what they want to do, not ours. But they were adamant. We've received the first installment on the donation, but we need to show some progress." Serena's pen tapped a quick staccato on the desk, another indication of the unrest she was feeling over a financial benefit that arrived with major conditions attached.

"I can go out again, but I really don't think he wants to see me. And I don't think that asking any of the guys in the program past or present to try and reach out to him would make a difference either. He wasn't rude to me, but he certainly doesn't seem to want me there. He slammed the door of that cabin on me the last time. He's making progress on that building, by the way. There's a floor over the foundation. So we know how he's spending some of his time. Can't see how he can do it, what with the heat everyday and no trees by the house." Eduardo shuddered – he really loved his air conditioning on hot summer days and Serena smiled at her friend's distaste.

The pen's tattoo of tapping moved to Serena's lower lip. Pretty soon, she'd be chewing on that pen – she knew Eduardo had seen it often enough when she was worked up. He'd judge that there was nothing to do but leave and let her work it through. And she knew he was grateful once again that he wasn't the executive director facing these kinds of problems.

For a split second, she wished they could change places anyway.

*****

Tonight it didn't seem to be cooling down. The usual breezes over the marshy delta in the Sacramento valley were missing and instead the heat continued to bake into the evening. The air shimmered with it. Breath rasped, heads ached, skin screamed.

Serena's historically styled bungalow was set up on the hill above Flynn's Crossing. As the town developed, people built their homes up the hillside, an easy walk to Main Street. Her place was one of a row of almost identical houses on a quiet street with a view of the town to the south and east below. At night, the lights of the town were magical. During the holidays, the colors made her smile. Tonight, though, the colors were only those of the signs for stores and restaurants and nothing seemed to light up with an answer to her current predicament.

She was content with her life most of the time. Serena had found her place here in the foothills in welcoming friends and a great job that made a positive difference in people's lives. As is true in so many small towns, everyone seemed to know everyone else, and everyone felt they knew everyone's business. If you wanted to be anonymous, you couldn't live in a community like this. On the outskirts or in the surrounding mountains and canyons, you could still disappear. But eventually, everyone needed to come to town for something.

Serena felt lucky to have her girl tribe, friends she made when she first moved up from the valley six years ago. She met Tess first, attracted to the flower shop for something to brighten her new home and finding instant friendship in its colorful owner. Tess's flowing black hair with its distinctive white streak and her chiseled Native American features made her a natural beauty. If she wasn't so gentle sweet in nature, it would be hard not to be jealous of her based on looks alone.

A Saturday night art walk with Tess introduced them both to DK as they visited a cooperative art gallery. Their new friend was so gifted, creating incredible metal sculptures. The pixie body hid strength that could bend metal. Her Irish coloring matched her temper, though she rarely gave in to it. She'd much rather create more art.

DK brought her to Roxy's for dinner and introduced her to the edgy chef, and before long, Roxy was a regular at their conclaves. Besides the magic she could perform with any cooking ingredients, Roxy was a devoted and supportive friend. There was a back-story that involved a man who broke her heart, but she was never willing to discuss it. In Roxy's opinion, which she shared often, all men were scum, none to be trusted.

Gabby was Roxy's polar opposite. She worked for the county in the business development department and she had helped Serena finalize the paperwork to open her nonprofit, Balance. Having lost her husband, the man she loved above all else, two years before, Gabby was now raising her son Jeremy on her own. Of course, the kid now had a bevy of aunts to boss him around as well, but he never seemed to mind. And romantic that she was, Gabby was convinced that all of them would find true love someday, just like she'd had.

All of the other members who touched the tribe from time to time had contributed something vital to her life here in Flynn's Crossing. Maybe she'd been naive, taking for granted that life would just continue along the same vein. It probably was more like a holding pattern, waiting for the next steps in each of their lives. While they all dated, none were married. The single moms in their group couldn't hang out as much as the others, but still, everyone seemed to gain comfort and stability from their extended friendships. Their jobs hadn't changed much, and even DK's growing public success didn't shift their dynamics.

But change might be happening whether Serena wanted it or not. As Balance's anonymous and generous donor, Vision Quest's contribution would help many vets, not just one. But it required Balance to help Dane, the Mystery Vet. Dane didn't want any help, and in fact didn't even want to see anyone from the organization. Ergo, Dane wouldn't be returning to an active role in society in the donor's probable opinion and Balance wouldn't be receiving the life-saving funds it needed.

And with that, she might have to close the doors on the majority of its programs. Case sounding disgustingly closed.

Serena sat on her porch and looked down to Main Street, distracted by her thoughts from what might be happening below. On a hot July Friday night, she usually would be hanging out with her girl tribe, hitting Roxy's restaurant for dinner or helping Tess transport flowers some place. DK might have an exhibit to share. Gabby would be raving alternately on the latest politics in the county or the latest romance of her friends and coworkers.

But tonight, she didn't feel like doing any of that. She needed time alone to think.

Okay, it was silly to feel like you were linked to the outcomes of another human being you had seen for what — a total of three minutes, maybe four? First the store, though that didn't count because he was hauling ass out the door and was gone. And then on his property. Yet something pulled at her. Serena stood and paced the short porch of the bungalow.

What had he said in his clearing?

"I don't get many visitors."

He tried to keep people away, from the unmarked driveway through heavy brush to the cold welcome once someone appeared. And yet, she recognized a longing in his eyes when he stared at her.

His eyes were the windows to his soul, and that soul desperately wanted to be part of something again.

Chapter 12

The heat was already oppressive with no dawn breeze coming off the mountains to refresh the early part of the day. The sun had come up orange through the haze of forest fires, and the hint of smoke was acrid even this great distance from any active blaze. Dane could hope that the afternoon would bring the regular wind up the canyon to stir the sludge, but he'd given up on hoping for things long ago. Best to accept things as they were and soldier on.

Selecting his next board, he measured and marked, turning to the table saw. And startled, he dropped the board.

She was standing at the edge of the clearing. He blinked a couple of times to make sure that she wasn't a mirage. Nope, still there. He took in the hiking boots, shapely bare legs, and shorts that really did live up to their name. Realizing that he was staring, he quickly checked her face. She was wearing a small smile, and she held a paper tray with two big cups of something and a bag in her hands. Whatever was inside that bag smelled good, and he slowly took off the eye protection and earplugs, turning more fully to face her.

"Good morning, Dane! I thought you might like something to kick off your day, though it looks like you've been at it for hours already." She looked at him expectantly. Obviously, she was waiting for him to respond.

Instead, he blinked a few more times and took a long breath.

Her smile faltered. Damn, he thought. He didn't want to hurt her feelings. She looked awfully cute in her hiking gear. But why would she stop by here? Dane guessed that it must be on her way to wherever her day was headed. He took a few steps to the side, ready to run across the clearing to the relative safety of his cabin.

And that's when he noticed the work gloves hanging out of her back pocket. What the…?

"I'm Serena, but you probably remember that. I thought you might want a second pair of hands. It's hard to hold those boards in place and nail and such. I know. My dad liked to build things and I used to help him. I'm pretty handy! I even did all of the renovations on my house. I brought breakfast too!"

Her voice trailed off and Dane found he couldn't move. He was sure that if there was something like a deer-in-the-headlights look, it was definitely on his face right now.

What was it about her? It wasn't like she was traditionally beautiful, but there was something in her face, her eyes, a knowing that both disturbed him and drew him in. Dane straightened and cleared his throat. He would have to say… something. She didn't appear to be put off by his silence, and she wasn't leaving.

Did she expect him to invite her to help, to stay, and what, break bread together? But that bag smelled good, and now that he was closer, he could see some kind of iced drinks in those cups. His stomach growled. At least some part of him had a clear idea of what it wanted.

"Aaahh, thanks. You didn't have to come or bring anything. And really, I don't need any help." Dane's voice croaked from the early hour and lack of use. The rasp was obvious. He cleared his throat again and hoped that he sounded more sure, more forceful, more determined. Determined to push her away. He didn't deserve any company, and certainly no woman who had that sure look in her eyes.

Back to his first assumptions. Maybe that would put her off. "Looks like you're dressed for hiking. It must be the hottest day of this summer. I bet that you'd rather be up in the Sierras this morning, walking along some cool stream. Right?" He stopped. He sounded stupid even to himself, but he needed her to leave and he didn't want to be impolite.

But damn, she looked even more inviting as he got nearer. Her body was shapely but muscular and filled those clothes to perfection. And as he got closer, he could see that her hazel eyes were solemn as she regarded him, even with that smile on her face.

"Really, I can help. Think of how much faster it will go today if I lend a hand. And then we can knock off when the heat is its worst this afternoon, because I don't think the delta breeze will be coming up today at all. Maybe we can go grab an early dinner, together."

She had the whole day planned, it seemed. He wanted to fight it. He didn't want anyone to get too close to him. Dane started to shake his head slowly, and then sniffed that bag again. He took a slow step closer.

What harm would there be in having a little breakfast, letting her lend a hand for a while? She'd get disgusted with the heat and sawdust and hard work. Then she'd leave, satisfied that she'd helped out, and she'd stay out of his hair.

Yeah, he had a feeling that wouldn't happen.

Shock ran through his system when his brain caught up to his body, his feet telling him to move forward, his hands ready to shake hers, his voice willing to ask what was in the bag. Some primitive part of him wanted to see if she smelled as good as the pastries. His brain still wanted to deny it and tell her to stay away.

This was probably going to be a big mistake. But maybe it was time for him to take a risk or two. Maybe he was almost ready. He took another step forward.

"What's in the bag?"

*****

The day flew by, and with it, a lot of sawdust, boards and fasteners moved too. Serena sincerely loved the work, loved the feel of raw wood in her hands, the precision of the cuts and the satisfaction of the frame taking shape. It had been a while since her last big project on her house, and honestly, she was out of major projects there unless she wanted to tear something out and start over. She'd have to find an outlet to do this more often. It was fun, and it reminded her of good times.

Dane was proving to be a surprise too. He had accepted her gift of buttery croissants and iced coffee with a torn look on his face. Then he shuttered it, and since then, he was quiet and directed and detached. Like her, he seemed to prefer the rolls oozing savory spinach and feta cheese for breakfast, and the others, stuffed with almond paste and topped with slivered nuts, were consumed for a late morning break. The water they tapped from the big orange jug throughout the morning was cooling, but nothing seemed to cut the heat.

Pulling her shirt free of the stickiness on her back, Serena let herself stare from behind her safety glasses, resting her gaze on Dane when he couldn't notice her examination. He definitely was a fine-looking specimen of man. Hard muscles rippled across his back, visible when he'd taken off his t-shirt, and what could be seen of his legs below long baggy shorts made his running routine evident. She wished for the same freedom to strip off a few more layers herself. Wouldn't that shock Dane out of his serious, business-like demeanor?

She caught herself musing on what his butt looked like under those shorts. Snap out of it, she thought, giving herself a mental head slap. You can't date a client – or at least she hoped he'd agree to become a Balance client.

She thought back to their attempt at awkward conversation as they ate breakfast. If she could get him to mention his military service, she could talk about her programs. Bringing up the well-worn combat fatigues he wore was too obvious. She tried to open a door to what he thinking, but the dialogue, if you could call it that was stilted and mostly on her side.

"How long have you had this property?"

Dane had looked around the clearing for a few chews of croissant, swallowed, and settled his stare back on her. She was struck by how the bright deep blue of his eyes had disappeared, replaced by an emptiness that made them seem almost scary.

"About a year."

She waited, but he wasn't sharing anything else willingly.

Hiding a sigh, she tried again. "How big a parcel is it?"

Long pause. "Ten acres."

Again she waited. Up here, once you got people talking about their land, there usually wasn't any stopping them. You'd find out where the boundaries were, any interesting stories about it, what they planned to do with it. People up here loved to highlight the virtues of their piece of earth.

Serena looked around, searching for something else that might inspire a response of more than a staccato phrase. Asking about the pines was a bit too obvious. Everyone knew about the huge ponderosas and grays that grew at this elevation.

"Tell me about the view. What can you see from here?" There, that couldn't be answered quickly.

She remembered how Dane had picked up the iced coffee and taken a couple of sips, looking out over the canyon. He seemed to be considering how best to answer the question. Serena was hopeful, thinking maybe the door would squeak open a sliver and they would have something that resembled dialogue.

Finally, he turned back to her and with his bright blue gaze again evident, he said "Peace."

Chapter 13

The vegetable garden was extensive, containing all of the usual suspects like tomatoes and zucchini, plus a whole lot of unusual varieties of eggplants, peppers, and herbs. Serena liked helping out once in a while in Roxy's garden. Keeping her hands in the soil and watching something grow was another happy link back to her childhood.

Serena wanted to plant a big garden someday, but land around her little bungalow was at a premium. The rock of the cliff she lived on did not lend itself to flourishing growth of much other than granite gravel, and what she grew at home she grew in pots. Here, though, she could get her hands dirty. Gardening was a terrific Zen kind of experience for her. It emptied her mind and let her think.

And she had a lot of thinking to do. Her day yesterday wasn't wasted, and she knew that she wasn't being overly optimistic about the results. Dane opened up, even if it was just a little bit. His comment about the view giving him peace, and the obvious reaction he had to it if the softening of his eyes was any indication, gave her an idea about how to approach him. Once he'd shared that, he'd promptly picked up his safety goggles and earplugs and headed back to the pile of boards, selected one, measured, and turned on the table saw.

Obviously, their discussion was over for the moment.

Roxy returned from her conversation with one of her two full time gardeners. Besides using this produce and the fruit from the surrounding trees and bushes for her restaurant, she often sold specialty items to other chefs in the area, to the hotels, and through her grocery store. Someone was working almost all the time, especially on the weekends when everyone seemed to need something, and this Sunday was no exception.

"Well thankfully, the heat's broken and the breezes are back. The tomatoes hate the heat. They don't set fruit, did you know that? And the extra water that's needed doesn't necessarily help the plants, because it can leech out the nutrients in the soil too. The plants can't take it up..." Roxy trailed off.

Serena wasn't in the least bit interested in the lifecycle of tomatoes. Deep in her own thoughts, she examined the greenery in front of her as if they were the most interesting things on the planet. What were they again? Oh yeah, cucumbers.

"Serena, yoo-hoo, what's going through your brain?" Roxy tried more softly.

She had to give Roxy credit. When Serena showed up unannounced at the garden this morning, knowing that part of Roxy's Sunday ritual was a trip through the beds planning her menus for the coming week, Roxy gave her a quick hug hello and let her wander. But Serena knew she had to talk sometime.

Roxy was the only person she had told before she made her visit to Dane's yesterday. A single woman needs to make sure someone would know she was missing if something went wrong. And Serena knew her friend was being very polite so far about not asking questions. But they were there on her face every time she glanced at Serena.

"It's... Bob." She caught herself in time to avoid using Dane's real name, and the pseudonym of Bob that she had shared with Tess seemed to have become the obvious moniker. She thought back over the day and tried to figure out where to start.

"It was a really good day. I loved to get my hands on all that wood and see the framing go up for the shell of the house. It's a very interesting design – courtyard in the middle, raised a few steps above the ground with a cellar underneath. It will have great views out over the canyon." And there she stopped and looked inward again.

Roxy continued picking her way through a row of okra. Serena knew she herself was different today from her usual determined and fast-moving whirlwind, more contemplative, detached, and not engaged with what was happening around her. This most of all would concern Roxy, as she was one of the inner circle who knew about Serena's demons and the reasons that she drove herself so hard. When Serena got quiet, this kind of quiet, it usually meant that something had taken her back to the past, to a place that held both great memories and great tragedy.

Perhaps picking up on Roxy's vibes of concern, Serena glanced up and shook off her distance. A half smile settled on her face as she regarded one of her best friends. "He reminds me of Dad in some ways."

*****

The weekends were always the best times, family time they all got to spend together. Dad usually had a project in the works, which meant a trip to the hardware store and maybe the lumberyard. Mom would be cooking something special. They had a traditional division of labor, but it was clear that it satisfied them both. Their bond and their love for each other were just as obvious.

For Serena, being the only child meant she lived in both magical worlds. It wasn't unusual for her to spend part of the day with Dad in the workshop-slash-garage, building something, and then travel to Mom's world in the kitchen and contribute her share to the orchestration that was a weekend dinner. Both places felt comfortable, and most of the time it was a good life. She was loved, she was happy, and the world was a very safe place.

But there were times when things got dark. Dad's eyes didn't smile and Mom's face became pinched with worry. Sometimes during those dark times, she would go to

Aunt Liz's for the weekend. She lived close by, and she would make sure Serena got to school on Monday. When she had to stay for the school days too, it was the worst. No one talked about it or tried to hide it, but she just knew. It had been one of Dad's dark days when things finally blew apart.

*****

"Serena, are you okay honey?" Roxy looked worried.

Serena had been so deep in the past that she didn't even realize she was now standing in the middle of the vegetables, a few feet away from where she started.

Peace. Dane's single word had gotten to her. It was the same thing her dad used to say when she asked him what he wanted for his birthday or for Christmas.

Peace. When she was little, she thought he meant peace like peace on earth and goodwill to all men. Maybe he had. But as she got older, old enough to recognize the dark times for what they were, she realized it was both more and different.

Peace.

"I think I figured out how to turn a corner with Bob, based on yesterday. I was just thinking about how I could reach out to him, to reach inside him, you know?" Serena busied herself pulling some miniscule weeds from the zucchini bed but knew she wasn't fooling her friend.

"And it all took me back to the past too."

Finally, Serena looked over to see Roxy's concerned but knowing look. Without a word, the two started for the covered patio at the edge of the garden and the table holding fresh lemonade.

Settling into a rocker, Serena accepted a full glass and took a sip, grateful for a minute to get her thoughts in order. She wanted to talk about it, the feelings that the day had brought up. There wasn't a logical place to start, so she began in the middle where she'd left off earlier.

"I don't always let myself remember how good building something from scratch feels. It reminds me of… good memories. But yesterday it was more than that. And the more than that part is… Bob."

She was going to mess up and call him by his real name one of these times. But he wasn't a client – yet. And in a small town like theirs, keeping secrets was hard. Most knew other people's business, like who was receiving services and who was providing them. But they tried to keep the confidentiality in place just the same. So Bob it would be, for now.

"Is he some kind of trigger for your memories?" Roxy had draped herself across a lounge chair with her own lemonade, but she had yet to take a sip and her laser stare was intent on Serena's face.

"His eyes, they go dark and blank when he doesn't want to talk about something. Dad was like that. It was his dark side. When I was a kid, I'd try to joke him out of it when it was happening. We could tell. Sometimes he could pull himself back, and other times, well, then I'd go to visit Aunt Liz."

In the silence at the end of the sentence, dragonflies buzzed by and two hummingbirds chortled at each other in battle over a flower. The breezes were back, and coolness in the shade comforted like a balm, calming so many things.

Her mind wandered back to other memories from yesterday. The way she and Dane set a rhythm in their work, Serena placing and holding the boards across the sawhorses for measurement, then helping Dane guide them into the table saw, and finally both of them, each with an end, placing them atop the framing, a drill with a screw head in hand to secure the wood. Up and down ladders, board after board. It became a sort of dance. They hadn't said much of anything after Dane's comment about peace.

And it had been peaceful. Yes, she had been sweaty and dirty as the day progressed, but it felt like honest work. Occasionally the rhythm was broken when Dane needed to consult the plans spread across a nearby table, and in those times, they both took long drinks from the orange jug. They discussed little other than the construction.

Mostly they just worked. And it seemed that perhaps an easy camaraderie was building between them, even if they didn't say much.

It wasn't only the work, though, that had Serena thinking it had been a good day. There was no mistaking it, Dane was a good-looking man and it was a pleasure to watch him move. The fine hands she had noticed on her first visit seemed to handle each board with gentle care. Even the work gloves did nothing to dispel that observation. There was caring here, something delicate and finely tuned. It was in his deliberate attention to the measurements, the placement of each board with purpose, the few times he stopped for an instant and looked across the canyon. It was like he was handling something precious.

What would it be like to be the center of all that care, that precious consideration? Instinct and heart agreed that they would love to find out what it was. But again, this wasn't for her.

Client, think client, she chided herself.

It had been a long time, though, since she'd had such a visceral reaction to a man. Her nerves tingled and her stomach took a wild elevator ride. The flex of his muscles, revealed when he shed his t-shirt in the sun, almost made her lick her lips. Heat that had nothing to do with the searing temperature on the thermometer left her flustered and jittery.

"Is that a problem?" Roxy's question started Serena back from her wandering daydreams of a hard body pressed against hers. Roxy looked questioningly at her, and there was a trace of a smile on her face. "Is there something else going on that I should know about?"

Serena swallowed and examined the last direction of her mind's meanderings. "He's good looking, in a rugged but gentle kind of way." Meeting Roxy's now huge smile with a rueful one of her own, she settled back in the chair. She knew she wouldn't get away with saying nothing more now.

"Apart from the brief glances I've been able to take of him at the store, I wouldn't know about that. So why don't you tell me more about him."

Roxy wasn't above living vicariously through her friends when it came to romantic interests, Serena knew. As luck would have it over the past couple of years, Serena hadn't been the subject of much scrutiny or good-natured ribbing about her romantic encounters since she'd had so few dates. She had male friends, but none of them brought her that rising tremble of heat that she felt yesterday around Dane.

"He has lots of great muscles under those fatigues, at least what I could see when he took his shirt off to work in the heat yesterday. I don't know what's behind the beard, but his eyes are the most amazing deep blue when he's not, he's not..." She faltered. What would she call that dark side that brought such a dead look to his eyes?

Yes, it was like her father had been, but also not exactly the same. She started again. "I'm guessing that whenever he flashes back to whatever hurt him so much, he's looking back at that and isn't in the present anymore, if you know what I mean. Whatever it was, it was bad. When he's not thinking about it, there's a gentleness to his look. He never smiled at me yesterday, but I think at least I amused him. I surprised him, that's for sure!" Her own giggle surprised her.

"What's so funny?" Roxy's mouth quirked into its own smile. Serena relaxed a bit and played with the idea that something could develop with 'Bob'.

"I couldn't help myself, I know I was chattering away sometimes. But I'd catch him looking at me and I'd swear he was smiling, at least a little bit. And I think he liked the fact that I could actually help. We got into a good flow. I asked him if the house was going to have a second story and what the plans looked like. He didn't seem to want to share that. I probably wanted more information than he wanted to give."

"It's a good thing he's building himself a house, right? People don't usually do something like that unless they see some kind of future. Where does he live now?"

"He has this little cabin on the property – looks like it's been around for a very long time. But he has electricity and running water and indoor plumbing. Really, it's a cozy little space, like something you'd see in those little vignettes at IKEA. You know the ones – you can fit your life in three hundred square feet. But a whole lot more rustic."

"I thought you said something about a tent."

"He has that too. He has a bed in the cabin. I don't know why he has the tent too, but it's probably too hot some nights to sleep indoors. Or maybe it reminds him of his military service. Some vets keep a talisman of their service, like their haircut or wearing fatigues. Maybe he just likes to sleep on the ground."

Serena's voice drifted off and she stared out at the garden without seeing it. In the quiet, the hum of insects became obvious again and she knew Roxy wondered where her thoughts had wandered off to now.

"So it sounds like you had a good day. Are you going to try to rescue him? Date him? Or what?" Roxy reached for the pitcher of lemonade to refill their glasses, picking out some mint floating on the top for each glass. Settling back, her razor gaze returned to Serena's face as she waited.

"You know the rules. I can't date a client – that's completely against professional practices and ethics." And fiddling with her mint, Serena looked everywhere but back at Roxy.

"Serena honey, Bob's not a client, at least not yet, is he?"

Chapter 14

The clearing looked different from before, and Dane knew he should be pleased with the transformation. Shrubbery along the driveway was cut back, leaving a much wider space through the woods. The former potholed track now had a thick layer of fresh gravel that trucks had already worn smooth in parts. The shield of trees between the little shack and the house site was gone too.

What was now visible was the house itself, and what he had envisioned was turning out to be so perfect. The structure was raised off the clearing floor. A few steps up led to a deep porch that wrapped around out of view on the canyon side. The roof had a gradual slope that would shed the snows of winter well. It looked solid already, and it didn't even have its roof on yet. But it had great bones.

The trusses for the roof were installed over the past couple of days. It was one of the few things Dane had hired out. Yes, he could have built them himself, but that would have meant another winter in the cabin, and it was starting to feel a little cramped. When he first moved here, the cabin felt safe, probably more like a womb than housing. He could walk from one side to the other in eight strides.

But lately it felt confining. He couldn't see the view from its windows, and while he was sure he'd find a use for it someday, right now he was ready for something more.

Maybe Powers was right, maybe he was healing. The nightmares were fading, at least not visiting him every night.

Rubbing his eyes, Dane thought about what had replaced them. Dreams of chestnut hair, laughing hazel eyes, shapely arms swinging a hammer. A curvy figure that wrapped around him in welcome, with skin soft enough to cushion a thousand tomorrows.

Shaking his head to clear his thoughts, Dane regarded the construction zone again with a tinge of amusement. Serena wouldn't take no for an answer and showed up to help for another weekend, this time both Saturday and Sunday. She had been game to do just about anything on the house, even the grunt work of clean up. Sometimes she chattered and Dane wouldn't respond, not because he didn't like to hear her talk, but because he couldn't think of what to say.

Yes, his social skills definitely needed some work. Before all of the craziness, he had been something of a ladies' man, his attitude of detachment exotically fascinating to beautiful women in major cities all around the world.

But now he felt broken, and he didn't think that any of those same women would want him. It wasn't only the scars on his body, but the ones on his heart and his soul. He didn't think those would ever heal. And those were the ones that drove everyone away.

Of course, whatever he exposed to Serena hadn't driven her away, at least not yet.

On that second Saturday, she'd looked around the construction zone with a puzzled expression. "Where is it?"

Dane frowned, unclear what she was referring to. Rather than say a word, he leveled his eyes on her and deepened his cloudy expression.

Serena put her hands on her hips, not appearing to be the least bit put off by his mood. "You know, the boom box, the music. Every construction site has one, though what's playing depends on who's working. What kind of music do you like?"

Perplexed at this conversational direction, Dane turned back to the board he was measuring.

"How about if I bring my iPod player tomorrow? It uses batteries. My taste is eclectic, or so I've been told by my friends, and I have a little bit of everything on there. You can pick the style of music."

When he ignored her, she got that pitying look on her face. That frustrated him even more. What did she think she knew about him and what he needed?

"Come on, Dane. It's only music. It can help, you know? It's part of what makes us a society, a community. Kind of like rejoining the human race."

He didn't want to rejoin anything. That was it. He wanted one thing and one thing only.

"I told you before, I want peace. That's why I'm here. That's why I don't have any music playing." He shook his head at her, realizing his loose ponytail of long hair didn't respond well to his vigorous denial of interest. "No music. Peace!"

The vehemence in his tone was evident. It was Serena's turn to frown now. But she dropped the subject, and he congratulated himself on turning out the lights on that idea.

But the next day, she brought the iPod, and shortly into their work for the morning, she turned it on. Rock and roll from the eighties and nineties came to life out of the small speakers. Serena bopped around to the beat, singing slightly off-key as she moved through her clean up. Dane grumbled, shooting her irritated looks. She smiled back at him, and sang louder.

Grudgingly, he had to agree that the tunes brought a different lively energy to their routine. He wasn't going to admit that out loud though.

And still, he'd like to think he was getting better, that time was in fact healing him in ways he had yet to recognize. He hadn't itched to pick up his gear, but he kept everything clean and ready for use. He was sure he would never be ready to work again. But old habits from years of service didn't disappear easily.

Moving towards the house, Dane's mind wandered back to Serena. She definitely stirred something in him, some need to feel better about himself. He hadn't answered any of her occasional questions about his past. She was curious, but she wasn't pushy. She suggested going out to dinner, not once but three times now. She wasn't giving up on him, which was interesting in and of itself. Why was she so persistent? And she seemed to respect the fact that he wasn't willing to talk about his past and not much about his present either. The future didn't even come up.

She brought up long-buried feelings, like the pleasure of having a nice meal with a gorgeous woman who also intrigued him. She brought a sense of recognition awake in him, a feeling he couldn't recall ever having before. Physical interest and a stirring inside made things more interesting, but there was also a linking of minds that he hadn't felt in years and thought he'd never feel again. Serena was under his skin, which alternately crawled with the exposure and heated with the thought of pulling her even closer.

But it wasn't for him. Relationships, even simple friendships, he didn't deserve. It was better that way, better that no one could see how easy it was for him to turn his back on human beings. He could walk away from family, or crawl away from friends during battle, and screw the consequences. It was best not to dwell on a future, other than building this fortress for his solitude.

And best to turn others, especially Serena, away before they learned about the real Dane, the man he was today and what he'd been willing to do.

Darkness returned with the thought, and he felt a deep ache of disappointment expand in his chest. Why her, and why now? Maybe things weren't really getting better after all.

Chapter 15

Dane could hear a truck rumbling up the new gravel on the drive. He wasn't expecting anyone today, and in fact, he didn't want interruptions to intrude on his current sense of pain and doom. It was a comfort to him, something he understood better than the pleasant thoughts of Serena he'd been harboring recently. Ducking into the cabin, he let the place go quiet.

The interior was dark and no one could see into the old wavy glass windows. Dane peered out a corner of the glass to watch his brother step down from the cab of a big company pick-up, logo emblazoned on the door, a huge smile on his face. And as if he couldn't wait to see what other surprises were waiting, Powers headed for the new construction with anticipation obvious in his rapid steps.

Since he was moving fast, Powers almost passed the cabin when the door opened. Dane didn't say anything, moving on leaden feet from the protection of the doorway. He knew his eyes were guarded, distant, and dark. He stopped a few feet short of Powers and stared, the smile fading from his brother's face and replaced by anger and uncertainty.

From the questions evident in his expression, Dane knew Powers was wondering how bad today was. It had been a rough couple of days when the depression cascaded over him like a tsunami, brought on by the earthquakes of feelings he was discovering he had for Serena. Dane had examined the haunted shadows under his eyes in the tiny mirror he kept in a cabinet. He was holding himself together by sheer will.

"Hey Dane, how are you?"

Powers neared two steps and Dane responded by retreating two steps back. They both stopped in unison. With a forced smile back on his face, Powers tried again.

"You've got trusses on the house. It looks great. You're making incredible progress. When does the roof go on?" His voice sounded too enthusiastic.

Dane knew what would come next, knew the direction this conversation with Powers would take. What he wanted to ask was how Dane was, if he was sleeping, if he was eating right. If the nightmares had stopped. If he had enough of everything, whatever that was. He knew he'd never get answers to those questions, but the house, news about the house should be safe.

Run or stay? Stay here or move? Dane needed to decide.

With a suddenness that made Powers jerk, Dane turned and walked towards the new house at a fast pace. In a second Powers was following him. Neither one said a word. At least he wasn't running back to the cabin and slamming the door in his brother's face, Dane reasoned. That was better, right?

As they got closer, the changes in the house would be obvious. Powers would see that the exterior walls were already up, and the interior was ready for plumbing and electrical work. Once the roof was on, the house would take shape quickly. Dane was working fast. At this rate, he'd be able to move in before the worst of the winter weather rolled in. He hoped that this was enough for Powers to leave him alone.

His progress on his own insides, on his heart and his acceptance of the cold emptiness of his remaining life, was at a total standstill.

Stopping at the base of the steps, Dane turned and looked hard at his brother. "Is there something you need, Powers? Something you want? Or just checking up on your crippled deranged brother?"

The level of bitterness in Dane's voice surprised them both. This was not progress. This was the same kind of hostility that had been evident when Dane was first recovering.

A bad day for sure.

He recognized disappointment in the bitter taste in his mouth. He wanted to get better. But it didn't look like things were moving in a positive direction right now.

He continued his angry tirade to the still-silent Powers. "I'm doing fine, and even if I wasn't, it's my business, not yours. You don't need to check up on me. If I need you, I know how to find you. What I don't need to anyone snooping around. I get enough uninvited guests as it is."

Powers remained still, accepting the animosity his little brother was spewing. Grief crossed his face, and he held himself in check with obvious difficulty, probably ready to say something vicious in return.

He wanted to find some link to his brother again. After their mother died and Powers started college, they had been distant for years, siblings living under the same roof but not really connecting. It had taken them a decade to get close enough again for civil conversations. Then the war and Dane's choices had driven them apart once more.

Instead of saying anything, Powers shoved past Dane and took the unfinished front steps of the house two at a time. He followed the porch around the house and out of sight. It was obvious that he expected Dane to follow him if he wanted to continue the battle. It was easier to give him time to explore the house and cool down before they both said something unforgiveable.

Grudgingly, he appreciated the fact that Powers kept coming back for more, even when his good intentions were shoved back in his face. It didn't used to be like this. They'd been decent to each other, not something that all brothers could say. Not friends exactly, but the events of the past two years had changed everything between them, perhaps irrevocably.

Holding still just in case he let out any of his tightly protected emotions, Dane breathed slowly in an attempt to control what felt oddly like tears. After his satisfaction with the look of the house morphed into daydreaming turned sour about Serena yesterday, the demons decided to pay another visit. It had been a restless night filled with dreams of blood and screams, and he'd woken up more than once with his throat feeling raw. He was sure that he had screamed himself hoarse in the night.

Some nights were just… unbearable.

He thought he was past the worst of it, memories of the Korengal, of Anderson, of his own actions that he tried to forget. The career he couldn't or wouldn't return to. It was another choice he'd made. He knew it all pissed off his brother. Powers wanted things to go according to some kind of plan.

But most of all, he knew his brother ached for him.

With a deep sigh, Dane put a boot on the bottom step. He was weary of the fighting, all of it, brawling with his brother, struggling against his own emotions, battling the depression that threatened to swamp him. He was at a crossroads and he knew it. He could either continue to turn away, or he could try to make some headway.

A picture of Serena suddenly flashed in his mind. Her smiling face, the satisfaction when she looked at the work they'd done together, the intent stare he'd caught more than once. There was an awareness there, an interest. She felt something too, that pull of intrigue that also kept Dane up some nights.

Another good reason to get his act together.

Rubbing his face and deep in thought, Dane encountered the beard he had neglected for so long. It itched. Maybe it was time for a little bit more change on a lot of levels. It could wait, though.

Stepping up on the porch, he dragged his feet towards the corner where Powers had disappeared out of sight.

*****

"I'm sorry, man."

Dane surprised himself with his words more than he seemed to shock Powers. His big brother was taking in the view overlooking the canyon off the house's incomplete back porch. It was spectacular. At least his brother could see what had attracted Dane to this plot of land in the first place. He'd always liked open spaces, letting his eyes wander on vistas and taking in the little details that other people missed. That was one of the very special things about his talent, his sense of a place settled in one rapid blink.

Powers turned and locked eyes with Dane for a few breaths. Concern and pain ravaged his face, an echo of the dark despair Dane knew filled his own eyes. It was hard to be mad at his brother when he was trying to wipe out immeasurable sorrow.

Seeming to search for the right words to say, Powers turned back to the view and sat down on the edge of the porch, his long legs dangling. "I can see why you bought this place. It feels like you're one of those buzzards making lazy circles on the updrafts, closer to flying than standing on land." He let the silence settle, as if he found some neutral subject, Dane would sit down too and they could talk, really talk, as they hadn't in a long time.

The silence stretched for a couple of minutes, filled only with the whisper of a slight breeze and the occasional bird cry. Giving up the stiffness and the desire to soldier on by himself was hard. Dane fought it, wanting to maintain the distance he so resolutely thought he needed.

How long would it take, he wondered, before Powers would tire of this and burst out with one of his platitudes again? 'Things would get better.' 'You just need to keep going and look at the positives.' 'It's time to get back to normal.' Not only had he heard them all before in the last two years, but he'd been hearing them for nearly his whole life since their mother died.

The weariness of battling on alone was crushing, but he thought it was what he should do. He'd taint anyone he let get too close to him. Of course, Powers knew the worst and kept coming back for more.

Serena was an innocent, and she needed to be protected.

Funny that she should pop into his mind right now, an uninvited and surprising addition to his celebration of self-loathing. If he wanted to be better for her, to see where that might lead, he needed to find his way back, step by step. It was like lining up that perfect shot. Sometimes you didn't get it right the first time. But you could always keep shooting.

Dane took a seat on the decking a few feet away from where his brother still stared out over the valley. The sun this morning was warm and gentle, not yet baking as it would in the later hours of the day. The two sat in silence, neither one willing to break the tentative truce.

"It still hurts, you know?" Dane's voice was muffled and hoarse. He was trying to hold back powerful emotions, memories that were never far away. After a couple of deep breaths, he continued.

"The physical pain in almost gone. My legs healed well, despite the extent of the original injuries. It could have been a whole lot worse. Now there are just the battle scars, but no one sees those. At least, not the ones on the outside."

Surprisingly, Powers held his tongue. This was the closest Dane had been able to come to describing how he was feeling. They'd had an emotional explosion after the bomb-related one, with Powers furious about Dane's professional and personal choices while Dane was sullen and hurting. Since then, the two had been polite but distant with one another. Powers certainly had no idea how Dane was really doing right now because Dane hadn't been sharing.

"How are you feeling on the inside these days?" Powers asked, his voice flat and non-judgmental.

Dane pondered this for a while. He kept his face closed and emotionless, but a small tick started near his left eye. He was agitated, but he thought he was doing a good job of hiding it.

"Some days are good – scratch that, there are more good days than bad days now. On good days, I don't think about anything at all. My mind's a blank. On bad days, I think about it all the time. You just happened to hit me on a bad day." He paused with a rough sigh. "A really bad day."

"What happened? Did something happen to make it a bad day? There's progress all around you. If you want some crews to come up and make the job go faster, you just need to say so." Powers was doing what he always did, trying to fix things and ease Dane's way.

"Just too much thinking time. Most of the time I can keep my mind a blank, but I was thinking about a future that's not for me. Remembering some happy times and some not so happy. It brought back the nightmares, and when that happens, sleep is not my friend."

A rueful twist stretched Dane's face now, and he tried to make it friendlier than the blank canvas he had cultivated a few minutes before.

"Are you getting any help, someone professional to talk to?" Powers turned to stare at Dane intently, and his intensity communicated itself across the feet dividing them. He seemed to expect much more than the simple question indicated.

"Someone stopped by, but I don't want to sit around talking about how bad it was in-country and how no one understands stateside what happened, the changes a man goes through. And I don't want to talk about what happened to me. It happened, I made my choices, and nothing can change that." He suppressed the surge of anger, though he realized that he might not be mad at Powers, but with himself. It would be something to consider later, when he had his solitude back.

"Maybe talking will make it easier. You know, get it out in the open so that it isn't so dark inside anymore."

Hell, Powers had no idea if what he was saying was the right thing, but he was being Powers and trying to fix things, as was his way, and at least they weren't currently fighting. Dane supposed he should be grateful for that.

"Talking just makes me think about it, and I don't want to think about it. End of story."

And with that, Dane stood up and turned towards an entrance to the house. His mask again in place and his emotions hidden, he asked Powers politely if he'd like a tour of the house before he left.

Powers stood as well and politely said that of course, he'd love a tour of the place, but Dane could tell that inside he was fuming. His fists tightened at his sides and he held himself ramrod straight, as if relaxing anything would allow his anger to escape. Dane often brought out that anger, though for a long time, they had been able to work past it.

They were never going to get past this, Dane realized with a shock. The feeling left him empty again.

"Are you sure you don't need some professional help? I hear there's a great organization in town, something called Balance. They come highly recommended." Powers stopped abruptly. Dane was sure it was his own cold dark stare that made him shut his mouth.

He stepped up toe to toe and nose to nose with Powers, and he could feel the simmering rage coming off his older brother. His own outrage was fueling him, but he was determined to keep it civil. Dane was certain Powers would try to fix this too, force him into some kind of treatment program when the only thing he wanted was to be left alone. Over twenty years later after their mother died, and Powers was still trying to run his life.

Unclenching his teeth enough to speak, he let his blue eyes blaze into dark browns and ground out each word with menace in his voice.

"I, do, not, need, any, help!"

Chapter 16

The e-mail on the screen laid it out pretty clearly. Somehow, Vision Quest knew that Dane wasn't receiving services. They were not happy about this. A Ms. Simpson, the executive director, was asking for a full report of all activities that the funds Vision Quest had donated were being used for, and particularly wanted a progress report on outreach and services for Dane. And she reminded Serena quite succinctly that the only real requirement tied to the funding was that Balance help this one man.

Eduardo summed it up pretty well. "Just who is this guy and why are they so adamant that the money came with these particular strings attached?"

Serena didn't have a clue. She was providing the biweekly funding reports required as a condition of the grant. That wasn't unusual, thought perhaps every other week rather than monthly was more frequent than other foundations asked for. But why would they be so specific about helping one individual in particular, by name, when the need was much broader in the community?

There were a lot of local vets, some of them from wars past and many more from the recent battles, who needed help. As often happened in a volunteer army, the ones who felt the call to action in this rural community were from salt of the earth families, farmers, ranchers, agricultural workers, and sons and daughters of career military parents. They attempted to resettle in this relative peace and quiet once their tours were behind them and they were thinking about what to do with the rest of their lives.

What they saw, even in the calmest theaters of action, changed them, and that change was permanent.

Some were able to keep their sense of humor and their ability to interact with society, and the changes weren't as apparent to the outside world. Others came back broken, sullen, and acting out at the slightest provocation. Most fell somewhere in between and sometimes what turned things for the worse was an innocent remark or a perceived snub. It didn't take much to be right back in the heat of things, dark things that no person should have to endure.

Balance helped them cope, to find a different way of dealing with the triggers that brought out the bad side. Most were able to get help and life went on. They had a much greater appreciation for the simple things in life than before their military days, and they could move past what they saw during their duty and have successful family lives and careers.

For a few, counseling was a continuous and necessary support so that they could function.

But it was highly unusual to find a funder being so specific about a single person, by name, granted by first name only but the other details had been specific enough for Serena to find him.

Sitting back in her chair, Serena thought again about the two sides she'd seen of Dane. There was the silent but seemingly upbeat Dane, the one whose eyes glowed blue and beneath that beard, probably smiled, at least a little bit. He was still quiet, but it was a friendly kind of quiet, or at least she thought so. He didn't turn away when she chattered on, even if sometimes it was nonsense coming out of her mouth. He put up with her and didn't seem to mind.

Then there was his darker side. His eyes were like coals then, dead and distant. He didn't tolerate anything well when he was in one of those moods, not even gestures of friendship. She hadn't seen that dark side when she'd kept their discussions simple. When she was there on business trying to help him formally or asked about his past, though, she struck a nerve. He didn't want her help in that way.

Sure, nailing a board in place or sawing something was fine. But don't talk about anything too personal.

"Where were you raised?"

When she'd asked it on Sunday as they broke for lunch, Dane frowned and turned a stony gaze in her direction.

The day before, she'd asked about his military garb. There weren't any patches on the shoulders, no insignias to mark his service unit.

His response had been to turn his back, put the plugs in his ears and power up the table saw.

On one trip down the ladder, Dane stumbled. The unexpected stream of curses shocked her into standing absolutely still. He massaged his thigh. She stared, wondering what it would feel like to comfort him with gentler caresses, the idea giving her chills down her spine even as her insides heated.

When she asked if he was okay, he turned dark and empty eyes to stare into hers and said nothing.

She wondered what had hurt him so badly.

And she wondered why none of the veterans' services agencies that usually reached out to Balance to help a soldier like Dane had been in touch. Either Dane had been involved in something that needed to be kept below the radar, or it was so bad that no one was willing to talk about it. But usually, good or bad, the soldier was cared for, particularly if he was wounded.

Maybe that's what it was, Serena pondered, the cycle of thoughts running round inside her head until she visualized an overactive hamster. Maybe he did something so wrong that he was dishonorably discharged and didn't want anyone to probe for the reasons. Still, he needed to talk about it, needed Balance's help.

She felt that stirring again, that need to make things right for Dane in a way that was much more than her usual compassion. It wasn't for Dane alone, but for the two of them together, to give them time to explore their mutual attraction and intense interest.

If he was a client, she couldn't go there.

Her personal feelings warred with her professional standards as she gnawed on the end of her pen and tapped out a generic e-mail response to Ms. Simpson. Hitting send, she leaned back in her chair and set her eyes blindly on the middle space of a poster of Lake Tahoe that covered the opposite wall.

She respected what Dane was doing in building his own house. She was curious about what he did for money, because clearly he had enough to afford whatever he seemed to need for the project. There was no hint of borrowed tools or waiting for cheap lumber to become available as a castoff of someone else's construction. He wielded the nail guns, drills, and saws on the worksite as if they were an extension of him.

"Where did you learn to build things?" The question was harmless enough.

He turned away and replied, "Hand me that board, would you please?"

"No really, I'm curious. You must have had some profession in the trades, right?"

He shook his head and measured twice, then drilled a hole through the board. He never answered her question, but it was obvious he was no stranger to the work.

She wanted what was best for him. Delving into what brought him to this point of isolation in his life was important for him to move on from whatever it was. He'd be healthier and perhaps happier if he got it out in the light of day where the demons could be seen for what they were, tricks of shadows and darkness.

But if she was honest, she also wanted him to feel better for purely selfish reasons. There was something about Dane that called to her, strumming along her nerves until she felt keyed up and antsy. She liked him. When they connected, she could feel the unrelenting pull of emotional magnetism when he turned warm blue eyes on her.

Those times were too rare.

The man he showed her on those occasions made her ache with longing. The woman in her appreciated the body he did his best to hide, even in the summer's heat. Client or not, she knew that the vague humming on both levels would continue until she did something about it.

But, as Roxy said, he wasn't a client right now, was he?

Chapter 17

Early morning sunshine streamed through the windows of the Brew Bank Bakery. It lit up the cases of breakfast muffins, cupcakes, and pastries in an almost holy glow. Almost everyone who walked into the shop left feeling like they'd had a religious experience too. There was something about the aroma of so much buttery, creamy goodness that could make any day seem divinely blessed.

Serena heard the familiar jingle of the Christmas bells hung inside the door quiet as she stopped just inside. Their cheerful notes brought Sarge out from the back, his stout middle-aged body dressed in a white shirt and apron. The color did nothing to hide the dusting of flour down the front. His face already smiling, he broke into a huge grin and clapped his hands when he saw who was standing in front of the full cases. Flour dust puffed around him and added a halo surrounding his round face and another layer of white to his bald head.

"Serena, Serena, Serena, you are still too skinny. Obviously we need to feed you more!"

Coming around the counter, Sarge grabbed Serena in a bear hug. After putting in his twenty years in the Army and seeing tours that covered every hot spot in the world during that time, Sarge had been one of the first clients of Balance. He returned from his tours confused, still hiding secrets about himself and trying to forget the worse parts of what he had done over the years. He credited Balance with helping him to find himself, find a life partner in his Stuart, and find an unlikely profession he loved, baking. It made Serena proud to see where he had taken his life and most of all, to see him happy.

"I don't think I can eat much more, Sarge! Even at this rate, I risk having to buy a whole new wardrobe every couple of months!"

Serena couldn't help herself, though, and soon she was closely examining the various goodies in the cases. Thoughts about taking a breakfast to the worksite expanded to snacks and dinner and dessert too.

"So what's happening? I hear from some of the vets that Balance is having some money trouble. Anything we can do to help? Sponsor a fundraiser or something?" Sarge already had a big box in hand, loading up a few savory pastries he knew to be Serena's favorites. Then he waited patiently as she tapped her cheek and stared, deep in thought at the decisions to be made.

What kind of pie for dessert?

"Thanks for the offer. You know that I appreciate all that you do for Balance and for our clients. Your pep talks to the current folks really help them see that there is a good life waiting for them."

While she had never taken her eyes off the baked goods, she knew Sarge would be looking concerned. He felt connected to Balance, as did so many of the vets and others in the community who had benefited from its services. She was grateful for that. If she could harness all of that positive thinking, all of the benefits that people had achieved, just think of how powerful it could be.

The 'before Balance', and the after.

She even had some of the pictures to prove it. When shootings in the mental health department of a neighboring county brought about a change in state law, Balance had needed to take photos for identification of their new clients before they began receiving services.

Those photos told stories by themselves. The pain, shame and confusion were evident in the lines on people's faces, the anger in the set of head on shoulders, the hurts they were trying to conquer in the grief in their eyes. The change, once they had come to terms with their pasts and learned how to deal with life's current challenges, was phenomenal.

If only there was a way to capture that visible change and tell their stories.

Lost in thought that didn't involve the pie options for tonight, Serena only came back to the present when the bells on the door jingled again for another customer.

"I'll let you know if there's anything you can do, Sarge, and I really appreciate all of your support! Now about those quiches…"

Chapter 18

The view from the drive up to the house was different today. New rocks crunched under the wheels of Serena's SUV, and she jammed on the brakes when she entered the clearing. The trees that had formed a barrier between the cabin and the new house were gone, and the view was stunning. From a distance, the house seemed to float at the edge of the canyon, with the interesting roof lines making it appear like it had grown from the very rock it was sitting on.

Dane lingered in the door of the shack. Her smile of greeting passed over him, intent on returning to her examination of the house. Her eyes snapped back to him quickly.

The ragged beard was now trimmed and his hair was shorter in his traditional ponytail. He'd replaced his usual fatigues with a white short-sleeve shirt that buttoned down the front, and shorts that were still long, but no longer camis.

She was excited by the changes to the house, but she was more intrigued and taken with the changes in the man. He'd moved away from the shadows of the cabin out into the sunlight. A shiver of something powerful ran through her and left her shaky. He looked good, too damn good for her equilibrium.

Flinging the door open, Serena tumbled out of the truck laughing, doing a little dance of excitement as she looked at the house.

"You've changed – you look awesome! And you're ready for the roof – it's ready for the roof!"

She yelled it all out in wonder as she ran to Dane. That feeling of delight in the progress was overwhelming, and she couldn't stop herself from throwing her arms around him.

And without a thought, she pulled his face down to hers and kissed him.

Another tingle of excitement that had nothing to do with the house shot through her. Unconsciously, Serena meant the kiss to be quick, a sign of friendship and camaraderie, shared joy in what the house was becoming. But once she had her lips on Dane's, the stirring of attraction, a rollercoaster ride in her stomach, took over.

She tilted her head and began to explore the contours of his lips, the slight rasp of the edges of beard and moustache on her skin a new sensation. He tasted of coffee and man, his scent coming to her in waves of soap and something else that was subtle, a fresh and earthy scent that she'd come to associate with Dane. He alone was enough to set her hormones humming and the rollercoaster went for another round.

Dane hadn't moved. His arms were still at his sides. Serena realized that at some level, he was probably in shock at her actions.

To some degree, so was she.

He wasn't resisting and wasn't jumping back, though, and finally his lips moved tentatively over hers. After a few moments, his arms came up around her in slow motion. They moved over her back, molding her form to his, and he tucked her in a little closer.

His lips began their own exploration in turn, subtle movement and delicious pressure, and soon he was taking and Serena was giving. He tasted deadly, feeding a craving she didn't even know she had until now. Serena felt her heart rate pick up and shivers of anticipation glided through her.

Dane abruptly pulled back and gave himself a shake. Setting his hands on her upper arms, he moved

Serena away from him. His bright blue gaze settled on Serena's wide hazel eyes for a second, long enough for her to see that his hunger matched hers. Then he took three steps back, turned away and strode quickly into the cabin, shutting the door quietly without ever uttering a word.

Standing rooted to the spot where he left her, Serena wasn't sure what just happened. For someone who always tried to be in command of her emotions, she didn't know what to do with this current sense of longing. It was just a spontaneous kiss. There was a hint of promise, a taste of wildness coupled with a yearning that made her hungry for more. Putting a hand to her stomach, she willed the rollercoaster to stop, but it was on wild ride and didn't seem to want to quit any time soon.

As a shiver ran through her again, she turned to look at the house. The trusses made a world of difference in turning what had been a simple framed structure into its future promise. Just like the changes in Dane's appearance gave some signs of promise too. He looked more controlled with his hair and his beard trimmed. The scruffy look before had worked for him. She'd been attracted to him, but she'd put it aside. The new appearance underscored his rugged good looks and brought her physical attraction front and center where she couldn't ignore it.

It was more than that, though. She sensed a deep pool of feelings in him. His sense of beauty and art was clear in the design of the house, one he said was his own inspiration. His appreciation of the vastness of the canyon below, and his attention to the very little things, like pointing out a hummingbird hovering over a wildflower or his little smile of joy as they watched a doe and fawn still in spots explore the edges of the forest, spoke of his gentleness without words. The tentative way he accidently touched her when they were working, like he thought her made of fine china, made her feel treasured.

Client? She didn't want him to be a client now for purely selfish reasons. She wanted him. Oh god, what had she done now?

With another harder shiver, Serena looked at the silent cabin with its forbidding dark door in indecision. She felt awkward. Go or stay? Stay and say what? Or do what?

Because there were plenty of things she wanted to do with the Mr. Mystery Vet.

*****

Dane leaned against the closed door, breathing hard. The kiss had surprised him. Shocked him. And while it stopped him in his tracks, it also pulled him forward. It had been a long time since he'd kissed a woman and much longer since he'd wanted to let the kiss grow into more.

He'd been embedded in country for only nine months, but since that fateful day when things literally blew up around him, his only lengthy female contact had been with doctors and nurses and therapists in the hospitals and rehab facilities. And frankly, when they were cleaning up after him early on, taking care of him after the surgeries, or putting him through his paces in rehab, sex was the last thing on his mind. He hadn't felt a stir, hadn't wanted to do much more than yell at them when they wanted him to work harder, or on those rare occasions, ignore them when they showed interest in him beyond his medical condition.

Since then, he hadn't felt a single nudge of interest. The oftentimes-gory curiosity some women displayed for what had happened to him turned him off. And since he began his self-imposed exile, he'd become the kind of man that women tended to look at with pity. Or they looked through him as if he wasn't there at all, and the feeling was mutual.

Until Serena.

Low and behold, his body today had a completely different idea. He looked down at himself, half-staff and tenting out his shorts. And he didn't think the cause was kissing just any woman, but specifically kissing Serena.

Thinking about her brought another stir. At least some part of him seemed to have a good idea of what it wanted. His bark of self-derisive laughter broke off on a curse.

His brain needed to catch up and make some of its own decisions.

Moved to action even if he didn't want to leave the safety of his enclosed space, Dane paced to the far wall of the cabin, turned and came back to the door. He sorted through pictures of Serena in his mind. The humorous Serena telling him funny stories about the various people in town, filled with obvious deep caring and respect for those she knew so well. The poignant tales she told of her Balance clients, always keeping their identities hidden but again, invested in their personal happiness and success.

Then there was the hard working construction goddess, covered in sawdust or wiping beads of sweat off her neck. His mind's eye fixed on the trail a droplet would take down her smooth skin. Damn. The stirring took the form of a full body shake this time, and he tried to turn his heated thoughts to the mundane.

She knew a lot about working with wood, and she'd been willing to follow his directions on the house, picking up on his rhythm in the building process. Without being asked, she took on whatever needed doing next. He'd worked with plenty of men growing up in his father's construction business who were wimpier than Serena. She soldiered on through the heat of the later part of the days without a single complaint.

This newly discovered sexy Serena, though, was a surprise.

Scratch that, he recognized she was good looking from the moment he'd laid eyes on her in Roxy's. If he was honest with himself, he realized that he recognized that pull of physical attraction in those first few seconds. Seeing her again when she first came to recruit him to her vets program only confirmed it.

The construction worker duds of shorts and sleeveless tanks had done nothing to hide her figure and her strength. But there was much more than the physical side of her beauty. She was beautiful inside too. All wrapped up in one terrific package.

For the first time in almost three years, fascination with a specific female was in the picture.

Tired of pacing, Dane stopped and rubbed his temples. His heart was beating too fast and the stirring he'd felt before had escalated to a full-fledged hard-on. He wanted to act on it, and it terrified him at the same time. Besides, in his experience, women who made the first move didn't take kindly to being tossed aside. By now, she'd probably driven away. That thought deflated him quickly.

He screwed this up royally. She shocked and surprised him, in a very good way. He reacted without any sense, running away when he should have stayed and made that lip lock the first of many.

Arousal stirred again as he thought about the kiss.

It was silent outside the cabin, no crunch or spit of gravel to mark Serena's flight. Truth be told, he was too wrapped up in sensations that felt foreign to be aware of much. Yes, she was probably long gone by now. He told himself it didn't matter, though the weird ache where his heart seemed to be and the reaction stirring in his shorts made him recognize that his head was lying to the rest of him.

He was already missing her.

It would be for her own good. Sever the attraction before anything started. He was still too broken to be good for anyone.

Damn it, but if it really was better this way, why did he feel this unfamiliar hurt inside? He put his back to the door again, confusion taking over as his reigning emotion, locking him up in a prison of uncertainty about what to do next.

And that's when he heard it.

*****

Serena wondered if he was ever going to come out of the cabin. She could hear him pacing in there, his boots thudding on the wood floor. A time or two, she thought she heard muttering and curses as well.

She'd crossed a line, not intentionally or consciously, but a hard line nonetheless. If she wanted to get Dane help, more help than she alone could provide, she'd have to set her own feelings aside. If he wanted help, he deserved it.

The thought made her cringe with regret, a personal loss that left her cold and clammy in the warm morning air.

First, she needed to get him out of the cabin. Maybe she could talk to him, let him know that, what, she was stepping back? Or maybe that Balance would be there for him, no matter what? That should reassure him.

The thought that she would be there for him too, no matter what, followed close behind.

The scent of savory quiches, still warm from the bakery, carried to her on the next gust of breeze. Breakfast. She eyed her SUV, its driver door still hanging open. The boxes with the quiches sat on the front seat in the rising sun.

Picking up the boxes by their neatly tied string, she walked nearer to the firmly closed cabin door and raised her voice.

"Hey, I brought breakfast, something different! How do you feel about quiche?"

For more than a few beats, she waited. The cabin door opened slowly. Dane stared at her, silent in the cabin's shadow. He nodded once and angled his body away from her to walk to the unfinished house. Climbing the stairs, he eased himself down on the edge of the porch and stared off into the distance.

Serena let out the breath she wasn't even aware she'd been holding. Damn, after that kiss, all he did was walk away, sit down, and expect her to bring breakfast to him. But then again, she'd offered.

Damn him. Damn her too.

*****

They shared the quiches sitting on the edge of the deck, looking north and west through the new clearing and back down the drive. After a few silent bites, he grunted.

"These are good." He paused, waiting a few beats. "Even if real men don't eat quiche."

She glanced at him sideways, puzzled. He'd never tried to make a joke before.

His beard didn't completely hide his grin, and her sudden answering smile had him stirring again. The sudden wash of gratefulness for her stubbornness, staying instead of leaving as he was sure she'd wanted to, chased his joy. He didn't want her pity, but damned if he could figure out exactly what he did want, other than another one of those kisses.

*****

By the time they tried their iced mochas, Dane was feeling talkative. Legs hanging, they discussed the house, how the roofing would be done this coming week, what they could work on that day, supplies that would be needed for the next steps.

They talked about anything but the kiss. When her thoughts wandered in that direction, she felt as awkward and tongue-tied as a teenager. Tension became heavy until they moved back to a safe topic.

A few minutes later, Dane fell silent, and his expression locked down into the blankness that shut her out so completely.

"What made you decide on a tile roof?"

Serena was determined to break his dark mood. She picked the last of the quiche crumbs out of the bakery box and made an elaborate effort to get every little bit of residue off her fingers with a balled up napkin. She'd only met his gaze a couple of times while they were eating. When she had, a look sizzled between them and they'd both turned away quickly.

Dane watched her intently as a crumb made its way from the box to her finger, then her finger to her lips, and he was slow to respond. Serena shivered at the distracted glare in his eyes, the hunger that was new and raw.

She'd love to satisfy that hunger. One kiss and she'd turned into some kind of sex fiend. She imagined him licking that crumb off her finger, off her lips. Heat hit her core and her breath quickened.

In the silence after her question, birds cheeped again in the trees. It wasn't an uncomfortable silence. It's like they both knew that eventually, Dane would answer. Serena looked down into the dirt, up at the sky, into the trees, everywhere but at him. But finally, she couldn't avoid it any longer.

Dane's vivid blue eyes were on her face, and longing and regret flashed in his expression before he suppressed them. His stare grew distant but he didn't break her gaze. A tremor passed through him, and then he broke away to look down the driveway with a sigh that seemed to bring him back from a place far away.

"It's safer from a fire perspective. It will keep the house cooler in the summer and warmer in the winter. And it fits the overall style. There'll be stucco on the outside and the courtyard in the middle. The tile works, makes it look like a Spanish hacienda, which was the style I was going for." His voice was a monotone, and he didn't look back to her.

Now it was Serena's turn to brood silently. The deep blue of his eyes and intensity of his look before had shocked her. It was such a contrast to his black emptiness. That intensity reached out to her, and she realized that her breath was coming too fast. The effort it cost her to rein in her feelings burned off all of the calories of her quiche, and probably more. And the neutrality of his response was a sharp contrast to his previous air of intense interest.

She tried to focus on safe topics again. "What's going to happen with the space in the middle, the courtyard?"

"A fountain or some kind of water feature. I know I want it there, but I haven't gotten to the point of knowing what 'it' is yet."

And he almost smiled. Still, though, he didn't look back at her, moving his gaze any place but towards her.

It was clear that the house, the idea of it both as a refuge and an outlet, made him happy. He seemed a lot calmer when he talked about it and when he worked on it. The restless thrum of energy without a channel was quieted when he was busy building.

Serena was surprised. Builder Dane was a very different from the one his neighbor had complained about. He didn't seem violent. He didn't seem crazy. She glanced around the clearing in the strengthening morning sun.

"Do you ever get any wildlife visiting? You know, deer, or foxes, or, uh, anything else?"

Now he definitely looked amused. "Are you afraid of something bigger than a fox or a bobcat surprising us?"

She thought back to the neighbors' reports of screams during the night.

"No, not at all, really not at all." But she looked over her shoulder again, and vowed to pay a little more attention to her surroundings. Anything could be lurking in the brush, causing the commotion at night. It didn't have to be Dane, right?

Dane picked up their boxes from breakfast, folding them flat and taking them inside the cabin. The quiet interlude was over, and it was back to the business of building. Serena rose too and, surprised at the moisture on her palms, she rubbed them dry on her shorts. She didn't usually get nervous, but the whole morning had been unsettling. First the kiss, then this pleasantly relaxed side of Dane, and then thoughts of what could be causing the screams.

Forget the rollercoaster. She had a whole damn amusement park full of rides playing with her emotions today.

Chapter 19

Everyone seemed to need a break this week, and rather than wait for Friday, they met up at DK's barn of a house on Tuesday night. Serena suggested it. In fact, she'd just about demanded the girl tribe evening. Gabby couldn't make it – the first parent-teacher night for the new school year required her presence. As a single parent of a very active young son, she missed their girl tribe meetings more often than any of the others. On the upside, Roxy's was closed as usual on Tuesday, so Roxy herself had a night off to enjoy.

"Come see the latest piece, the one I'm doing for the new winery owners at Witch Hill. They want to unveil it at their first crush event next month." DK grabbed Serena's arm and headed for the old barn that served as her studio. Tess linked arms with Roxy and they strolled more slowly behind.

"So tell me what Serena said," Roxy whispered to Tess when they had fallen behind.

"She's not saying much, which is not like her. Something about how odd the weekend was. Then she was quiet until a client came into her office and she got all business-like and signed off. But she was the one who wanted to get together tonight. She seemed kind of – I don't know, urgent – about it too."

"Maybe she got some additional funding for Balance."

"Or maybe the board pulled the plug. She doesn't seem like she's upset in that kind of way though. If it was Balance, I think she'd be nervous or jittery or chatty. It's like she's holding herself still instead."

Serena heard their furtive whispering as DK guided her around the metal sculpture's pieces, explaining what still needed to be done. DK's black lab Fusion was sitting patiently to one side, seeming to observe the work as well, until Serena stopped beside him. Serena looked as directed, nodding, exclaiming over the work. She patted Fusion's head absently.

Inside, she was far away, the slide show playing in her head very different from the view of the hundred-year-old barn filled with metal and welding equipment.

"Hey, that's really coming along! Look at the detail in these grape leaves!" Roxy clapped her hands in excitement at the almost completed structure in front of them. Tess joined in the noisy oohs and aahs. DK pointed and explained and pointed some more, and there was a flurry of activity when the top portion of the installation was discussed.

DK's need for input on the piece she was creating ruled the loud interchange. Serena listened with only a fraction of her usual attention. Something about lust and sexy and needing some passionate inspiration. Her mind locked on the memory of the kiss, the searing quality of Dane's lips on hers. His abrupt departure and his later bright blue stares were sending mixed messages. The tingles brought on by those memories had her breathing fast.

Tess started them all for the house with laughter and big grins. That's when they seemed to notice that Serena was with them in body only. She stood to the side and stared unseeing at the work of art taking shape in front of her.

They glanced at each other, then frowned as one and turned to Serena.

"And so I'm planning on putting a couple of giraffes copulating on the top of it, to show what too much wine can do to a creature," DK said, watching for Serena's reaction.

When all she got was an absent-minded nod and no comment, she threw up her hands in frustration and grabbed Serena, turning her around to shake her.

"Okay, what gives Serena? You were the one who demanded we get together tonight. But now you're someplace else completely."

Quieting her voice a bit in case the news was bad, DK's tone grew more sympathetic to soothe whatever it was that was bugging their friend.

"Is it Balance? Did something else happen?"

Serena's mind snapped back to the present like an over-extended rubber band, letting her mouth quirk at the wry humor of her situation. She focused on each of her friends in turn, finally settling on DK.

"You said you needed ideas about passion to finish your work. Maybe I can help, because ladies, I'm in serious lust, and it's a very bad thing."

*****

"Let me see if I can get this straight." Their whoops of joy for Serena had turned to serious talk when she hadn't celebrated with them.

Roxy repeated the summary. "You're attracted to Bob. You kissed Bob. Bob kissed you back. Bob seems to be interested in you. He isn't turning you away. You haven't run – yet. So what's the problem again?"

Serena nibbled on her lower lip and took another slow sip of her wine. Her girlfriends were all staring at her with differing combinations of happiness mixed with concern. They didn't get it.

"He's a client, or at least he's supposed to be a client in order for Balance to continue to receive funding from Vision Quest. They're very clear about that. I think he could use our help, if he wants it. I don't know why Vision Quest is focused on him, or who he is. Maybe he did something very courageous, or maybe something bad, because none of the branches of military have claimed him. I don't even know his last name."

"But the kiss fried your brain. And you haven't had your brain fried in – how long, anyone remember? Serena?"

Of all of them, Roxy seemed to be the least concerned about the whole client thing, more inclined to counsel Serena to go for it. Tess was the most concerned, and it showed on her face too. DK seemed to be arguing both sides of the debate. Only Serena wasn't listening to any debates at all.

"Look, if something happens between us and he becomes a client, and I really think we can help him so he should be a client, it's going to be a problem. I can't have a relationship with a client."

"But if you already have a relationship with him, what does it matter? You're not going to be his counselor, are you? And you don't have to discuss his case with whoever becomes his counselor, probably Eduardo. And we all know Eduardo could keep the secrets of the pope, he's so discreet." DK knew Eduardo better than any of them other than Serena, since they had worked together to form the art therapy program a couple of years ago. "He wouldn't tell you anything about what's going on with Bob."

Serena rose to pace the patio around the pool in DK's backyard. "But that's just the point. I want to know what's going on with him! He won't talk about his past so I have no idea what happened. At least he doesn't slam the door to his cabin now each time I try to ask a personal question. He just picks up a drill or a board and goes back to work. End of discussion, such as it is."

Tess tried a different tactic. "But if he starts talking in counseling, he'll probably be more willing to start talking to you too, right? I'm betting he'll be willing to tell you a whole lot more once he gets started."

"But what if it all backfires? What if, knowing that I head up Balance, he clams up in counseling? He may believe that no matter what, I'll know exactly what he's saying."

It was a big risk, she knew. It wasn't a secret to Dane that she was head of Balance. As much as she could assure him about client confidentiality, there were things she had to know.

"Will you?" DK raised the obvious question.

Serena was silent for brief moments. "I have to write the reports every other week to Vision Quest. And since they're adamant about Bob getting help, I'll have to report something, like if he feels it's helping or not. That's specifically something they asked for, his testimonial about his progress. I'll know."

She felt the support in the other three women's eyes on her.

"You don't think he'll understand? He can give you something to put in the report." Tess paused. "Or is it something else?"

Turning to DK, Serena's eyes were troubled. "What if he thinks that the only reason I'm interested in him is because of what he can bring to Balance? Do you think he'll trust me? After all, that's why I went out to his place initially. He might not understand. Things have... changed for me."

Serena poured her commitment and her love into Balance and into her friendships, celebrating her friends as they found love and their versions of forever, but she never seemed to believe that she could have a happily ever after ending of her own.

That was, until now.

DK's voice was softer now. "You've earned some happiness too, you know?"

Roxy jumped up and snorted, not comfortable with all of the coddling. "Look, if you're interested and he's interested, you both deserve to give this a chance, funder or no funder. Besides, Bob is not currently a client. What would it take to get you to try it, to open the door to the possibility of a relationship?"

Moving slowly, Serena walked to the end of the pool, pausing to look down into the water and its tickle of ripples from the breeze.

"Maybe I could ask Eduardo to go out again and see Bob, ask again if he wants to join a program. If he does come in, I'll continue just being his friend. Maybe someday he'll graduate from counseling and then we can explore what we might feel for each other, if he feels anything at all."

A plan of action made her feel better, even if it hurt deeply. Serena settled into a chair and looked around at her friends.

"And what about you, Serena, what do you want?"

Tess's question was hard to consider.

"Whatever he decides is fine, because it will be his decision. You know, it will be what he wants." Smiling a bit too brightly, Serena knew she wasn't fooling anyone.

"How do you feel, Serena?" Roxy was more direct. "What do you want for you?"

Pain warred with hope, impatience with fortitude. The battle had her exhausted and vulnerable.

Finally, with a deep sigh, she spoke. "I want Dane."

Chapter 20

"I think he might be ready, Eduardo." Serena motioned her head vet counselor to close the door for their morning status briefing.

"What makes you say that?" Eduardo trusted Serena's instincts, but she knew from experience that he would want to hear it from the vet directly.

"Our Mystery Vet is moving forward. There's progress on the house, and there's the fact that Dane now holds complete conversations, at least with me. His beard is no longer the unkempt mess it was. It's like he's taking the time to care about things again."

Eduardo was watching her carefully, like there was something else, he could tell. But Serena wasn't sharing that. All he knew for sure was that Serena had seen Dane over the weekend and she thought that he might be ready, or at least willing, to get some help. That's all he would need to know to make a visit to Dane and talk to the man for himself. Besides, some things were too personal to share, even with a good friend.

Her mind wandered back to the kiss and she shivered.

"Serena? Earth to Serena, come in please."

She let go of the burning memory to see Eduardo staring at her with a hint of amusement. "What are you not telling me?"

She was shaking her head even before he finished the sentence. "Nothing, really Eduardo. Just thinking about the weekend and my, ah, conversations with Dane."

He smiled now but said nothing more, and after a brief pause, he returned to the subject of their meeting.

"I hope you're not expecting too much. I know from both my own experience and those of our clients over the years that not everyone wants to air whatever problems they have in a group session or even one on one. Sometimes secrets needed to stay secrets."

"I don't think it's like that. Dane's opening up. I believe that if we can convince him to come into the center, we can help him to talk about whatever bothers him so much."

Silently, she added, of course, when he's a client, I'll have to step back, way back. The thought depressed her, and she tried instead to concentrate on the victory of getting Dane the support he needed.

Eduardo was shaking his head again. "Remember the Belton Brothers? They lived on a small place with two rundown trailers off the main road. Every day like clockwork, you could drive down that busy two-lane road through South County and see them walking single file. One way, and they were headed for the corner liquor store, the only establishment at that remote intersection. Coming back, they were toting their treasures, bags of chips, a bottle of cheap whiskey and a 12 pack of beer, and usually they each had an open container of something in a paper bag, taking swigs as they trudged back to their little slice of heaven."

Serena did remember. When they'd come to counseling, they never talked. In fact, they could be downright spooky. They each sported long white beards and dark glasses, looking like members of a hard rock band rather than the navy vets they were. They'd each seen a lot of action, and when they got out, they became recluses.

They never did talk in session, and after three months, they stopped coming.

"You remember that I went to the trailers once to see what was happening with them? They were polite but adamant. They didn't need any damn counseling, thank you very much."

Smiling as he shook his head at the memory, Eduardo continued. "I had to give them credit. They knew what they wanted, didn't bother anyone, and lived their lives their way. What more could anyone ask for, really?"

She knew he was right. Some people, even when they seemed to be willing to take the next step, never raised that foot off the ground.

They were content with the status quo. But things were different with Dane. She was sure of it.

"He's making so much progress on the property. The big potholes in the driveway? Gone now under a fresh layer of gravel. The trees that blocked the view of what Dane was building are gone too, and you can see the big clearing and the structure. The trusses are up, and Dane said that the roof would be going on this week."

She paused, realizing that the words were coming too fast and her enthusiasm was showing. She considered the pen she was playing with thoughtfully. "He seems almost, I don't know if it's the right word, normal now."

*****

In front of him, trucks from one of the local roofing companies blocked most of his view of the house. Not that it mattered. Dane knew what it looked like, and the vision of it with its tiles in place was one that would soon move from imagination to reality.

His attention focused on the roofing company chief supervising her crew. Few had given Genie credit when she took over her father-in-law's roofing business a few years back. But she had gone head to head with every other company in a three county area and hers was a growing business. She was the best, and he was lucky that a cancellation created a hole in her schedule, allowing her to work on Dane's job right now.

Genie noticed him watching and came over. "Looking good, huh boss?" She smiled up at him and Dane almost smiled at the tough little pixie in her hardhat and well-worn jeans, all of five feet tall and yet towering over her crew by will, determination and experience. They worshiped her, and she took very good care of them.

"It's everything I envisioned and more. Your people are making good time. You work hard."

With a derisive sound, Genie waved off his compliments. "You get what you pay for, my friend, and with us, you paid for the best!"

She chuckled, and Dane felt himself grin more easily in response. Yes, he was lucky to be able to afford the best. At least he wasn't hurting for money, and he forced away the reason for that, trying not to spoil the good feeling of seeing the place come together.

Sometimes, he almost felt like a normal person again. Not that he really was, but it was nice to fool himself into thinking about it occasionally.

Soon, this would be his refuge. That thought wasn't bringing the same solace and comfort that it once had though. Still, it was all his, and as long as he was able to live here, he could protect himself from the attentions of that dangerous bigger world.

Dane stopped outside the range of the crane lifting tiles to the roof and admired the house. The structure was substantial, settled and stable and one with the mountains.

"You certainly know what you're doing and how you want it done." Genie had come up to where Dane stood studying the house. "Those tiles will shed the snow and any fires that might come up the canyon. The stucco on the outside and that fire suppression system piped on to the roof and under the porch will help too. We're doing lots of interesting things on this place." And with that, she broke into a huge, appreciative grin as she looked at the house with something akin to fondness.

He stepped towards the structure. "If you need me, I'll be working on the interior – so don't drop anything!"

*****

"Hey, anyone home?" Dane wasn't sure he'd heard something or not over the din of boards being laid for the roofing base and clatter of tile placement. He felt a pair of eyes on him rather than heard him or saw him. Some remnants of his war duty didn't ever go away, which was probably a good thing. He turned slowly to see who was causing the interruption.

Standing in the doorway was that counselor Eduardo, leaning casually against the bare wood jamb. Dane pulling the name up from the man's previous visits. He didn't appear to be a threat, like he was trying to make himself smaller than his stature allowed. And he had a smile on his face.

Dane didn't want any help or any interference. In fact, he was going out of his way to make everything appear normal. Fake it 'til you make it, as they say. The counselor watched him, his expression assessing even as he grinned, which made Dane more guarded. The man's smile seemed to become more genuine as he stuck out his hand and moved slowly towards Dane.

"Hey Dane. I heard about the great progress out here, and I wanted to see it for myself."

His hand was still out, but so far, it was only gripping open air.

"And who keeps sending you out here?" Cautious, Dane hadn't moved from his place in a doorway leading to the back of the house. Granted, he hadn't walked away, but he wasn't ready to be friendly either.

"Serena – we work together." Eduardo's hand finally sunk slowly and his face became neutral. See, I am not at a threat, was all Dane could think he was trying to convey. Clearly, though, this was official business. Why would the guy come out here to check on him if Serena hadn't told him to, if she still didn't want him to get into a counseling program?

Dane turned and ducked out of sight through the doorway. He hadn't said anything, and for the time being, Eduardo seemed to be taking this as an invitation to follow. Dane was sure he'd been asked in before with less welcome. At least there was no door to slam in his face, and the opportunities to block his access in the construction area were non-existent.

Stopping on the other side of the doorway, Eduardo let out a low whistle of appreciation. "Man, this is some space! What is this, the great room?" He followed Dane into the open area and craned his head around, trying to take it all in.

Dane felt a small surge of pride at the effect of the room, open and running the width of the house. Heavy beams supported the ceiling and new tile roof, and at one end, there was a large fireplace box and chimney.

But what made the room spectacular were the views of the canyon and the ridge to the south and the high peaks of the Sierras to the east. The far wall overlooking the canyon was ready to accept floor to ceiling windows and sliding doors. Eduardo moved to what would one day be a bank of glass and stood looking across the canyon.

"This view is incredible. How did you find this place?" The counselor's eyes stayed on the view.

It was an obvious question, equally obvious that he was trying to start a dialogue. Dane didn't feel like talking. Then again, if he was going to try for normal, he needed to decide to engage in conversations with normal people again.

He moved to stand next to Eduardo at the window openings.

"I visited this area a few years back. It was time to settle." It wasn't the whole story, but he wasn't going to give out any information unless and until he was ready.

"You made a great choice. And you've got Genie doing your roof – her crew is the best! So really, who designed this place for you?"

He considered answering. Feeling his way along the lines of safe topics was sometimes tricky, but no trickier than feeling his way along dusty back streets in desert compounds.

Dane continued to look out over the canyon, staying still. He scanned the distances with only a small turn of his head. He knew his stillness could be spooky and unnerving, and if it wasn't for the continuing noise from the roofers, one could assume that for a moment or two, everything stood still. It was how he survived, being able to do his job until his mission was accomplished without anyone noticing him.

It took him back again, back to the seconds before the bomb blew up and everything changed. It was one of his personal demons. Maybe if he'd moved, attracted attention, made himself visible and obvious that day, things would have turned out differently for his friends.

The thought made the sun seem dimmer, and Dane knew that the pleasure of the day, the joy in the roofing and in reaching for some semblance of normality, was over.

He shoved away to a pile of copper tubes in a corner and a work in progress, ignoring Eduardo. He didn't say anything. Maybe the man would get the hint that the conversation was over. Dane tried to forget that Eduardo was there.

To his credit, Eduardo stayed where he was. Dane was sure the man had worked with vets for too long not to recognize the dismissal. As all of the counselors during his physical rehab had said, a dismissal wasn't so much a 'leave me alone' as a silent cry for understanding and help. If he was right, Eduardo would continue to talk, like maybe he could get Dane to accept him being there.

Walking across to a sheet of blueprint hanging from interior framing, Eduardo examined the maze of lines and attachments. Dane had the drawings open to the plumbing plan page. It looked complex and impressive, though Eduardo didn't seem the type to know what he was looking at when it came to construction.

"This is something. Serena said you're doing most of the work yourself. I'm guessing that you worked in construction before. Where'd you learn the trade?" His features schooled to targeted interest, Eduardo turned back to Dane and waited patiently for a reply.

Building someone's confidence back up after it had been shattered, Dane thought. Nice try, but the best already had with poor outcomes.

Dane continued to turn a cutter around a piece of pipe, and eventually the piece separated into two pieces. He measured another length, and started the process again. He didn't feel compelled to fill the silence, and Eduardo appeared to be ready to out-wait him. It wouldn't be the first time. He'd gone through whole hour-long sessions during rehab without anyone saying a word.

Another piece of pipe joined the ones on the floor, and Eduardo walked over to the pile, crouched down, and began sorting the pile by length. "Hey, this is copper, right? Any problem with anyone stealing it off the site, since it's so pricey these days?" He looked up at Dane, trying to make himself smaller again.

Again, Dane recognized the tactic, the man's position on the floor making him appear to be less threatening in the hope that Dane might open up a bit.

His patience was wearing thin now. He just wanted to be left alone. Continuing the turns of his cutter on another pipe, Dane avoided glancing at Eduardo, his gaze concentrated on the work in his hands. He said nothing.

Eduardo shifted position, moving so close that Dane couldn't set him outside of his line of sight. Invasion of personal space, something designed to either comfort or push that final button.

"Look, man, I've been where you are. You saw things, experienced things, did things that most people can't even imagine. You come home and it's hard to relate the hell you were in to the calm around here. Whatever problems these people have, they're minor when compared to what you've seen in war. They don't understand, they just want you to be normal, whatever the hell that means, and you get tired of explaining, so tired that you shut up and find a place to hide." Eduardo paused. "But it doesn't need to be like that. We can help."

Dane felt his anger rising, and it was only through years of training to hold his feelings inside that he kept up his casual and deliberate routine - measure, cut pipe, stack.

Eduardo stood up and moved a pace away, beginning again. "Balance has programs that have helped a lot of people and we can help you cope too. Serena thinks it would help you. You can come in, meet some of the people, and talk about where you've been. They've been where you are." He hesitated. "It's a military benefit, man. You're covered – you don't have to pay anything."

Dane was surprised the other man couldn't hear the irate pounding of his heart over the roofers' noise, as fast as the blood was rushing through his veins. Military benefit, yeah, right. He stopped moving, still clutching a piece of pipe. He didn't lift his eyes from the work in his hands, didn't meet Eduardo's gaze. A slight tremble moved through his body.

With a suddenness that he knew was unexpected, Dane jumped in Eduardo's face, anger blazing. To his credit, Eduardo didn't step back, though he flinched when Dane charged him.

"You have no idea what I've seen, what I've experienced, what I've done," Dane bit out, his fury even more evident because he spoke so quietly. "If I wanted help," he nearly spit out that last word, "I'd go looking for it. And I doubt very much that Uncle Sam would pay for me. You can't help what I've seen, what I've done. No one can."

Some of Dane's anger faded on that last sentence. Just as fast as the anger had engulfed him, it shifted as hopelessness replaced it. Dane did not want to let on how much he was hurting.

Eduardo was watching him carefully, probably for any little tell that would let him know what Dane would do next. But he'd played all of these games with the counselors before. One more wasn't going to shake him.

Stepping back and taking deep breaths, Dane looked down at the pipe in his hand and wondered briefly how it got there. "You can tell Serena thanks." He spat out the last word. "I don't need her help with my problems." Now he made the sarcasm deliberate. "And I don't need her help on the house either."

The pipe dropped from his hands and clattered to the floor, chiming against the other pieces Eduardo had so carefully been sorting. Without a glance at his unwanted visitor, Dane disappeared around the corner that led to the porch. Eduardo moved fast to follow.

"I'm sorry, man, really. Just trying to reach out and help a fellow vet, ya know?"

Right, a fellow vet. The guy had no clue what had happened, what he'd done. Eduardo probably felt sorry for him. He had his pride, that and the right to some space to keep his feelings to himself if he wanted.

They moved fast across the clearing towards the little cabin. Dane wasn't running, but Eduardo needed to work hard to keep up. When Dane reached the cabin, he finally looked back at his unwanted visitor.

"One vet to another? Are you serious? You have no idea what you're talking about! Go to fucking hell, dude, and tell Serena she can do the same!"

And with that, he slammed the door in Eduardo's face.

Chapter 21

"And then he slammed the door in my face." Eduardo sat across the desk from Serena. He hadn't wanted to relate the whole experience to her, but she'd been insistent.

Serena had been feeling positive about Dane being ready. She was surprised – no scratch that, shocked – that he'd been so vehemently against it. And her own annoyance was building as Eduardo described Dane's sarcasm about her willingness to help.

"So what does he think, I was only working on the house to get in his good graces? So that I could – what – ambush him into counseling?" Annoyance was changing to anger. It so rarely came to the surface that its sudden appearance would have shocked her if she'd taken a second to recognize it was there. Only when something cut very deeply did it ever get the better of her.

Hurt coursed through her just under that surface too. Did Dane think she was trying to manipulate him? Was that he thought of her? She felt something different in that one kiss, the edge of potential as well as a hint of fear, and she could swear it wasn't just on her side.

Did Dane discount the meaning of that too?

"He doesn't want to come in, Serena, and pushing it will just make him dig in his heels. When he's ready – if he's ready – he knows where to find us. He definitely knows where to find you."

She knew that Eduardo could see the anger continuing to build. It was probably fascinating to see the hurricane of her feelings gaining strength. Now he'd know that something else was definitely going on, but she doubted he'd call her on it. Eduardo hadn't survived years in war zones without recognizing when it was a good time to take cover and wait for reinforcements.

Standing and backing up to the door, obviously realizing that retreat was a better option, he said, "I'm going to head into the next group session. Is there anything else you need from me right now?"

"No! I'm going to deal with this myself! Just who the hell does Dane the Mystery Vet think he is anyway?"

*****

At some level, Serena realized that she was probably too angry right now to confront Dane. She'd be better off cooling down, letting her objective rational self do the talking instead of this whirlwind of intense feelings and piqued fury. But if she let go of the indignant anger, the hurt surfaced. And she didn't want to go there, now or ever again.

The work site was quiet now. The roof was completed and the place was looking like a real house. A dusty new-looking pick-up sat next to the cabin now. That was different. She hadn't seen it before. She'd assumed that Dane had some kind of truck, since he picked up supplies for the construction on a regular basis.

And the tent – the tent was gone.

Serena was only slightly interested in the changes she could see because for the most part, all she could see was red. She hated letting her negative emotions get the better of her like this. It made her too vulnerable, and she hated that feeling most of all. But right now she was only dimly aware of what was roiling beneath the surface.

How dare Dane think that she was only out here with him for any reason other than she wanted to be, enjoyed his company, and loved to see what they were building together?

Her foot hit the brake at the same time that her feelings caught up to her thoughts. Enjoyed his company?

Yes, she definitely did, and she had other deeper feelings waiting just outside of her reach. Loved what they were building together? That made her stop mid-reach turning off the ignition.

Together. She hadn't been inclined to think about together with any man in quite a while.

She hit the key. In the stillness that descended with the SUV's motor silent, Serena rested her forehead on her hands where they were gripping the wheel. Anger, hurt and confusion were at war to see which would come out first and move her forward. Best to hold on to the anger. Best to remember that Dane just thinks of her as a manipulating... a manipulating – what? That she was only befriending him to get into treatment, a treatment that her nonprofit would get paid for.

That the kiss meant nothing to him.

Going with the flood of anger was easier than admitting the pain that the feelings she had thought were behind the friendship, the camaraderie, the kiss, weren't real. With a shake of her head and a surge of determination, Serena threw open the driver door and put boots on the ground to confront the enemy.

*****

The routine was calming. He hadn't done it in a couple of days, hadn't felt the need and frankly, with the roof going on, he'd been busy. It had been good to feel that connected to something other than the past. But the past had come roaring back to him with his morning visitor.

So Serena had been sharing a discussion with this Eduardo character about what was happening between them. Reporting back that he seemed to be opening up? Maybe that he was primed for an approach? Maybe that he seemed to be willing to 'come in'? Just what the hell did coming in mean anyway?

He cleaned the equipment in his hand with a lot more effort than needed. Putting one segment back in the case, he picked up the next piece. The routine didn't require conscious thought.

And just what was happening between them? He had been enjoying her company. Serena was funny and upbeat, even dealing with the occasional pitfalls on a construction site like this with humor and a big grin. She made him laugh more often in their days together than he could remember doing in total in the past few years.

She was caring too. The way she talked about her work, about the people her company helped, her friends. Serena had a big heart and a deep pool of emotions for others.

And then, there was the kiss. Just thinking about it made his gut clench. It was so sweet, so promising, and so full of hope for something that he no longer had any right to. Whatever anger he had left at Serena for sharing what they had discussed with a stranger dissipated in the pain of realizing that he had been fooling himself to think she was coming to care for him. He didn't deserve it, and she didn't even know why.

It was the right thing, pushing her away.

But then why did it hurt so much? He had forgotten this kind of emotional pain existed, the kind that settled in deep and ached like it was never going to leave you. He deliberately avoided it since the incident, and if he was honest with himself, for years before too. Love 'em and leave 'em smiling. Keep things light by keeping the women at a distance. It seemed to be safer somehow.

Placing the last bit of gear in the case, he let the pain throb through him. Maybe it would cauterize the wound, get him used to being alone again. Serena would get the message through Eduardo, and that would be that.

The idea made his soul ache even more.

Damn, it had been good to feel some hope and caring again. But no one would condone his past actions, and because of that, he was better off alone. If they knew about him, knew what he was capable of, people would be shocked and they'd turn away. Just like his brother had.

Staring at the gear with only a vague idea of what he was looking at, Dane thought over the past two years. Scars ached. He was back in the dust and the blood again and he felt his mind empty just like it had back then. His hand reached to touch the contents of the case.

And with a bang like a rifle shot, the door to the cabin burst open.

*****

Serena took in the tiny space in a second. Dane, sitting at the table with some kind of black case in front of him, the case she had noticed under the bed before. He was staring at her, and reaching inside for something. A gun? There were rags and other supplies on the table. Had he been cleaning guns?

Her common sense should have told her to run back out the door and not stop until she had her SUV down the driveway, but right now, anger was winning out over common sense.

"What the hell did you think? That I was out here because it was a means to an end? That I was manipulating you so that I could, what, use you? That I was only trying to get you to trust me so that I could make money off you? Do you think this is all about you? Don't you think I had some personal investment in all of this too?"

Marching three steps forward in the small space brought her to the edge of the table. Her glance at the case didn't give her anything to go on – the lid blocked her view. Besides, she was so mad that even if it contained an arsenal, she probably wouldn't have backed down. What would he do, shoot her?

God, she hated getting so mad that she let her emotions rule her good sense.

Dane was frozen. His eyes were seeing something else even though he was staring right at her. He didn't move, his hand still hovering over something inside the case. It wasn't indecision holding him back. He seemed to be stunned into inaction.

"What, nothing to say to me? I thought we had a good solid basis for friendship! I came here because I enjoyed getting to know you, and I had fun on the work we were doing. I am not a manipulating bitch!"

Serena heaved deep breaths, riding out the anger. One more phrase burst out of her.

"You made me feel things!"

Dane still hadn't moved, though at least he seemed to be staring at her rather than through her now. There was profound sadness on his face as he turned away. Withdrawing his hand, he slowly closed the case, snapping the clasps in place. With a quietness that spoke volumes about how tightly he was controlling his emotions, he got up like a defeated old man and lifted the case to its storage spot under the bed. And straightening, he finally looked her directly in the eye.

"You don't know who I am or what I've done. You don't know anything about me. And you don't want to know. Because if you did know, you'd be heading down that road as fast as you could drive it. Stand down, Serena. You don't want to be involved with me." His voice was quiet, as muted as his hooded expression.

"You're right, I don't know much about you. You don't share anything about yourself, and when I've asked, friend to friend, you've turned me in another direction or given me the silent treatment. And I've respected that! But don't you think that by now, you could open up a little bit? Hell, I don't even know your last name!"

The last words were bitten out and Serena realized in disgust that she was a hair's breadth away from letting her own hurt push the anger aside. Hot tears were welling up in her eyes, and she'd be damned if she'd let him see her cry.

One of them had to back down. Standing not three steps apart, it felt like there was a canyon of space between them, a canyon with no bridge across it. How important was it that one of them wins? Serena wasn't sure, but she knew that she was already losing. Her heart was cracked in two. Where did that come from? She hadn't had a chance to recognize how deep her own feelings for Dane had become.

"I said, get out Serena!"

Rage bubbled up in Dane so fast that Serena blinked in surprise. From a tired old man to a volcano in no time flat. If she had been able to examine it, she would have been impressed that someone else had a well of emotions as deeply hidden as her own. She stepped back from the anger and felt the rejection cut deep.

"You don't know me - you don't want to know me. Have I made myself clear?" Dane advanced two steps, then another, putting them face to face.

She could clearly see the deep blue of eyes, could feel the flame of rage. She didn't think it was aimed at her, and while she should have felt scared, she wasn't. Odd that the dangerous rage didn't bother her, but Dane telling her to go sure did.

Moving around her, Dane strode out the open door and stopped in front of her SUV. His voice was low and quiet, contrasting so much with his words that Serena had to strain to hear them. "Get out. Get in your truck, drive away – fast. Don't send anyone out to see me again. And don't come back yourself."

And with that, he turned and headed off into the woods.

Chapter 22

"Basically, he kicked me to the curb. He was so angry, Tess. He said I didn't know him and wouldn't want to. And he really didn't want to know me."

Serena sniffed into the tissue. She hated crying. Luckily, her tears held off until she was safely back in town.

She'd taken Dane's word as command and driven away fast. At a wide spot a few miles past Roxy's, she pulled over and sat in shock for a time. The depths of her own feelings were just beginning to make themselves known. She needed some sympathy and comfort, and she punched the speed dial for Tess on her cell phone.

Twenty minutes later, she was curled up in a deep armchair in the second floor expanse that served as Tess's living room above the flower shop. A pint of pralines and cream ice cream sat on the side table next to a big box of Kleenex.

"And I really don't know him," she continued. "But I thought I was starting to."

With a deep sigh, she picked up the bowl and filled it to the top with ice cream. After a couple of spoonfuls, she lost interest in it, leaving it to melt. Tigger the kitten jumped up on the table and eyed the bowl with eagerness.

"Is it the kiss? Is this turning into something a whole lot deeper than you thought?" Tess sat in a matching armchair across a woven rug, ever watchful, stroking a purring Penelope curled in her lap.

Serena nibbled her lower lip and played with the melting comfort food. Some things couldn't even be solved by ice cream, sad to say.

"I have feelings for him, Tess. Feelings that I really shouldn't have, and not because I think he needs to be a client of Balance. Feelings that I shouldn't have because I haven't known him long, and other than the work on the house, we really haven't spent any time together. I haven't been to dinner with him – those meals I've been bringing out to share don't count. I don't know what he did before the military, where he's from, how he came to know so much about construction, even if he's gone to college. I don't even know his last name."

She hiccupped back a sob and wiped at the new tears, furious with herself for caring so much.

"Is any of that important right now? Are you willing to throw away the possibility just because you haven't read his full resume yet? Would any of the rest of that matter, given how you feel about him?" Tess always was the voice of reason, the calm center in any storm.

"No, you're right." Serena smiled a little at her friend, and gave a final sniff before setting aside the bowl and the tissue. Stretching in the chair, she shook her head. "I haven't felt like this about a guy in – god, how long has it been, if ever? But he doesn't seem to want anything to do with me now."

"Give it some time. Maybe he'll come around. Or maybe he'll find that he misses you. You have feelings for him and you deserve to act on them, wherever that takes you. You can't live your life by stepping back each time some guy you might lose comes too close. There are a lot of men out there who don't live their lives on the dark side, Serena."

Tess paused and stared hard at Serena.

"Not all of them are like your father."

Chapter 23

The day was dragging by so slowly, Serena swore that the clock had stopped. She checked it more than once, looked at her cell phone for confirmation, and then checked the computer too just to be sure.

Work was going slowly too. It was time to fill out the biweekly report to Vision Quest, and while she had great things to report on every other use of their donation dollars, she didn't know how to approach the issue of Mystery Vet Dane.

After their confrontation, Serena ground through the week. She thought about Dane often, replaying conversations they'd had, viewpoints they'd discussed, things that had happened. It was amazing how much they had packed into those few weekend days together, she thought now. She knew a lot more about him than she realized, or at least she assumed she knew things. Sometimes she wasn't so sure.

She missed him, which should have been silly considering how short a time they'd known each other. But as Tess noted, what did that matter? If Dane didn't, say, go to college, would she drop him? Did it matter where he was born, or what he'd done before his military years?

No, because she had already come to know a lot about the man inside now. Besides, he stirred her to the core, and she hadn't felt that kind of heat, if she was honest with herself, ever in her life.

That hadn't made the waiting any easier. Each night, she'd called a different one of the girl tribe to talk her out of heading to Dane's to get things out in the open. The facts, in her mind, were that they had many things in common, at least from what they'd talked about. They got along well, or at least they had been. And they had some other layer of things going on, some feelings that she thought it would be worthwhile to explore.

Because she, at least, hadn't felt any stirrings like this in a very long time.

Each night, her friends had cautioned her to wait. If Dane wanted to get in touch with her, he knew where she worked. He might not be ready yet.

Tess warned that he might need time to come to his own terms about what he felt, that sometimes men took longer than women to figure things out.

Gabby softly suggested that perhaps he might not feel as strongly as she did, and asked if she was willing to let things go if it was all on her side.

DK said she hoped that he came to his senses and got with the program, warning that otherwise Serena would need to move on.

And Roxy reported no sightings of him in the grocery store, and being her usual tough and edgy self, told her that just about any man wasn't worth the hassle.

Still, Serena couldn't let go. Friday morning seemed to be three days long. Though it had been only five minutes, she checked all of the clocks again. She still didn't know what to put into the report, and she typed, backspaced, and typed again, trying to find words that indicated some kind of progress without saying anything that wasn't true.

Could she honestly say that he was sharing more of his feelings? Yup, that she could do. Anger, mostly.

The buzz of her office phone was a welcomed relief. Even if this call was about a difficult APS case or another major challenge, it would be easier to handle than the report on her screen or the thoughts filling her mind.

And that ache in her heart that just didn't seem to go away, that could use a distraction too.

"Balance, this is Serena. How can I help you?"

Silence greeted her on the other end of the line. It wasn't dead, because she could hear whomever was there breathing slowly. And there was noise in the background, outdoor sounds. But whoever it was didn't want to talk.

She tried again. "Hello, this is Serena. Can I help you with something? Is someone there?"

Again the silence. She didn't want to waste time, but something kept her on the line. Curious, she looked at the caller ID and didn't recognize the number. It wasn't local, and she didn't know where it came from. No name appeared, only a notation for 'mobile caller'. Sometimes clients didn't like to talk right away and you had to be patient when they called. But she couldn't remember anyone having a phone number with this odd area code.

One more try. "You've reached Serena, the executive director of Balance. I'd like to talk with you, but right now this is feeling one-sided. I'll need to hang up now. Please call back when you're ready and I'll be here for you."

Getting ready to click off, Serena heard a male voice as she moved the cordless handset closer to its cradle. Quickly she put it back to her ear. "Yes, I'm sorry? What did you say?"

The voice paused again. Then it started slowly. "It's Ashland. My last name."

Serena knew that voice, and the shock of hearing it come through her phone had her sitting absolutely still. "Dane?" While she had been willing him to get in touch with her all week, to take the first step, now that he had and was calling her, she was at a sudden loss about what to do next.

"Yes, Dane Ashland. That's my name." He paused again. "You said you didn't even know my last name, so I'm telling you." He stopped again, waiting, it seemed, for her to reply.

Serena wiped a hand across her eyes and blinked a few times, but the phone was still in her hand, and there was Dane on the other end. She didn't think she had willed a dream into reality. And she didn't think she was asleep, so this was probably real.

Her heart started a faster beat and she felt a little flash of excitement settle under her belly button.

"Dane. I'm so glad you called! I've mi- I mean, I've been worried about you." God, she had nearly told him she'd missed him! Talk about jumping right into the fire.

"I'm sorry, Serena." Dane's voice sounded rough, like he hadn't used it much lately and was out of practice. "I'm really sorry. I shouldn't have yelled at you. Sometimes, well sometimes I'm not a very nice person. Most of the time, actually." He fell silent again.

Serena put both hands on the phone, wishing she could will him to continue and yet at some level, she was worried about what he might say. Was he apologizing, only to then tell her he didn't want to see her again? Realizing that she'd let the silence drag on for too long, she cleared her throat.

"I'm sorry too, Dane. I shouldn't have raged at you. I hate it when my temper gets the better of me. I don't let It happen often because I hate how ugly it gets when I do. I was really poking into your business, a place I didn't belong. I'm sorry."

Only the breeze whispering in the trees in the background of the call let Serena know they were still connected. Dane didn't respond.

She really screwed things up this time. She knew she shouldn't do anything when she was that mad. It was always a mistake. She had blown another relationship, setting her expectations too high and then chasing someone away with those self-same expectations.

She was thinking about apologizing again when Dane's voice came back through the line.

"Would you have dinner with me tonight?"

The uncertainty in his voice came through to her. He wasn't sure either, and that gave her hope and a sense of protectiveness as well.

"Dinner, tonight? Sure!" God, she sounded as eager as a high school sophomore being asked to the prom by a senior! But the glow inside was starting to spread and a big grin filled her face. Trying to calm down her racing heart, she tried again for a more sedate tone. "I'd love to have dinner with you tonight, Dane."

A sigh on the other line ended with what could have been a small chuckle. "Good, really good."

"Where are we going to go?" she asked. She quickly cataloged the usual casual places nearby, trying to figure out what to suggest so that Dane would feel comfortable.

"Why don't you meet me at the house? We can grill, if that's okay with you. Salmon is in season. Do you like salmon?"

"I love salmon!" Okay, she really needed to get a grip on herself. Soon she'd be swooning with enthusiasm over a side dish. She needed to project the right tone, not too needy and not too grateful, though she was damned happy he'd called.

Inside, though, she could still do her happy dance.

"Ah, alright. I can grill the salmon for us, along with all of the sides." He paused again. "Is that okay? I'd like us to be able to talk, or rather, I'd like to tell you some things, and I'd rather not do it in public. Say six-thirty?"

Serena's heart gave another little jolt. Dane wanted to talk to her about 'some things', and because of where they were in their relationship, if it could be called that, she had to assume it was things about his past, about him and his moodiness. Those were the kinds of conversations usually best conducted in private.

And the thought of having Dane cook for her seemed like such a delicious novelty. She assumed he could cook, since he rarely seemed to go anywhere. Roxy's staff said he bought great things at the store, never anything premade or packaged. This man didn't eat out of a boil and serve box.

"That's fine. What can I bring? Dessert? Some wine?"

"Dessert is good. I'll take care of the wine. Just dress comfortably, because you know I don't have much to offer it the way of furniture."

Serena could swear she heard the rustle of a smile in Dane's voice.

"Comfort it is! I've got some camp chairs I can bring along too. Do you need anything else? Dishes, glasses?"

Okay, slow down girl. This was a little grilling and a little dinner, not a full buffet service. But come to think of it, she wasn't sure Dane had more than what he needed for himself alone.

Now the smile thrummed in his voice for sure. "I've got that covered. Just bring the dessert." His voice grew more serious again as he paused. "And you."

She could hear him pull in a long breath.

"And Serena? Again, I'm sorry. Thanks for being willing to be my friend despite it all."

And with that, the line went dead.

Serena sat with the phone to her ear for a full minute before she could put it down. Her grin spread from ear to ear.

The day was really going to drag by now. She had a date.

Unable to resist, she jumped up out of the chair and let the happy dance take over her little office.

Chapter 24

Even though the early evening was still a bit warm, Dane pulled on jeans. The air would cool as soon as the sun went down, and if he was lucky and Serena didn't run away when he told her more about himself, they'd still be talking when the stars came out. Tonight was the peak of the Perseid meteor shower, and he hoped that she'd stick around for that too. He didn't want to hope for more.

Dane had been thinking a lot these past few days. Mostly, he was thinking he was disgusted with himself. He'd acted like the worst kind of monster, taking Serena's offer of help and throwing it back in her face. And then he'd been indignant that she was mad at him. What right did she have?

But he'd come to realize that maybe it was because she cared, and because she had felt that same jolt of something that he had. Maybe she was acting out of some new feelings and sense of future, rather than greed or anything else.

He cautioned himself not to get too far ahead of things. She might not like what she hears. She might not like him all that much once she knew him better.

She might not like his cooking, but he figured that alone wouldn't be enough to scare her off.

He had to laugh. It had been a long time since he'd had a sense of humor about his own actions. Besides, he didn't think Serena scared easily. Still, he'd taken great care with everything tonight.

He'd actually gone to a barbershop and had his hair and beard trimmed by a professional. Of course, the old man harrumphed when he'd seen him and hummed when

Dane had said he just wanted things shaped up and trimmed, not shaved completely, but soon he was happily telling tales about the history of the little town along the major road to Flynn's Crossing. Dane himself hadn't had to say a word.

Then he stopped at Roxy's for supplies. The freckled redhead did a double take when he looked at Dane at the checkout counter, his smile wide and genuine as he said, "Thank you very much for your business, sir!"

Salmon, salad fixings, and sweet potatoes for dinner went into the paper sacks. And he bought ice to chill the wine – a nice Oregon Pinot Gris he remembered from a few visits to that winery. Hell, he even bought a big bowl for the salad and some wine glasses. He was making something of an investment here.

But it was worth it. Serena seemed to have forgiven him, or at least she was willing to discuss things over dinner. She hadn't even balked at the request to have it here, with him cooking. He'd taken the time today to look at some of the old pictures, the pictures from his life before things went completely wrong. Hopefully he could explain something about himself – without giving everything away – and restore their friendship to its previous level.

And lay the groundwork for it continuing in a completely new direction.

Yes, Dane thought as he washed vegetables for grilling, he seemed to be ready for something more normal in his life. At least he told himself he was ready. He wasn't ready to tell all yet – or maybe ever – but he thought that perhaps they could work past that. He hadn't been interested in any woman the way he was in Serena for a long time. If he was honest with himself, never exactly like this. She stirred him, body and soul, and his groin tightened with memory and anticipation.

Yes, he was ready for normal.

He turned to the fire pit he'd built in the gravel area in front of the house. He started the wood half an hour ago and now the coals were beginning to break down and create a good hot bed for grilling. He had a big metal frame ready to place over the grill and was thinking about setting it over the coals when he heard the crunch of tires on the gravel.

His gut clenched.

Ready? Not hardly!

*****

Serena took ten seconds to appreciate the tight jeans and t-shirt on the spare but well-muscled frame before her eyes moved up to Dane's face. Her delighted surprise must have shown, because as she was jumping out of the SUV, Dane seemed to shake off some kind of tension and he smiled at her.

That smile did her in. It lit up his whole face, his whole being. Her insides did an excited back flip and she realized she was staring. Damn, he cleaned up so well! He'd trimmed his beard and his hair, while still on the longish side, had been shaped up too. This wasn't a do-it-yourself job, and she wondered if he was trying to impress her. If he was, she wasn't going to tell him that it was working, at least not right away.

All the same, she was glad she'd taken the time to dig the push-up bra out of the back of her underwear drawer for tonight. This was the one place her curvy figure left her feeling under-endowed, and Gabby had talked her into the enhancement the bra promised. She wasn't sure if it really worked, but it did boost her confidence. While Dane had seen her in a tank top before, this should provide him with something new to consider.

She picked up the two boxes from the bakery and pushed the door shut with her sandaled foot before turning to cross the drive. And her gaze ran straight into Dane's warm stare. The sense of sexy appreciation and hint of something stronger in his smile sent a frisson of excitement through her. It made her step falter for a moment while her answering smile moved from tentative to full blown delight.

*****

Damn, but Serena was looking incredible. Dane was glad he'd taken the time – with everything. He stepped forward to greet her and felt a clutch of desire so strong that it rocked him to a stop. This was like high school, he thought, and had to allow himself a wry smile at his own foolishness. They were both adults. This was a date, not a life and death situation. He'd been through blood and guts and this should be a piece of cake by comparison.

Shaking off the dark direction his brain wanted to go, he started up again to meet her.

"Two boxes? What, couldn't make up your mind?" His smile was real and as big as hers as he took a box from her. They were wrapped with knotted string, reminding him of the bakery boxes his mom used to bring home for special occasions when they were kids. The happy memory calmed him. And Serena's open smiling face inspired him.

Not waiting for her answer, he leaned forward and brushed a quick kiss of greeting across her lips. His movement stilled her, her eyes flickering shut as she swayed into his embrace. She tasted better, much better than whatever was in the boxes, and something pushed him to kiss her again, this time lingering a while and moving his lips gently over hers. His free hand came up to cup her cheek, brushing fingers down her jaw until he held her chin. The skin was so soft under his fingertips. Her lips moved under his.

Before things went deeper, they needed to talk. He needed to explain. He broke the kiss and stepped back on a sigh while his body began a drumbeat for more.

Serena's eyes fluttered open as she swayed once and she raised her confused gaze to his. Dane watched her carefully, wishing that he could tell for sure what she was thinking. She had responded, and he could swear she enjoyed it. Did she feel the same pull of desire that he did? Hopefully she would still want something to do with him when he'd had a chance to talk about his past and his present.

"Um-ah... yes, I, ah, I couldn't make up my mind." Serena seemed to shake herself back to the mundane, still holding up the second cake box by its string in explanation. "One's this incredible carrot cake – four layers with these whispers of cream cheese frosting between them and a thick layer on the outside – and nuts, lots of pecans. And the other's a flourless chocolate ganache with white chocolate mousse on the top. I kept going back and forth for so long that Sarge made me take both."

God, she was adorable, with that sheepish look on her face that did little to mask her delight in their dessert choices, while her confusion over their kisses still lingered in her eyes.

She looked like an excited kid in a candy store. And like candy, he'd found, incredible sweet to the taste too. If they didn't move, he was going to kiss her again and this time the cakes might not survive the encounter.

"Either one – or both – will go great with the rest of our meal." He turned and took Serena's free hand casually to pull her the rest of the way across the drive to the fire pit and his impromptu seating area.

"What's this – a futon couch? I didn't know you had this." Serena plopped down as Dane put the boxes in the cooler away from the fire.

"I didn't – had to drive to other side of Sacramento to find it. I wanted something I could use for temporary seating around the place while I'm working on it. And it has a bonus for tonight – it reclines out to a bed."

Her sudden stillness made him realize that this had come out all wrong. Taking a couple of verbal steps back, he added, "Tonight we can lay out here and watch the

Perseid meteor shower – it's the peak night and it's a whole lot easier to watch laying down than sitting up with your neck in a crick from leaning your head back."

He wished he remembered something of the smooth moves he'd had before things blew up. Conversation had never seemed to be so much work. He was clearly out of practice, and he was making a hellish mess of it.

Serena's expression was impossible to read, things were moving so fast across her face. Confusion, doubt, joy, desire. Sometimes she was hard to read and sometimes she was an open book, but he wasn't sure he understood the language. He'd like to learn it, though, much more than he'd imagined.

After a moment, she glanced up at the setting sun with a smile and responded, "That sounds like fun. I got to watch another set of meteors late last fall at DK's place. It was amazing! It seems like every year, either the moon's full or the sky's hazy with smoke at this time of year. I've never seen Perseid before."

Dane smothered his sigh of relief. He seemed to be forgiven for his faux pas. Something was going to betray his rising desire before the evening was over. It was a race to see if it was going to be his body or his words.

*****

Turning to the cooler again, Dane pulled out a selection of vegetables. It gave Serena a few seconds to enjoy the sight of his backside in snug jeans. He had a great butt, much more obvious now in tight denim. Her heart rate picked up a few more beats, not that it had dropped at all since the welcoming kisses.

She ran a trembling finger over her lips in memory. There wasn't a blaze of passion and heat in their lip locks. It was a long slow simmer instead, the kind that promised and enticed. Until something flashed. Serena's heart kicked up even faster at the thought. She needed to change the direction of her mind or there would be no dinner on the menu tonight.

"What are you making?" She rose from the futon to come around the other side of his makeshift worktable. His hands were competent, and she wondered what they would feel like running along her skin. She shivered from her imagination alone.

"Roasted vegetable salad. I'll grill these first, and when they're cool enough to handle, I'll cut them up and we'll toss them with oil and vinegar. We have sweet potatoes that will bake in the fire, and salmon – from Oregon, no less – to grill at the end. I hope you like the fish." He stopped his work to look at Serena and questions formed on his face when he found her staring at him.

She shook her head to clear the visions of the two of them together.

She started to babble. "You can cook! I'm not a good cook. It's not that I burn things and I can boil water, but I really have no sense of what goes together. I end up with some odd recipes. Roxy calls me flavor-combination challenged."

Dane grinned at her. She could see his smiles now that his beard has been trimmed.

He had a terrific smile.

"So what do you do? Order take-out? You seem to talk about food a lot." His indulgent look took any sting out of his words.

"I rely on Roxy – a lot – to tell me what to prepare. And I admit I buy restaurant food or the meals from her grocery. I just never learned. My mother didn't really cook, and we survived for a long time on things like ramen noodles or skillet suppers from a box or fast food. Or cereal for dinner. That's still a favorite comfort food of mine."

Serena stopped, not believing she was jabbering so much or that she had brought her family life into the discussion. She never talked about her family unless she'd known someone forever. It was a very uncomfortable subject because it always rolled around to questions about her father, and then if she didn't stop it there, the 'incident' as she thought about it in her impartial mind, and the subsequent changes to her family life.

"What about you? Where did you learn to cook?" There, a safer subject, safer direction.

Dane paused, his hands stopping for a second. If she hadn't been looking at his hands, thinking again how artistic they appeared, how gentle, she would have missed it. Maybe not such a safe subject after all, for him.

"My mom. And my dad too. Mom made sure that we all knew our way around a kitchen. She said that as long as my siblings and I knew how to cook and do our own laundry, we were well prepared to function as adults no matter what career we chose." He looked out over the clearing but was seeing something else, some happy place based on the reminiscent smile on his face.

"And what did your dad like to cook?"

Serena was fascinated with the mix of emotions playing across Dane's face. He hadn't opened up like this before. Before, it was like he realized he was heading in a personal direction and he shut it down. But he wasn't doing that tonight. What had changed?

"He loved to grill. He had a gas barbeque and a wood smoker. But his favorite was this big fire pit he'd built in our backyard. He tried everything on it – meat like they do in South America and Aussie-style shrimp on the barby. But his favorite, no doubt about it, was fish, fresh local fish. He'd do salmon on planks and halibut on skewers and just about anything you can imagine that once lived in rivers or seas." Dane's grin was huge now in his reminiscing, more happiness than she'd ever seen him display, and his gaze returned to the vegetables he was prepping.

He chuckled. "It took him a while to figure out the fire in that pit. It would flare up and completely burn the fish. Or it wouldn't stay hot enough and the fish would dry out before it would cook completely. But he made sure we all knew how to cook on it too."

Silence followed. Neither of them felt any need to fill it, and that was comfortable. Like Dane, she was inside her own memories and thoughts.

Her family, at some point she'd need to talk about them. And they were… complicated. It might be more than he'd be willing to take on.

Of course, she knew nothing about his family either, other than his last name, and now, that his parents had taught him to cook. And he had siblings. It was a whole lot more than she had known this morning.

Clearing her throat, Serena decided she needed to feel useful. "I can to do something, if you tell me what you want done."

Stirring the burning wood in the pit, he glanced back at her over his shoulder, his eyes locking on her intent expression. His own eyes widened slightly and he licked his lips. Her vision focused on the tip of his tongue and goose bumps raised on her arms.

"Why don't you open the wine? It's in that bucket by the couch. The glasses are in there too."

Chapter 25

"That was an amazing meal!" Serena sat back on the couch and watched the dying fire with a deep sigh. "I can't cook, but I do love to eat. And you, my friend, can cook!"

Dinner had been a huge success. He'd set up a card table and folding chairs on the unfinished back porch, taking in the view of the darkening canyon. They kept the banter light. The salmon was succulent, well matched to the sides he'd selected. The wine complimented the meal, and the desserts proved to be so delicious that they had to share them.

"No, you have to try some of this. Here." Her fork was poised in the air between them, the chunk of chocolate cake nearly falling off the tines.

He was sucked in by her sheer exuberance. This was a piece of cake, after all, but she was treating it like one of the seven wonders of the world. She was full of passion for so many things, and he paused only long enough to fork some carrot cake and stretch it out to her in return.

Dane kept his eyes on her as he tightened his mouth on the chocolate. When her lips wrapped around his fork and she closed her eyes, oozing appreciation, he was glad that the table blocked her view of his lap. The tip of her tongue coming out to run over her lips only made his jeans more uncomfortable. He was surprised he hadn't bent her fork, since he was still biting down on it so hard.

Their discussion over the meal ranged from books to music other forms of art. They had a lot in common, with some amusing contrasts too. Serena was a diehard rock and roll fan, while Dane's taste in music fell more towards the New Age and classic end of the spectrum.

"I can't believe you enjoy classical music. What perks you up?" Astonishment at his taste, or maybe lack of taste, was evident in her face.

Right now, you Serena, but he kept that thought to himself.

After pouring the last of the wine into each of their glasses, Dane folded himself down on the opposite end of the futon and turned towards her. Thinking back to the few times that Serena had laid a hand on his arm to make a point, Dane had to admit that the desire that he was trying to hold at a distance was growing with each passing minute. He wanted to move closer and explore her mouth again. Fingers, tingling with the memory of her soft skin, wanted to explore new territories. His body was campaigning for a whole lot more. But first, they needed to talk and he wanted to delay the inevitable pain his story would bring.

Taking a last sip of his wine, Dane decided to take the opening Serena's comment about cooking and family provided. "You mentioned your mom before. Do you have any siblings? Tell me about your family growing up."

Serena's face shifted from a dreamy gaze into the fire to a sharper and sadder stare. Maybe the topic was a bad idea. But he wasn't willing to jump into his past right away. And besides, he wanted to know all about her.

"I'm an only child. Mom and I were on our own. Dad died when I was twelve, killed in an accident. It took Mom a long time to get back on her feet again and she never really smiled or laughed much after that." She sipped some of her wine and continued to stare into the fire, not meeting his eyes.

"You must have gotten close, since it was just the two of you."

The myriad expressions playing across her face were fascinating to watch. Unconsciously he moved a little closer on the couch, intent on catching every memory displayed on her features. The remnants of the fire threw everything into a deepened glow and her contrasting contours were in sharp relief. He took a mental picture of her like this to roll over in his mind later when he was again alone.

Shifting in her seat, Serena still didn't look at him. "I wouldn't call it close. Mom had, well, she had problems afterwards. She didn't bounce back well. Dad had been her whole world. I was on the outside looking in – they had that kind of special relationship. He was a free spirit, kind of wild according to my grandmother. He still rode a motorcycle – Mom would never get on it. And I never could, that's for sure. I adored him though." She fell silent again, her face pensive in the shifting amber glow of the last of the fire.

"What kind of accident took him away from you?" Dane could see that this still hurt, and he wanted to know what was causing her pain. He had a sudden urgent need to wipe that pain away.

Serena sighed and dropped her gaze to the glass, twirling the stemware in her fingers. "He wanted to take a motorcycle ride up in the mountains – we lived near the Oregon border then, near Mt. Shasta. Mom didn't want him to go. It was Saturday, and she wanted us to do something as a family. He got in these moods, these dark funks when he just had to get away."

She stopped, looking at Dane. There was something assessing in her examination, and he tried not to squirm. Even he could recognize the comparison she must be making.

She looked into the fire embers again as she continued. "A devil would take over my funny, happy father. He was determined that day, determined to get away. They were arguing over it, and then he just – left." She stopped, the scene probably replaying as the sadness crossed her features once again.

God, she was beautiful. He never wanted anything painful to put that kind of damper on her usual shimmering excitement.

Clearing her throat, she raised her eyes to his. "I was peeking out of the kitchen into the living room and heard them fighting before he turned away. They said some terrible things to each other. He stomped out the door, Mom stomped upstairs. Hours later, Dad was riding on a twisting two-lane road up east of Redding, and he was passing a logging truck. The load shifted on the truck, and the chains broke. The logs came crashing down on him. He was killed instantly."

She was still looking into his eyes, her own dry but incredibly sad. And he couldn't help himself. He moved forward into the silence and gave her a quick hard kiss, just a fast meeting of lips to let her know he wanted to honor and share her grief, evident even after all this time.

Her eyes stayed open and when he began to pull away, he realized her eyes were a whole lot wider now than they had been.

"I'm sorry for your loss." The words always seemed so inadequate.

Blinking a few times, Serena didn't immediately look away. A quick flash of something like wonder crossed her expression. Then she dropped her eyes to the fire again. She sighed.

"Anyway, Mom never recovered from it. She and Dad had fought and they never made up before he left. Their last exchange had been angry, and she never got a chance to tell him she understood what happened when the dark side drove him away, and she was sorry. She kind of, well, kind of fell apart after that."

"The symptoms," Serena's voice changed, becoming more distant and professional, "were very much like post traumatic stress disorder, though no one really recognized it as such at the time. Mom couldn't function for a while, and according to the doctors, she was severely depressed. My Aunt Liz, my dad's sister, lived nearby and did what she could, but she had her own family issues to deal with. Mom's mother, my grandmother, came from Arizona for a while to take care of both of us. When they finally found the right mix of medications to keep her moods stable, Gram went home. And it was Mom and me."

Sitting forward and cupping the empty wine glass in her hands, Serena's voice grew quieter. "I think that's when I realized what I wanted to do, to help people who'd experienced painful things in their lives and needed help to move past them. You see, Dad would never go to a counselor, and neither would Mom."

She shifted again to move closer to him. "And I'm not sure why, maybe Mom felt she needed to punish herself for surviving when he was gone because they'd parted on such bad terms. I know now that talking it out would have helped her. Survivor's guilt, or PTSD, or something else, but working with a professional would have helped her to see that it wasn't her fault and she could safely move on in life."

Serena looked up into his eyes. "Maybe it was the rural area we lived in – maybe there weren't any services available. But there should have been somewhere she could have gotten help. And that's why I run Balance today, so that someone else doesn't have to go through what Mom did."

She stopped and looked away again.

Dane was afraid to move, stilled both by her words and by the deeper implications her past had for their own relationship. Her gorgeous face in profile was lit by the dying fire, and he captured a picture in his mind.

But it was her words most of all that held him quiet. There were so many parallels to his own life. What would she think if – or when – he shared his own experiences of the last two years? Would his dark side be too much for her? Or would she feel the need to fix things for him beyond anything else?

*****

Serena was surprised. She usually didn't share her life's little tragedies until she knew someone very well. Opening up about it was always hard. But there was something about Dane that made her feel safe and comfortable, like they'd been together longer than a couple of months.

Like they were a couple, period.

Shaking herself and trying to redirect her thoughts, Serena pasted an upbeat smile on her face and turned to Dane. "It's in the past and I've learned to work through it, even if it still makes me sad. So what about you? It sounds like you come from a big happy family, doing things together. Are you close to your siblings?"

Dane was staring at her. "Just wait one second," he said, raising a finger as he set his wine glass aside on the ground. He moved closer to her, close enough for her to see the bright blue of his eyes even in the waning firelight. His hands came up to caress her cheeks gently, his fingers just a bit rough to the touch, and he moved in so close that their breaths mixed.

Her eyes dipped closed, falling into the light touch of his lips to hers. He was both questioning and demanding, and she leaned forward to get a better angle and raise her hands to cover his. With a sigh, she shifted nearer, feeling the heavy heat of thigh against thigh through their jeans.

Dane used his tongue to tease her lips, running it back and forth across the seam until she parted them for his advance. Serena pushed forward as well, exploring the shape of his teeth, tangling tongue to tongue. A low moan escaped her, and the deepening kiss caused her heart to pound as a shudder of excitement shot to her core.

That rollercoaster appeared again, and she was more than ready to hop on for a long wild ride this time.

He broke the kiss first, hands on her shoulders gently moving her away with obvious reluctance. As he stared at her face and traced the shape of her lips with a thumb, Dane continued to stare into her eyes. His own wary gaze was unblinking and held tremendous sadness, and she longed to wipe it away and give him some joy to hang on to instead.

She raised a hand to scratch at his beard. It was rough, and she smiled. Her heart gave another little lurch. What was she doing?

The only thing she knew with great certainty was that she wanted the kisses to continue, and she wanted a whole lot more.

Chapter 26

God, what was he thinking? Dane couldn't move away, and he didn't want to look away from the hope and desire he saw in her eyes. It paralyzed him.

Serena hadn't moved either, watching him with a ghost of an expectant smile on those lush lips. He filed this moment away to take out and treasure when the nights were long and dark. It was the thought of those times that finally broke through his immobility and with a sigh, he tucked her against him and turned them both towards the embers as the moonless night deepened.

His heart was stuttering in his chest. He gulped in air to calm himself. Their silence stretched as nothing could draw any words out of him.

She fit so perfectly under the drape of his arm, the perfect height, her body molding easily to his. Dane closed his eyes and took in a range of sensations. The whisper of the late breeze coming up from the canyon stirred her hair and brought it across his face, another caress. The hint of wood smoke was overpowered by the scents of her, some crisp shampoo leaving her hair fragrant under his chin and a deeper fragrance that he came to recognize as her rising desire.

His heart steadied, a wave of serenity moving through him. He wanted to capture this moment forever. It had been a long time since he'd felt so calm. The woman was magic, a balm to every disappointment and hurt he'd suffered over the years.

Serena finally stirred against him. "Okay, your turn. I showed you mine, now show me yours." Her light teasing tone eased a smile out of him. "Your family story can't be as gruesome as mine."

Dane kept her tucked against him when she would have looked him full in the face. Some things are best explained under the comfort of darkness. He stroked her bare arm and felt goose bumps rise. "Are you cold?"

"No, just liking your touch, that's all." Her voice was husky and low, and more than anything, he wanted to turn her in his arms and tease her mouth open again. He wanted to run his hands down her curves and cradle her length against him and gently remove that tempting top to see what was underneath.

But first, he had to tell his story, and hope that she would understand.

Pressing her head to his shoulder, he cleared his throat and matched his low tone to hers. "Gruesome, no. Difficult, yes." He tried to think about where to start.

"We weren't what you'd call a close family, though we seemed to be together a lot. It was expected. Dad built a construction company with his father. They were both... brusque, I guess you could say. My grandfather thought that hard work was all that was required to solve any problem, no matter how hard a challenge it was. He demanded a lot of Dad, and Dad grew up into the same kind of man, demanding with high standards and big expectations and little patience for emotions."

Thinking back, he reflected on the dinner discussions, the probing questions about grades, the obligations his father wrung out of him to try harder when he got B's as compared to his brother's A's. His sister, being a girl, hadn't had those same educational expectations placed upon her. Their mother had been much more subtle in guiding them.

"But you sound like you have some affection for him. When you were talking about grilling with him, I mean." Serena nestled against him and put an arm across his waist to hold him closer. It was a very comforting position, that feeling of safety and warmth surprising him because it was so unexpected.

"Using your words, Mom gentled him. He'd come home with a thundercloud on his face and she'd have him chuckling and grinning in no time. She'd tease him until he couldn't resist, and he'd do anything for her. And she'd convince him that he was the best griller in the world, the best builder in the world, and the best in everything. Together, they were really something." He fell silent for a moment and let his cheek drop to Serena's silky hair. It smelled like flowers in the cooling night air.

"Mom had this way of making you think – no, making you know – that what you were doing was terrific and important and the best thing that anyone ever accomplished. And she always did it in such a way that you were happy and content and secure. You wanted to try harder because of her. She was our anchor, our rock, and our inspiration."

His voice trailed off. Even the woods became silent, listening to his story.

"You said 'was'." Serena's voice was gentle and she rubbed a hand over his heart, as if she knew something still hurt.

"She died too young. It was cancer, something she ignored. She kept telling us it was just fatigue or something. Dad took her at her word and if he pushed her to see a doctor, we never knew about it. By the time her pain made a doctor unavoidable, it was too late to do much, though they tried all sorts of treatments. Through it all, she kept her sunny disposition, kept insisting we do things as a family, like those barbeques. That was a mainstay in our activities. Weekends were sacrosanct, particularly close to the end. All of us wanted any time we could have with her."

Serena kept her hand over his heart, and he dropped a kiss on the top of her head in thanks. She seemed to understand his need to talk this out.

"Two weeks before she died, we had our last grilling event together as a full family. Mom could only sit in a chair in the shade, gentle still, directing us all as we put everything together, as if we hadn't been doing this together forever." His lips quirked in memory. The picture of that last dinner together was one that would stay with him forever. "And she made us promise, each of us, that we'd continue this tradition of building our meal together often after she was gone. She seemed to know that once she was gone, things would get damn difficult."

Serena shifted against him again, putting a gentle hand against his cheek. "How old were you when she died?"

"I had just turned thirteen. Amanda was fifteen and Powers was eighteen, already working part time in the family business."

"That's a hard age for a boy to lose his mother."

He pulled her closer, tangling his legs with hers.

"And I didn't handle it well. I went a little wild. Mandy was absent a lot of the time, spending most of her days with her friends. Powers became a younger version of Dad overnight, brusque and demanding, getting on my back all the time, a real control freak about everyone and everything."

"Where are they now, your sister and brother?"

He toyed with her hair absentmindedly. "Mandy, I don't know. She disowned us years ago. Said she didn't want anything to do with us anymore. It was like she was perpetually mad and blaming us for something, but we never could figure out what it was." Regret never left him over that.

Serena toyed with the cloth of his shirt. "And your brother? It sounds like you must have some conversations with him."

Dane guffawed, a bitter sound. "He went on to college and an engineering degree and then grad school, and eventually he took over a big chunk of the business from Dad after our grandfather retired. He runs the family business now, and reminds me as often as he can about how I should be running my life. He's turned into a real control freak." Dane fell silent again.

"And what did you do after your mom died?" Serena delivered her probing question gently in the black night.

"I got into trouble in high school on a regular basis. None of it was major – I never got picked up by the law or anything that severe, but I never seemed to do anything right. I was in trouble all the time from Dad – and from Powers. Never could satisfy either one of them in whatever I decided to do. But those damn family dinners – they continued. Depending on what was happening, they were either silent, or one or more of us – usually Powers and I at a minimum – were yelling at each other. When Dad bellowed, we all shut up. I tried college but it wasn't for me. I had other ideas on who I was. I found other outlets for my energy."

"Is that how you ended up in the military?" Serena's question was innocent, and yet he knew why she was asking it. She was trying to find the link to what he must appear to her, a veteran of war who was damaged goods and needed fixing. It was easy to let her believe that. He'd rather skip over the middle of his story anyway since it didn't matter anymore.

"It's how I ended up in Afghanistan two years ago, the beginning of the hardest time in my life. My unit was on a counterinsurgency mission – clearing the people away from the insurgents by stationing soldiers with the people. The lieutenant of the platoon, my buddy Anderson, was working with the local elders to get medicines the people needed. We were making sure people were compensated for their losses from the war. We distributed materials and supplies the locals needed to get on with their lives, and

Anderson was helping them form a local government structure too. We worked with the kids, building trust and helping them to smile again. And we were trying to get the word out that the face of war had changed. The Afghan people for the most part trusted us."

Dane turned Serena's face to his and placed a soft kiss on her lips. He wanted to be looking into her eyes, trusting her with his memories. She held his gaze and placed her hands over his on her face.

"Anderson was a great guy, talented and compassionate and an inspiring soldier. He had those three great characteristics of leadership – competence, caring for his people, and courage and conviction in the mission. He was near the end of his tour, scheduled to come home in three more months and spend his leave with his wife and his three boys." His voice broke, and there was no way for him to stop it. "Everyone looked up to him. I know I certainly did."

Serena shifted and pulled his mouth down, her kiss as gentle as his had been, tender and supportive. She deepened it by sending her tongue into his mouth. For a moment, all he could think about was how right this felt, being held by her and finding the sweetness of the moment in her lush taste. Her tongue mated with his and their dance made his heat rise. His groin tightened and he groaned, hopefully only in his own mind. He still had stuff to get out, things to tell her, before this went any further.

Moving his hands to her shoulders to set her away from him, Dane held on to Serena's eyes with his. "The event occurred in the Korengal Valley in Konar Province, near Asadabad, a place we knew as A-bad. Our platoon came under fire while we were patrolling a neighborhood that was supposed to be safe. We approached a house that had been cleared before. I can still see it in my mind, a courtyard with some piles of trash, the ever-present haze of heat and dirt, the empty darkness of holes that were once doors and windows of someone's home."

He forced himself to keep his gaze locked with hers, even when he wanted to look away. Hell, he wanted to run away. The need to dive deep inside himself overtook him as it always did when he got to this point in his memory. The pain was overwhelming.

"The area was booby trapped by insurgents while we were trying to build a rapport with the locals. Sometime between when the area was swept and when we got there, bombs were hidden – no one later was sure where, in the debris or under the dirt of the courtyard, but someplace or somehow we tripped explosions. Eight soldiers died right away, blown up initially or killed by collateral damage. There was blood and dust everywhere, it was hard to see."

He closed his eyes briefly because the next words were so hard to get out. Serena placed a hand on his face, stroking his beard and cheek, tracing his jaw, as if she was easing him through it. She didn't say a word, and finally, he was able to open his eyes again to find her watching him with damp-eyed compassion.

"It's okay, you don't need to tell me if you don't want to." Her quiet acceptance and understanding eased something inside Dane. He felt the death grip on his heart start to lessen and realized that perhaps getting this out was a good idea after all.

Inhaling the night's freshness, he continued. "It's hard to get through sometimes, the pictures of this. He was such a good friend to me, closer than I'd allowed myself to get to anyone in a long time. Anderson, he was right in the middle of the courtyard. He, ah, he didn't die, not right away. The blasts took off his legs, and he was screaming for help. I couldn't tell what was happening, if there was gunfire or if that was part of this series of bombs the insurgents had rigged."

He swallowed the bile that rose in his throat.

"What did you do?" Serena's voice was husky and so low that he thought he was hearing it as a whisper in his mind. His brittle bark of a derisive laugh might have surprised her, but she didn't turn away from him and didn't pull back. He took that as a good sign.

"I didn't do anything to help him. I fulfilled my mission, my duty." He just about spit the last word out.

"Were you injured then too?"

Dane set her aside now, a little roughly, angry with himself for the past. He rose so quickly to move away that Serena ended up sideways on the couch. He started to pace at the edge of the fire's pale light. He could see the concern for him in her expression. It calmed him. Running a hand through his hair and then rubbing his face, he stopped in front of her and dropped down to squat on his heels, taking her hands in his.

"Yes, and I didn't realize how bad until I was in Germany. There were surgeries, treatments, rehab. They took care of most of it, though the scars won't ever completely go away on the outside."

He traced the mounds and valleys in the palms of her hands with rough thumbs. She gripped his fingers, giving him the strength and desire to continue.

"It's the ones on the inside that hurt, though. I won't ever be able to forget the look on Anderson's face as he lay there in his own blood, dirt on his face streaked by tears and his look enraged at the unfairness of it all. It will be with me, always."

Serena tightened her hands in his, as if she was trying to take some of his pain into herself.

"You survived, and that's sometimes harder. Based on what you say, there probably wasn't much more that you could have done for him. His injuries sound like they were too severe. You were a soldier and you did what you had to do to survive a war. You were badly injured. What did you expect of yourself?"

While her question was gentle, he could sense a defensive shift in her tone. Was she trying to defend him? If he wasn't so torn up inside, he would have examined that idea further. As it was, he was too disgusted with himself to appreciate the irony.

"Oh, I expected better. I benefited from Anderson's death, profited you might say. I could have gone to him, friend to friend, eased his pain as he passed. But no. I kept myself distant, did my job, and later on, much later, I not only survived but I thrived from all of this."

His self-loathing came in waves, his words doing nothing to hide it. He could barely stand to be in his own skin when he thought back to everything that had happened. He would have walked away into the darkness, but Serena had a tight grip on his hands and pulled him forward.

"You did what you had to do. You survived, and that's the important thing. You were a soldier, and you did your job. That's all."

Her acceptance irritated him. She didn't understand, not yet, because he hadn't shared it all. He couldn't - at least not tonight and maybe not for a long time.

Dane rose from his crouch, pulling Serena up with him, and yanked her into his arms, his mouth already aiming for hers with angry desperation. This was the closest thing he'd felt to forgiveness, to redemption since that fateful day. And he couldn't stop himself from taking what he needed for that next step in the journey.

Chapter 27

Serena didn't even have time to pull in a full breath before Dane's mouth crushed hers. She tasted desperation in his kiss and her compassionate heart ached. He'd felt so much pain. And while she wanted to wish it away, it was an important part of who he was today. She opened her mouth to his and felt the immediate demanding dart of his tongue searching for hers. His arms banded around her and a whisper of a groan escaped him as he held her tighter still.

Her thoughts scattered as he took more from her, a hunger in him calling to an answering craving in her. She let her hands bunch in his hair, feeling the coarse curls around her fingers just as his tongue curled around hers in their mated mouths. His hands eased on her back and started to move in slow motion up and down her back, tracing her spine.

Dane massaged her neck and lingered in her hair for a time, his other hand exploring the curve of her waist, his thumb tracing a rib under her skin as if imprinting her shape in his memory. Serena felt her nerves tighten even more, and the jolt of energy sent tingles of expectation up her spine to spread throughout her body. She was lightheaded and grounded at the same time, an unusual feeling of being both in her body and out of it all at once.

And it felt incredible.

When Dane suddenly pulled away, the coldness despite the warm evening air was a shock. He didn't let her go far, staring into her eyes, questioning. Serena shuddered, the wave of desire and pleasure so overwhelming that for a moment she forgot where they were. With a shake of her head, she reluctantly eased her hold on him, and he didn't hide the disappointment in his eyes.

Yes, she wanted him, but she also didn't want him coming to her out of hurt or despair. Her core ached, a raging heat making her wet with need for him, and glancing down, she could see from the erection his jeans couldn't hide that his desire for her was just as intense. Now didn't seem to be that time, though, not until they were both wanting from a perspective in the present, not trying to hide from the past.

"Wow," she said with a shaky smile. After a brief moment, he rubbed his hands up and down her arms and grinned sheepishly before stepping away slowly and turning to the remains of the fire. His back hid his expression from her. She wondered if he was as moved past just the physical by what had happened between them as she was.

Serena took a deep breath and thought she should try again. Dane tended to get quiet when something got too close to the edge of his emotions, and she didn't want him stepping back now, not when they had come so far together.

Looking up, she realized how dark the night sky had become. No moon hid the stars tonight, and the Milky Way arched and branched overhead. The breeze blew away any summer haze that might have lingered, and there were so many stars that it made picking out the constellations almost impossible. And just then, she saw it.

"Look, a shooting star!" She grabbed Dane's arm and turned him to her, pointing upward. The quick movement initially caught him by surprise and she could feel the tension in his muscles under her hand. He looked up to follow her finger skyward to the northeast. And just then, another brief streak dashed across.

Dane grinned now, his teeth shining white in the darkness of his beard. "It's the beginning of the meteor shower. Things should be picking up fast now. It starts slow but gets lively quickly, and you can see dozens of meteors an hour."

Together, the two of them stared up at the night sky, oohing and aahing when streaks of light, sometimes white and often other colors as well, danced across the sky. After a few minutes, Serena shifted her shoulders to get the kink out of her neck.

"I think it's time to let this futon do its thing," Dane said, placing his hand on her neck, rubbing out the stiffness that the unnatural position brought on. "I'll lay it out flat and we can stretch out, watch the shooting stars from relative comfort." His quick kiss held friendly promise, but none of the heat of a few minutes ago.

Serena rubbed her arms, wondering at her sudden disappointment. Maybe she had called a halt too quickly, she realized. She missed him already across the small distance between them, that space taking on a whole new significance. Her heart gave a little nudge that she chose to ignore. Now was not the time.

*****

Dane found the latch that held the couch upright and pulled the futon down to a flat surface. He was kicking himself. He'd moved too fast, but he'd felt such a need to have her in his arms, tight against him. Maybe in that moment she had been his life preserver when he was drowning, but he felt fairly confident that he could tread water safely again.

It had been cathartic, all of that talking about the past, talking past the pain of it. She had been right, he did need to discuss it. But he didn't want to talk with a bunch of vets who didn't know him or to a counselor who was paid to care. He wanted to talk about it with Serena. He wanted her to care.

The jolt of surprise at the thought stopped him mid-step for the space of three seconds before he was able to put a foot down to move forward.

He was coming to care deeply, perhaps too deeply, for Serena. He wanted her to think well of him. Hell, he wanted her to think about him becoming something more than a friend. And that scared the crap out of him.

Dane shook as he moved to his makeshift table and grabbed the pillows and blankets he had left there earlier. What would she want with a broken down mess like him? Granted, he was better – a whole lot better – than he had been, even just a few months ago when he'd started rebuilding something of his life. But he'd never be the same as he'd been before.

Circling the almost extinguished fire, he realized that maybe him not being the same would be a very good thing.

*****

"How do you know so many constellations?" They were laying side-by-side, pillows under their heads staring up at the continuing light show. Serena smiled in the darkness at his question.

"I was brought up in the country, and we always had stars to watch. My dad showed me a lot of them when I was little, and I just remembered. Those were times when I felt the closest to him. He'd be sitting in the backyard in the dark, looking up, and I'd go out and crawl in his lap, begging for attention. I'd ask him what he was looking at, and he'd point out a constellation and then tell me a story about it. I just loved to hear him talk, knowing that he was focused on me in those few minutes."

Serena was aware of a small sigh escaping her as she thought so fondly of those nights. "After he was gone, I used to go outside at night and look up at the stars, and pretend he was up there, riding one of the mythical creatures he used to build into my stories. And when I grew older, I got curious about the stars on my own. I learned about them, about the myths and the fables, but none of the stories were as good as what Dad used to tell."

In the silence, Serena felt Dane watching her. Despite the lack of a moon, there was enough light to see shapes and spaces, and she was intent on trying to read his face with what little night vision she had. His mouth was set in a soft expression, of sympathy or pity, she wasn't sure. But now he was sad for her, just as she had been so sad for him before. She could feel it.

His concentrated stare didn't make her dwell on the past. In fact, she forgot completely what she'd been saying. The magnetism in his eyes drew her forward. He was leaning on one elbow, looking down at her, and she shifted to mirror his position. Almost nose to nose, they continued to stare into each other's eyes.

Funny, she thought, there was enough light here at night for her to see the growing glow of passion. His blue eyes were beginning to blaze, and she knew that an answering fire was building in her own.

Now, now it was time. Even if it wasn't for him, it was for her.

Chapter 28

She wasn't sure if she was leaning towards him or if he was coming for her, but either way, Serena was ready to feel those lips on hers again. This time, she had an awareness that added a spice of danger. No one was hiding from the past or reacting to it. It was just now, just right under this blanket of night with the rockets of shooting stars overhead.

When their lips met, she opened hers immediately, ready and welcoming for the invasion of his tongue and the searching suction his mouth provided. The bolt of energy shooting through her was immediate and her craving for him followed right on its heels, hardening her nipples and setting her core throbbing. Like a meteor, the desire spiked and flashed along her nerves until she couldn't wait for gentle and nice and dug her fingers deep in Dane's hair to pull him closer.

Rolling them both, Dane settled on top of her, holding himself up just enough to keep from crushing her with his weight, letting her feel that his desire was rising to match hers. His hands moved blindly over her face, tracing bone and feature as if imprinting them in his mind. His kiss changed direction and deepened, his breath catching.

Then he moved off her lips to let his tongue trace a path to her ear. He took her lobe gently in his teeth and sucked on it, sending another flash of energy through her. She had to move.

The surge of power she felt would have surprised her if she'd been capable of thought. Her hands couldn't be still, and they roamed over the cotton on Dane's back to explore the shape of him. His muscles felt like steel and molten heat came off him in waves. But even that wasn't enough, and when she reached his waist, she yanked the t-shirt free and set her hands against his bare skin.

Dane jolted over her, seeming to feel the flash of her power just as she felt it rise within her. One hand stayed on her face, guiding his mouth back to hers in a kiss that now had a new sense of urgency to it. The other molded down the side of her body to her hip, lingering there for a few burning caresses before moving back to the side of her breast. Despite their rising excitement, she felt his intentional gentleness under the pressure.

She lifted off the couch as his hand softly shaped her breast through the bra and tank top. She tensed, wanting a more intimate caress. The heavy weight of him pressed her back into the futon, and his arousal pressed into her, notching up her needs even more.

Serena let her fingers play up his back, tracing his spine and the contours of his shoulders. She knew from their days working on the house how his bare back looked in the sun. Now she realized that she'd evidently spent a lot of time staring at it, because in her mind she could imagine just what the skin and tendon and muscle looked like in each place where her fingers now wandered.

Dane's mouth was on her neck, pressing his lips to the fast beat of her pulse just below her ear. The scrape of his teeth made her nearly levitate off the couch as it seared her. She moved her restless mouth to his ear, nipping at his neck in turn, wanting him to feel as driven as she was.

The hand on her breast tightened and his hiss of breath let her know that, bingo, she'd hit the mark. Fingers came around to tease her nipple, and she shifted with each new edgy sensation, wishing that the layers of cloth between them would disappear. The sizzle she was feeling was definitely hot enough to burn them off.

Abruptly, Dane pulled back and removed his hands, swinging his legs over the side of the futon to hit the ground, each foot with its own distinct thud. Serena blinked through her confusion at the sudden loss of his heat. It took five big gulps of air to steady her heart and find her voice.

Putting a shaky hand to his back, she said had to ask, "Dane, what is it?"

*****

What was it? He wasn't sure he knew how to answer that off the top of his head. Things were moving fast, and he wanted them to move faster. He also thought that he and Serena should probably slow down. As it was, he could barely sit for the tight strain of his erection inside his jeans. It had been so long, too long, and he clearly hadn't thought through how far things might go tonight.

"It's, ah, it's been a while." His voice was gruff and hoarse with need, and he tried to clear his throat again. "I'm not exactly prepared for this, didn't think we'd…" He trailed off, waving a hand to indicate the general state of things.

God, this was embarrassing.

"It's okay if it's been a while." Serena's voice was soft behind him and her hand was gently rubbing his back, now on top of the t-shirt again. He missed the warmth of her skin on his already.

"We can take things slow or fast, that's okay. We have all night. No rush, or all the rush in the world."

Dane had to smile. She was so understanding. Of course, she'd undoubtedly heard it all before from the men she counseled. Maybe the women too, but he had no way of knowing. But that really wasn't the issue.

Turning to her despite his embarrassment, Dane grabbed her outstretched hand and placed a lingering kiss to her palm. "I am not exactly a good host tonight," he said as he traced the outline of her thumb with his fingertips. "Not exactly a good boy scout."

Serena was puzzled. "Not a good boy scout? I don't get it."

Sighing, Dane took her hand in both of his, feeling how small the shape was compared to his larger ones. "It's been a long time, and I haven't been with anyone else in, well, in over a year. I've been checked out and I'm clean."

He was grateful for the lack of light. She couldn't see the blush of shame on his face. But she was still waiting. He cleared his throat again.

"But the boy scout part refers to my lack of planning about condoms."

In the thin light, he saw a smile start on Serena's mouth and reach her eyes almost immediately. Then her expression turned sheepish too. "It's been quite a while for me too, and I can say ditto to the clean bill of health. And I'm on the pill."

Her gaze gentled and she caressed his face, feathering her fingers through his beard before giving it a little tug. "And I don't mind if you don't."

*****

Dane froze in place, and Serena wondered if she had said the wrong thing. Was she being a slut? But it had been a long time since her last relationship too, and she didn't go to bed with any man to satisfy an itch. There had to be a bigger something happening, a connection of mind and heart as well as their bodies.

Besides, she knew she wasn't the only one feeling this incredible need to mate under the stars with the streaks of fire overhead echoing the ones inside them both.

Then there was nothing but movement. Dane turned and dropped over her, his mouth coming down on hers with a hunger that was so strong, she thought he would eat her alive. And she really didn't care.

Gentle? What had she been thinking? And then she really didn't want to think anymore.

Her own desire surging to meet his, Serena yanked up his t-shirt and Dane lifted long enough to toss it over his head into the darkness. His hands reached for the edge of her tank and she rose in turn to give him access. That too went flying off into the night.

The air, which should have felt cool, just fueled her own flames higher.

Tongues mating, she could feel the waves of heat coming off Dane, his breathing as ragged as hers. His mouth lifted and began a swift search down her body to her breast, licking the nipple through her bra and causing her to arch against him. His hands moved to the center clasp and he fumbled with the release for a heartbeat, too long in her opinion. She was ready to shove him aside and take over the errant hook when it finally came free to his groan of satisfaction.

The sensation of his beard on her already aroused breasts was staggering, sending another shock of energy through her. His lips tugged and sucked at her nipple before he moved across her body to give the other the same attention. The bolt this time went straight to her core and she couldn't help but cry out.

Dane froze again, setting his forehead against the side of her breast. He was panting. So was she. And she didn't want him to stop.

His voice was muffled. "I'm sorry, I'm being too rough, too fast. Give me a minute. I'm sorry." He didn't raise his head and his hands were still.

"You haven't been too rough. Or maybe it's been way too long for me too." Serena tunneled her fingers scalp deep and pulled him up so that his eyes couldn't avoid her stare. "I want you, I think as much as you want me. There's nothing to apologize for in that."

Keeping her eyes open on his, she pulled up to kiss him, a hard lip lock that had him sucking in air as his eyes continued to burn into hers. His hand moved between them, cupping her heat. Her body flexed in response, wanting that more intimate touch again without the weight of denim in the way. She heard herself whimper and didn't even bother to bite off the sound.

Her hand began its own slide down his bare chest. The flutter of muscles as she crossed his belly let her know that he was just as anxious, just as ready. She cupped his erection and he groaned. His hands dug into her waist to move her further away. She wanted to complain until his fingers moved to the button of her jeans, wrestling once again with uncooperative fasteners.

"Damn it!" His frustration at the difficult clasp had her laughing, low, until he closed his lips around a nipple again and the laugh turned into a gasp of pleasure. She caressed the hard shape of him through his jeans, and he cursed again.

Her impatience was growing along with her aching need. Pushing his hand away and rolling out from underneath him, Serena swung to her feet. With fumbling fingers, she finally opened the button on her jeans. When she would have gone further, Dane's hands stopped hers and he yanked down the zipper, pushing his hands inside to cover her buttocks and shove the jeans down her legs. She sucked in air when his beard tickled her belly and he dropped a fast kiss right over her heat, the panties offering no protection against the intimate gesture. And then her jeans and her panties were gone off into the night with the rest of her clothes.

Serena swayed with the speed of her accelerating desire. She was hot, wet and ready, and Dane still had too many clothes on. Her knees were shaking, and as if knowing that she couldn't stand any longer, Dane pulled her down on the futon and stood to get rid of his last barriers. Before she had time to fully appreciate his silhouette against the stars, he was on top of her, his hands linking with hers as his mouth sealed against her lips.

The kiss was luscious, ravenous, and hot, way too hot to last very long without burning them both up. Dane released a hand to run down her body, reaching between them to find her wet folds in a rough caress that had her arching up beneath him. Desire was spiraling up so fast she was surprised she didn't explode with it.

His voice was in her ear. "I want to take you slowly, but I don't think I can, not this time. I'm sorry, sweetheart. I want to be gentle with you."

She could hear the strain in his words. It made her heart flip to realize he was trying to hold himself back for her.

"Come inside, Dane. I need you just as much as you need me."

*****

For a split second, Dane's mind went blank, thinking he hadn't heard her right. She was hot under his fingers, his hand continuing its caress because she was so responsive. He thought he could stay like this, watching passion chase across her face under the stars, for hours on end.

Then Serena surged against his hand, crying out, and he was losing any ability to think.

Her openness was incredible, as eager as he was, and he cradled her mound for a moment before he moved to brace himself over her. Her legs and arms wrapped around him and he found her eyes in the darkness, glowing with the light of desire that loosened something in his heart. He was poised at the entrance of her heat, and she lifted her hips to forge the connection.

Just the feel of her, tight around him and so ready, killed any lingering consideration of going slow. His body reacted, withdrawing almost completely before plunging deeper. Serena gave a gasp of pleasure and that single sound made any remaining rational thoughts shoot out of his mind.

He linked his hand with hers and she responded, tightening her grip on him. He cradled her head as he drove into her. She shifted beneath him, taking him deeper with each thrust. Her free hand rubbed at the base of his spine, pulling him closer still.

Damn, it had been too long. He wanted to linger here, watch Serena's face, and see the expressions dance across it with each sensation. He wanted to hear her cry out again as she came. This pitch of ecstasy and agony was something he could enjoy forever, he was sure of it. But not today, not right now.

Never letting his eyes leave hers as he gave her a final hard kiss, he moaned and shuddered as he exploded inside Serena, taking her with him in a flash that rivaled those shooting stars above them.

Chapter 29

Her first conscious thought was that it had been ages, if ever, that she felt this loose and easy inside her skin. Every nerve ending was finely tuned to the rhythm that she and Dane set throughout the night.

After their first frantic round, they'd laid in each other arms, not speaking, watching the meteors dancing overhead. Dane had gently run his hands through her hair, over her body, and Serena was content to nuzzle his neck. The scent of him wrapped around her, lulling her into a peaceful haze.

She had no sense of how much time passed. Billions of stars blazed overhead, streaks of the meteor shower wove in between constellations. Then Dane lifted his head, and all she could see was the glow of his eyes on her.

Passion rose again, much slower and sweeter this time. Dane kissed his way down her body and back up again. Each square inch of her skin felt like it had his personal attention. Then he moved to her core, sucking and licking until she climaxed again with a shout of joy. This time, when he'd entered her and started that steady rhythm, the pace was slow. They'd risen up together and peaked, staring into each other's eyes in the muted light of the stars.

Sleep finally came for a brief time. As the eastern sky started to lighten, Serena took her turn, tracking the shapes and contours of Dane's body. She moved a gentle hand to feather a stroke up the inside of his thigh and halted abruptly when she felt a tough ridge of scar tissue. His hand stopped her when she would have explored it further.

It felt like it must have been painful, and she opened her mouth to ask about it when Dane put a finger to her lips to silence her. He used that finger to pull open her lower lip for the exploration of his tongue.

She decided that conversation could wait.

Stretching on the memory of that last climb to another incredible joining, Serena put a hand across the futon for Dane, only to find it empty. The sun was up, and she squinted around, realizing that she was alone – and still very naked – under the blanket. She had a moment of panic until she realized that it was Saturday, and no contractors would be appearing on the jobsite today.

But where was Dane?

*****

There were some things that needed to be prepared a certain way, and for Dane, one of those things was coffee. He'd had some truly rot gut brew in his travels, and the military version was probably the worst of all. Now he could enjoy that morning cup of espresso, and he'd treated himself to a good machine when he settled into the cabin. Roughing it did not mean deprivation. That first pungent aroma of good coffee in the morning always brought the day into sharp focus.

He had to smile as he waited for the steam to heat in the espresso maker. Reflecting back on the night, he was amazed that his desire for Serena hadn't lessened with each sensuous coupling. In fact, he felt a stir below the beltline even now with the thought of finding new ways to please her. Watching her cry out under the light of the stars was a picture that he would never forget. She was fire to burn him and earth to ground him, letting him soar and then taking him through gentle waves of building pleasure. She was all of the elements, all that he needed.

It startled him to realize how large that need was.

The machine hissed and he let out his own hiss to match it. He still hadn't been honest with Serena, still hadn't told her about his past, not completely. She thought he was an Army vet who had been wounded in the line of duty. And that wasn't it at all.

He didn't want to go there, the place where he had to discuss his shame and his self-loathing. The past was the past and he wanted it to stay there, even if it still influenced everything he did today. He was no longer the man he had been a couple of years ago, full of adventure and a need to make a difference. Now, he wanted peace and quiet and anonymity.

If he told her the real story, he was sure she'd keep his secrets. But was that fair to her? She had expectations of him, and he wasn't sure he could meet them. And in his newfound peace with her, he feared that if he told her everything, she'd run as fast as her long legs could carry her.

*****

Serena sat up and looked around the open area, taking stock of how far away her clothes might be. Her jeans were almost next to the futon, but her bra was a distance away, only missed being tossed into the remains of the fire last night by inches. That would have been a show!

She was contemplating how to get out of the futon gracefully while wrapped in the light blanket when the cabin door opened and Dane appeared carrying two steaming cups of coffee. She could smell it from here – strong and vibrant, just like the man carrying it.

With a shiver, she let her gaze ride up from the worn and tight jeans to his bare chest to his eyes locked on her. He was a very potent combination of strength and intellect that she was quickly becoming addicted to.

"Good morning sleepyhead," his voice rumbled low and a small smile tugged at his lips under his beard.

Obviously she didn't look bad in the full morning light or he wouldn't be looking at her like that, blue eyes flashing a fresh level of desire.

She'd have thought she'd be exhausted. The shock in realizing that they hadn't worn each other out last night sent a heated blush up her cheeks. His desire struck a chord in her, sending a spurt of energy from head to toe and making her nerves hum in anticipation.

"Good morning. That coffee smells incredible." He handed her a mug and she sniffed appreciatively at the rich aroma, taking a tentative sip. It was perfect, as smooth and warm as their night had been. "And here I was thinking I'd been doing you a favor bringing those mochas from town."

"Nothing wrong with a good mocha or latte, but a man's got to survive and good coffee is one of those survival requirements." He smiled again, a grin that reached his eyes and made her heart beat faster.

She patted the couch next to her. Sitting on the edge of the futon, he reached out to play with a lock of her hair, then traced the line of her jaw. His face grew serious and his eyes were sad.

She wanted to wipe that expression off his face, never letting him feel sadness again. She had a feeling he'd seen too much of it in his life.

His hair was damp, so he'd obviously had a shower already. That sounded good, but her stomach growled loud enough for him to hear. And that brought the grin back to his face. She smiled a bit sheepishly in response and dropped her eyes.

"I guess I, ah, burned off a lot of calories last night." She looked at him through her lashes and was relieved to see that he was now chuckling.

"I think we both did." He took her hand and turned it over his, bending to kiss the palm and then close her fingers around the spot.

Something inside her tingled in response and she had to stop herself from levitating off the couch.

"Last night, this morning, were incredible, Serena. You are an amazing woman." The serious look was back on his face, and he was examining her expression closely.

"It was amazing for me too," she said, suddenly feeling a bit shy, which was so unlike her. She was always one for bold and brazen, and this emotion was so new that she didn't know what to do with it. It was like he was looking inside her and examining her soul. His assessment paused at her lips and he lingered there for a bit.

He stood up abruptly, turning his back as he busied himself at the makeshift table and rummaged around in the cooler. "Why don't you have a shower while I fix us some breakfast? Omelets with vegetables and cheese okay?"

He still hadn't looked back at her, and Serena was surprised at the disappointment she suddenly felt.

Pulling the blanket closer around her, she stood up and wobbled, smiling inside when she realized that she was sore in all the right places and the feeling was fabulous. But it wasn't just because it had been a long time. She'd never had her needs cared for with the degree of dedication that Dane had shown last night. It was like he was tending to her.

Coming up behind him slowly, she tentatively touched his shoulder, willing him to turn around. All his actions halted as he felt her hand, then he slowly turned around and looked into her eyes. His were now unreadable. She reached up and placed a small kiss at the corner of his mouth, and he turned his head to return it full on, seam to seam. Even gentle like this, it seared her to the core.

Her heart stumbled in her chest and jumped to her throat. What had she gotten herself into?

Chapter 30

The shower felt wonderful, even in the confined space of the cabin's meager bathing facilities. It was like an RV shower built into the corner of the single room. Ingenious, but small. While she would have loved to have Dane come in and share it with her, there was barely space for her to turn around alone.

Toweling her hair while sitting in one of the few chairs, Serena idly thought about the day ahead. She was meeting the girl tribe tonight, and she wouldn't throw them over for a man. Granted, Dane was an incredibly hot guy, and a passionate and caring lover. But still.

Plus, she had a lot to process, and they would help with that. Maybe they could make sense of the rightness and something much deeper that was building inside her for Dane.

He would probably work on the house – he worked on the house just about every day. And it was coming along so quickly now. He'd be in it before the weather turned nasty, even if it wasn't completely painted and finished inside. This was his goal, to be living in the house before the rains started in another couple of months.

The cabin was cute, though, compact and orderly. It would make a good office for someone. It was the right size with basic amenities, and character whispered out of the old wood and simple design. She hoped he wasn't going to tear it down once the house was complete. She'd have to ask him about that.

As her eyes traveled around the small space, she spotted something that looked like an artist's portfolio, the large folding kind that people used to carry drawings or plans. It was open, braced up against the cold woodstove.

It appeared that Dane had been searching through it recently as well.

She'd never seen the full blueprints for the house, and she was curious about how he planned to finish the various rooms, particularly what the kitchen and bathrooms would look like. A corner of white paper that looked like a blueprint copy poked out of one side.

It would be amazing to see his full vision for the place. Standing, she moved over to the folio and picked it up, careful not to spill the contents out of the unzipped sides. It was heavy, a lot heavier than she expected it to be.

Maybe she shouldn't open it.

On the other hand, Dane had been very open about his house plans. He'd answered every question she had. In fact, he'd offered to share more about the design with her on a few occasions.

"How will the kitchen be laid out? And how are you planning to use all of the rooms?" They'd been taking a break on the interior work, the same day they shared that first impulsive kiss over the trusses and the upcoming roof.

"Remind me, I'll get the rest of the plans from the shack. I only keep what we need for the current phase of construction here. I have it designed down to the facings on the cabinets. You can give me your opinion." He'd seemed relaxed and comfortable with her interest in what came after the more mundane plumbing and electrical work.

He wanted her to see the plans. There wasn't anything secret about it, after all. And he was busy fixing them breakfast.

Her curiosity got the better of her. After everything they'd shared, she doubted that he would be angry with her nosing around, particularly into something he planned to share with her. It was standing open, after all.

Carrying the black folio to the large worktable, the only flat surface big enough to accommodate it, she let the hinges fall open.

Serena's gasp rang out so loudly in the confined space that she expected Dane to hear her and ask what was wrong. After a guilty flick of her eyes to the closed cabin door, she moved closer and ran a tentative finger over the contents.

It was full of pictures, big format photos specifically, amazing photography that made the animals and people in the shots seem to come alive and crowd the small room. Did he take these? He'd never mentioned any interest in photography. Or maybe they were a gift, maybe prints he planned to frame for the walls in his new house.

Whatever the reason Dane had for having them, she couldn't tear her eyes away. They were magnificent. The detail, the layout, the colors all popped out to meet her.

And as she paged deeper into the stack, some of them dropped from her shaking fingers with another startled cry as she glanced outside to where she'd left Dane.

*****

He sliced and diced a selection of vegetables, the simple action of food preparation allowing his mind to wander. He wanted to tell her about his time in the war zone. He felt that he owed her that. She had been open with him about her family, the tragedies, the need to build her nonprofit, the happiness along with the challenges. He shared enough to let her know something about what had happened.

But it wasn't the whole story. Did he owe her that too?

Dane was afraid, painfully afraid, that if she learned all about him, she would no longer look at him with the longing, amusement and something more that her eyes held only a few minutes ago. He wanted more of that, and more of her in his life.

Where had this come from so fast? If he was honest with himself, though, it wasn't that fast. They'd shared a lot over the time they worked together on the house, and the weeks had flown by. More than a month had passed by now, and he'd spent more time with her than with most of the women in his past. In fact, this might be a new world record for him.

That was the other thing in his past that he didn't necessarily want to think about or discuss - the women. There had been quite a few, casual friends with benefits. They had jobs like his that took them around the world for brief stopovers in various cities or outposts. Sometimes it was just a night, sometimes a whole weekend. But none of them ever mattered to him the way that Serena was beginning to matter right now.

And that scared the hell out of him.

He beat the eggs in two separate bowls, probably beating a whole lot harder with the fork than necessary, but it gave him an outlet for his disquiet. He had an urge to run into the thick of the woods so that he didn't have to face Serena.

He had a stronger desire to go into the cabin, take her in his arms, and hold her tightly to him until the fear drained away.

What he didn't want to do was tell her anything else, at least not right now. He wanted a few more days or weeks of this newfound happiness before things blew up in his face, another incident in the making. And that made him feel incredibly guilty.

*****

One hand tucked protectively over the smartphone in her back pocket, Serena walked slowly over to their little campsite. She'd taken pictures of some of the photos, both the pretty ones and the ones that disturbed her. They were all sweeping and breath taking, but in totally different ways.

She wanted to say something to Dane, but what would that be? She'd pried into his things, even if he had left it in plain view.

Well, not exactly. She did have to take the portfolio to the table and open it.

But did he take those pictures? Did someone else give them to him? Maybe he was going to put them up as décor in the new house.

That didn't explain the bad ones, though, the ones with gore and blood, agony on men's faces. Looking at them, she had a new appreciation for the incidents the vets she worked with described in sessions. Their words painted pictures that were awful enough, but when viewed in larger than life shots of living color, the horror that turned people's souls inside out was impossible to downplay.

Dane's back was to her, intent on his cooking, and as she got closer, she noted a tension in his shoulders and neck, an impression more than anything concrete. Or maybe it was just because she was feeling so guilty for prying.

She came up to the camp stove, clearing her throat so that she wouldn't surprise him. If he had lived through those kinds of events, she could understand his jumpiness at sharp noises.

"That smells amazing again. You really are a great cook. You and Roxy will have fun exchanging foodie ideas." She put a smile on her face as he turned to her.

There was a flash of something in his expression, an impression of guilt. Was she projecting again? She should have left well enough alone and not touched that portfolio. She should have asked him if she could look before she did.

Just as quickly as she noted it, the guilt she thought she saw on his face was gone. Had it ever been there? A look of wariness replaced it, and when she kept smiling at him, he finally relaxed and grinned back. It wasn't a full smile and it didn't reach his eyes, but at least he wasn't looking like he'd jump out of his skin.

"Like I said last night, in my family everyone was expected to cook. You didn't get a specialty. You had to be able to cook everything. I can even make a mean biscuit, given the right circumstances." He gestured to the fire and a cast iron skillet. "These aren't quite right." His smile got easier and his eyes seemed to brighten as he watched her.

He turned back to a small camp stove and set a pan with the vegetables on the table, replacing them with small fry pans. He swirled butter into the pans and when it sizzled, he added the scrambled eggs and deftly whirled them around the pans to form egg cakes.

Serena watched with something akin to awe. Omelets. And he was making them under what amounted to back country conditions. She would have to take a few cooking lessons just to make him dinner at her house. Or maybe order in. That would be safer.

Dinner at her house. Followed by incredible sex in her big bed and a shower together in the morning. Maybe a trip to Brew Bank for breakfast goodies. Her mind wandered to a pleasant concept of a next date.

And came to a shrieking halt. Date. She was dating, and what's more, sleeping with someone who she had been thinking of originally as a client of Balance. Damn! She gulped and took a long cleansing breath.

That now was clearly not going to be happening. In the heat of the moment, or to be honest, quite a number of moments, she's forgotten about professional rules, objectivity related to clients, and the ethics that had been her foundation for so many years. Just up and broke them, drawn in by the feelings she was developing for this mystery man.

Damn, what was worse? Having to tell him she'd cross professional boundaries last night or coming clean about seeing those heart-wrenching pictures?

*****

"Do you need anything else with these eggs? I have some potatoes I can fry up or there's bread." Dane turned to find Serena staring at him with a weird look on her face. It was a cross between shock and dismay. He stopped, wondering if he'd said out loud any of the guilty thoughts he'd been carrying in his head this morning.

Shaking herself, she came back from wherever she'd been and smiled at him again. Granted, it was a bit tentative. But she didn't look mad, nor did she look disgusted with him. He sighed inwardly and put a big smile on his face for her.

He considered her very easy to smile at.

"No, that looks fine just by itself. Do you have any hot sauce, like Tabasco?" She took the plate and fork he offered, tore off two paper towels for napkins and gave him one, and sat down on the edge of the futon, now returned to its upright couch shape.

"Hot sauce I have, quite a selection in fact. Let me get a bottle from the cabin."

"Oh, that's okay." She suddenly looked worried, glancing back at the shack.

"No, really, it's no big deal to get it. I want some too. I didn't know you were a hot sauce junky." He tried to keep the tone light because he sensed something was wrong. A distinct tight frown puckered Serena's brows.

He turned for the cabin, feeling Serena's eyes on his back. It was funny how quickly he was picking up this sixth sense about her.

Or maybe he was being ultra-sensitive because he knew he was keeping secrets from her.

Grabbing a couple of different heats of red sauce from a shelf above the woodstove in the cabin, he returned outside to their impromptu dining room. She was sitting in the same spot, eyes on her plate, shoulders hunched over defensively. She hadn't taken a bite yet.

"Would you like to eat at the table we used last night? We could enjoy the view. It might be more comfortable…" His voice trailed off as she turned to him.

Damn, she was upset about something. Thinking back frantically, he tried to figure out if he'd said or done something to put that look there. All he could think of, though, was the heaviness of his own guilt and lack of admissions.

"Ah, no, this is fine." She added a few shakes of hot sauce to her eggs but still hadn't taken a bite. Clearing her throat, she added, "Dane, I broke a few rules last night."

He'd broken a few himself, like keeping himself distant from any entanglements because it hurt too much when those people were no longer there. Like keeping the sex easy and unencumbered. Like not falling for a woman just because, well, just because she stirred everything up in him and made him want to come clean and be a better man.

Shit.

Keeping his tone light, he looked at her with an easy smile as he sat down on an overturned bucket to face her. "There are rules about eating salmon under a meteor shower?"

The frown hadn't left Serena's face but at least her tension eased.

"About work." She stopped, pushing eggs around her plate.

She still thought that he would come in for counseling. The jolt of that realization had him boggling his smile. He didn't need counseling. He just needed to come clean to her and then he'd be okay. Somehow he knew it, though he wasn't sure how.

Was he pinning salvation on Serena? That wasn't fair to her, and it was unrealistic for him.

Shit again. He was really screwing this up now.

He set his plate aside on the ground, rapidly becoming as uninterested in the eggs as she appeared. He moved the bucket forward and took her plate from her hands, setting it next to his. Not letting her go, he looped his larger fingers over hers in a tight grip.

"I'm not going to become a client, Serena," he said gently. "I don't have any problems that talking will fix, at least not talking in a group or with a counselor. I just need time, time to heal and time to take things at my own pace."

The words surprised him. He hadn't realized that this is what he had been feeling. Time, they kept telling him when he was in rehab, would help put things in perspective.

Maybe that healing was finally happening.

He lifted his eyes to find Serena watching him cautiously.

"I'm sure you've seen things, done things, that were, ah, difficult." She seemed to be searching for what she wanted to say next. "Things like that can change a person. One day everything's great and then the next it's dark and scary. People can feel very alone when that happens." She stopped, watching him closely. "Your scars…"

Letting go quickly, he stopped her with a raised hand. "I told you last night, I was in an incident, an explosion. I was injured. They put me back together and got all of the parts working again. End of story."

She shredded the paper towel in her fidgeting fingers. Dropping it abruptly, she leaned forward, clasping her hands together on her knees. She looked so earnest, yet another quality in her that he admired.

It was a turn on too.

Dane moved forward so that they were almost nose to nose, his hands surrounding hers. Swirls of conflict and concern shown in her eyes, and he appreciated the fact that she was so worried about him.

Softer now, he continued, "Undoubtedly I've changed. But time does heal. They kept telling us that in rehab, and it is true. My scars are as good as they're going to get, and I've been able to build up the strength and stamina that I had before." He stopped, intent on leaving it there.

"People change on the inside too, though." Serena's soft voice mirrored his, her eyes shining with something that looked suspiciously like tears.

"I'm fine on the inside, and getting better every day. The man I am today isn't only the product of that incident. I've been the way I am for a long time, decades in fact. Ask my brother, he'd tell you." Or maybe don't ask him, he thought, since Powers still thought of him as broken and needing fixing.

She turned her hands so that she could squeeze his and stared deep into his eyes. "Just know, Dane, that I am here for you. Not in a formal counseling role. But as your friend."

His heart lurched a little and a voice in his brain added, a good friend, I hope.

Chapter 31

Serena knew she was late, but she'd helped Dane on the house until the midday sun grew too intense, and then she came home to soak in a cooling bath, contemplating last night and this morning.

After breakfast, she volunteered to clean up so that Dane could get started on the day's construction work. Their conversations finally became light and easy again, the tension of their breakfast lost in the pace of their work, a sense of fun and each other. The occasional brush of a hand led to a kiss, and each kiss got steamy before one or the other of them would push back, laugh, and make some comment about their lack of progress on the house.

It was wonderfully playful and it made her heart sing.

Her solo afternoon drifted away as she tried to concentrate on paperwork, but her thoughts were distracted. She kept touching the cell phone, looking at the pictures she'd taken in Dane's cabin that morning. When she finally realized the time, she knew that everyone else would be in the pool and they would be full of questions for her when she finally arrived.

And so they were, when Serena opened DK's front door and listened. Voices came from the backyard, clustered on the deck surrounding the pool. She passed through the house and all conversation stopped when she reached the French doors to the patio. She examined their knowing smiles and expectant looks, trying to figure out why each was looking at her with such anticipation, even DK's dog. She frowned and they giggled, then went back to what they had been discussing before she came in, giving her a moment to settle.

"Here, try these dumplings. They're part of the vegetarian dim sum appetizer plate I'm bringing out next week at the restaurant." Roxy moved from woman to woman, handing out napkins and offering a plate holding three kinds of small snacks.

"I still can't get over it, DK. You live in a wonderful barn, and you work in yet another beautiful barn. You have a ton of land just for you, and this pool." Gabby sighed in appreciation.

DK laughed at the expression of awe on her friend's face. "Really, maybe you need to consider getting a larger place, Gabby. That condo isn't big enough for you and Jeremy, and he's growing like a weed!"

Gabby groaned. "I know – he goes through clothes so fast that I think time must be flying by at the speed of light. Between soccer and track and everything else he likes to do now that school's back in session, I barely have time for laundry anyway. I need more balance in my life." She stopped and looked around, the picture of innocence. "Speaking of balance, how are things going, Serena?"

Roxy added quickly, "And why were you so late?"

Tess came out of the kitchen with another plate of food in time to hear the questions. "Now don't go prying. She called and said she would be late. Something about working on the house today." And then she smirked.

DK smiled knowing. "She's building something alright. But I wonder just what?"

"Don't tease her," Tess scolded. "It's been a long time between relationships for our girl, you know."

And all eyes returned to Serena. She fussed as she settled herself into a chair, not meeting anyone's stare.

No one said anything, each waiting expectantly while Serena played with the piping on a pillow. In contrast to their relaxed poses, she felt uptight, itchy and ready to explode. There was so much that had happened in less than twenty-four hours. Had it only been a day since Dane called her at work?

In her mind, she replayed the easy comfort of most of their conversations, the sense of play today as they worked side by side. On her skin, she could feel every sensation of his touch last night. Her eyes closing, she could still feel each nerve and tendon stretch with each orgasm she'd experienced.

She didn't realize what a dreamy expression settled on her face until the silence was broken.

"Wow!" Gabby sat up straighter and stared at her.

DK followed close behind. "Damn! I want whatever she's having!"

Thankfully, Tess hadn't joined in their gentle caring jabs. When Serena looked at her, she saw both speculation and concern on her best friend's face. They all cared. But Gabby and DK couldn't resist poking a little fun at her. And grudgingly, she knew she'd do exactly the same thing in their place.

"Dane and I had a good time last night. It was a very – special – evening." She had to search for the right words. Too much enthusiasm and she'd be bombarded by questions.

"Ah, so now we know his real name, the man you've been spending so much time with," Gabby crowed triumphantly.

Damn, another professional rule broken. So much for confidentiality.

Gabby continued her prodding. "So tell us all about it. Me, I want to know every little detail that put such an out of this world expression on your face because I don't have time to date until forever when Jeremy's in college, and then I'll be too old and exhausted."

Serena stared at her hands, gathering her thoughts. What exactly could she tell them? What should she tell them? And what about the pictures?

Tess brought her a glass of wine and she murmured her thanks, her thoughts chaotic. This feeling of restlessness was usually something she reserved for business emergencies, when she wanted to take action but she didn't yet know what action to take. Now it was spilling over into her personal life.

It made sense, though. Her personal and business lives were now completely enmeshed, and she was afraid that one would certainly suffer in the outcome. But which one would it be?

She sighed and raised her eyes to her friends. "We had a wonderful evening, a wonderful night, and a wonderful morning." She stopped. Maybe not everything was perfect, but the majority of it was.

"Dane cooked salmon over an open fire. We watched the meteor shower. We slipped between the sheets. He's a gentle and amazing lover. We got up. He made breakfast, another tasty meal. We worked on the house."

She felt rather proud of herself for summing things up so nicely.

"And the sex. Was the sex tasty too?" This from Roxy, who was looking like she couldn't wait for the answer.

"Yes, Serena, tell, tell! Was it scratch the itch sex or curl your toes and blow your mind sex?" Gabby was clearly living vicariously through her.

"You do realize, don't you, that you had more last night than any of us have probably had in the past year. So details, sister, details." Tess's tone was gentle, even with the teasing glow in her eyes.

Serena sighed. She was going to have to give them more, much more, to satisfy their ravenous need to know.

*****

"There's so much to him, so many layers."

Throughout the meal, she related the history of her relationship with Dane, from that first sighting at Roxy's store to today at midday when she'd kissed him goodbye at the house site. She skirted over their nighttime activities to the degree they'd let her, but it had been enough to make each of them sigh.

As they picked up their dessert plates and seated themselves around DK's living room, she added the last – and biggest – kicker to the story.

"There's one more thing." She played with the confection on her plate, unseeing. "This morning, I was, ah, looking around in his cabin while he was making breakfast. There was a portfolio open and I thought it was some of the house plans. I was curious about what the kitchen and bathrooms were going to look like, so I opened it up."

"Snooping around, huh? This doesn't sound so good." DK leaned forward.

She really felt bad about what she'd done. It sounded even worse as she was explaining it. But what she'd found...

Pulling her cell phone from her pocket, she brought up the picture album function and paged through to the shots she had taken that morning. She started with the nice shots, the ones of what looked like an African savanna with all sorts of wildlife.

Handing the phone to Gabby, she explained. "This is what I found in the folio, large format prints of these incredible photos."

Tess, Roxy and DK rose to stand behind Gabby, all four of them squinting at the display. "It's kind of difficult to see on this little screen." Gabby had her nose close, and then moved back, still screwing up her eyes and trying to make out the specific forms.

"Send me the album, Serena. I'll project it on my flat screen." DK was already moving to her laptop, and with a few keystrokes, she had the computer linked to her TV.

This might be a bad idea. She'd taken pictures of some of the nice shots, but the battle ones were disturbing and she was sure they wouldn't make good viewing for a relaxing evening with girlfriends. But she needed input.

Forwarding the album to DK's e-mail, she tried to put things in perspective.

"It might be nothing. He might be planning to frame these pictures for the house."

"There we go," DK said triumphantly as a savanna shot came to life on the screen. "They won't be perfect in terms of what we see because they come from a camera phone, but it's a whole lot better than the small screen."

"Wow, these are incredible!" Tess was fascinated by a herd of elephants that seemed to come alive, their motion obvious even in a still shot. "Did he take these pictures?"

"I don't know."

All four women stopped their examination and turned to Serena as one. She felt disgusted with herself. Chicken, she had been too guilty about snooping to say anything to Dane about finding the pictures this morning.

"You don't know, as in you didn't ask him." It was a statement, not a question, from Roxy. Serena nodded.

"I probably shouldn't have been snooping. I didn't want him to think I was, I don't know, prying into things he wasn't ready to share with me."

"But what's wrong with asking about these pictures? The ones of the soldiers and children are just precious. If he took them, he's incredibly talented!" Gabby's face carried the same confusion as Roxy's.

"Here's why." DK was staring at the screen in a mixture of awe and horror.

All eyes turned to the TV and gasps filled the room. The screen was filled with a very gory shot of soldiers on the ground, a haze of dust hanging in the air. Whatever had just happened made the extreme shock on the faces of the men and women apparent.

"It gets worse. You all might not want to see these."

DK continued to advance the shots, and the intakes of breath were the only sound for a time as they watched the agony, determination and sadness apparent in every shot. And fear. That was there too, though the resolve to overcome it was just as evident on the soldiers' faces.

"God, these are awful! I mean, they're incredible pictures but what the soldiers went through..." Gabby's distress curdled her voice.

"It's no wonder that so many come home with such burdens to carry, so much healing to do inside even if they were never physically injured." Tess wiped away a tear and turned back to Serena. "And that's why you didn't want to ask about them, isn't it?"

"If I tell him I saw them, how do I say that I only saw the nice ones and not the battle shots? Originally, I thought maybe he had these blown up to frame and put up in the new house. That is, until I got to the gruesome ones. He doesn't want to discuss what happened to him during his time in Afghanistan, he's made that clear. I think that if he ever tells me, it's going to be because he wants me to share things at a deeper level. And we're definitely not there yet."

DK flipped back to a shot of lions and antelope and rose to stand in front of the screen, head cocked to one side in deep consideration.

"There's something familiar about these pictures." She frowned. "I don't know what it is." She advanced to a war shot that had them gasping again in the sharp contrast between the calm and the storm. She continued to stare. "I wish I could remember where I've seen them before."

"Do you think he might have gotten them as, I don't know, remembrances of what had happened?" Tess searched for an out.

"I don't know. He told me about the incident where he was injured, in general terms. That could be the war shots. That last one, of the bloody soldier on the ground who's screaming, that could be his friend Anderson. If it is, what a terrible thing to see, your friend cut in half in front of you."

The women sat in silence, eyes turning back to the TV and the mid-shout – or maybe mid-scream – on the face of the man on the screen. The agony was almost too much to tolerate.

Serena finally cleared her throat. "If he was there, it explains a lot about why he's turned into a recluse. How do you let go of this kind of horror?"

Chapter 32

The past few weeks had been amazing in Serena's opinion. She and Dane had seen each other almost every day. Nights were magical, finding new ways to please each other, even if it meant only snuggling under the stars at the new house or spooning in her big bed.

He'd finally agreed to an evening at her place, and the result had been magical. He still hid his scars from her, telling her they were too ugly and he didn't want to scare her away.

His laugh was forced each time he used that same line.

Despite that, it was surprising to her how quickly they had grown closer. It was like the night of the meteors had moved things forward in huge leaps. Sharing about their families, their pasts, had opened both of them up.

Except for one thing hanging between them. The pictures.

When she thought about them, she felt both guilty for prying and sad for Dane, heartbroken that they probably cataloged his memories. He still hadn't mentioned anything about them and wouldn't get specific about his past. But that, she hoped, would come in time.

DK continued to search, trying to figure out why she recognized the photography. She had asked for a picture of Dane, and on one laughing date night at the construction site, Serena brought her little point-and-shoot camera and snapped off a few quick ones. He wasn't exactly pleased when she'd been taking them, but she teased him back into a good mood.

She was a little hurt that he didn't ask for pictures of her in return. But she could keep their relationship friendly, right?

Her heart was another story. Each layer of Dane that she got to know made him all that much more appealing. It took her a week of convincing to get him to agree to a dinner out in a restaurant, and then he only wanted to go to the tiny sports bar near Roxy's, a dimly lit place with TVs in every corner. He looked around warily when they entered, and then settled them into a booth with a view of the door and his back to the wall.

He never completely relaxed, eating quickly, and he was impatient when she didn't follow his lead. The energy, the tension, came off him in waves. He was eager to leave, his eyes moving restlessly around the room. Once they were outside and back in his truck, he turned to her with a hard fast kiss.

That night as they'd camped out on the futon in his house, he had been almost frantic in their lovemaking. There was a desperation as he loomed over her, propping himself on an elbow to keep his weight off her smaller frame. He brought her up quickly, not that she complained about it, and sheathed himself inside her just as fast.

He'd looked into her eyes long afterwards, seeming to examine the depths of her soul.

Later when the lack of a moon made the darkness feel dense, he'd screamed out during the night, held in the throes of a dream that had him twisting the sheets and struggling against Serena as she tried to hold him. She had a hard time waking Dane up.

"What was it? What was in your dream?"

He stared at her with wide dark eyes, all hint of blue missing and the whites showing in the light of her flashlight. It took him some time to return from wherever the nightmare gripped him, vise-like and unyielding, until his breathing gradually slowed and his gaze became less frantic.

"Dane, it might help to talk about it."

He shook his head, not saying a word.

"Does this happen often?"

His affirmative nod cut her deeply. His frantic heartbeat took a long time to slow, throbbing against her back as he curled her tightly against him. She doubted either one of them got much rest that night.

At least she now knew what the screams the neighbors heard were all about.

She hurt for him. He was still dealing with issues and she ached to help him. The door was open. He just had to walk through it. Occasionally, she'd head the conversation in a direction about the war or his past, but he recognized what she was doing. Sometimes he gently turned their talk in another vein with a small smile, and sometimes he was gruff and adamant that he didn't want to talk about it. The only reason he would give was that discussing it took everything out of him.

But at least he was now a bit more willing to get out and do things. They had ventured to a couple of other restaurants. He was relaxing more with each public appearance, the wariness lessening with each new place. But sometimes…

"Let's go to Roxy's. The food is amazing and she's dying to meet you."

He laughed, running his hands down her hair. "I'm not quite ready yet to run the gauntlet of your friend's scrutiny."

At least he was laughing about it.

Setting the table in her little dining room, she thought with a smile about their lovemaking. There was so much emotion in their actions. Fast or slow, gently or hard, it spoke volumes about what they had come to mean to each other. The love she felt for Dane surged with each moment that passed.

And there she stopped.

When had she started to think about this relationship in terms of love? It had come up slowly, warming with each new laugh, story, and shared intimacy both in bed and outside of it. It had been nearly three months now since she first saw him at Roxy's, and it was almost as if he was a different man. He was still cautious, but he was opening up, and his brooding silences when he'd turn his back on her were now few and far between.

There was still a separation between them though. When she would have had the lights on as they made love, he continued to insist on darkness with only enough of a glow to see each other's faces. When she explored the contours of his body, he stopped her each time she visited the scars on his legs. When she'd wanted to return the favor of her mouth on him as he'd so often given to her, he jerked her up his body and distracted her until she forgot for the moment what she'd been planning.

Soon it would be time, she hoped, to move out of that darkness into the light.

Tonight was going to be special, she just knew it. She wanted to come clean about the pictures, because the guilt of knowing about them and not saying anything was weighing her down. Dane noticed when she got quiet thinking about them, and he did his best then to cheer her up. He didn't realize the cause. But once she told him, she could also feel free to tell him what she was feeling in her heart.

*****

He almost didn't recognize himself. It had been a long time since he'd shaved completely, and the bare face in the mirror was still something of a shock. Just who was this man now?

He'd told Serena that he was busy with some critical things on the house the last couple of days, things that took his work into the evenings. Their phone time was nowhere nearly as satisfying as sitting side by side, watching the moods chase across her face.

She had the most expressive face, and sometimes he ached to capture it.

But that wasn't for him anymore.

Or was it? He'd made a lot of changes in the past couple of months. Some of the barriers he had created between himself and the outside world were no longer necessary.

But a lot of it had to do with Serena herself. She was bringing him back out into the warmth of caring and laughter, a place he wasn't even aware that he'd been missing in his self-imposed isolation.

His heart stirred. He didn't have any experience with love, the all-enveloping kind that meant a lifetime of commitment, but he imagined that this is something of what it would feel like. It was an ache to make every moment of sadness disappear. It was the need to share every moment of happiness with her. It was the joy he felt when he could slide her from one shrieking orgasm to the next, giving her physical pleasure akin to what she gave him.

And it was the fear, the fear that someday, she would know what he'd done and she would send him away, revolted. His brother had been disgusted, refusing to speak to him for the first few months of his rehab. His agent got over his aversion once the money was rolling in. He grimaced at the greed and insensitivity, ashamed at his memories of his own actions.

What was that saying – feel the fear and do it anyway? Two days in the sun had given his newly shaved face some color, enough to make the contrast between pale and tan less stark. He felt naked and exposed. This might have been a bad idea. But if he was going to open up to Serena and explore these tentative feelings that might be love, he had to open up completely.

And that meant he had to stop hiding.

*****

He rang the doorbell. Serena had given him a key, kind of a first step towards a level of greater commitment, but he refused to use it. Each time, he rang the bell as if he was still a polite visitor to her home. He hadn't earned that level of intimacy.

"Hey, you can always use that key, you know, I wouldn't..." and she stopped, door swung open, gaping at him.

His mirror told him what she was seeing. His beard was gone, his chin pink from unaccustomed exposure to the sun. The jagged white scar that ran from the base of his ear down his jaw line and disappearing under his chin was thrown into sharp brutal contrast.

She finally raised her shocked eyes to his after a lengthy examination. Color drained from her face so quickly that he worried she would faint.

"Damn, I knew this was a bad idea!" Dane moved fast, upset and angry with himself for startling her like this. He should have warned her. He was sure that the scars on his face looked gruesome to someone who was unprepared.

"Serena, I'm sorry. I should have explained beforehand so you had time to get used to the idea. Or maybe I shouldn't have shaved at all. Damn it all!"

He scooped her into his arms, tucking her face into his shoulder and pulling her full length against him as he walked her backwards into the living room and kicked the door shut. He felt a spurt of panic. He had to make this right. He'd scared her.

He never wanted to scare her.

Pulling away, he looked down into her eyes. Tears, big drops that hung at the corners, perched ready to fall. One silently slipped down her cheek as her wide gaze focused again on the ridge that ran down his jaw. A hesitant hand came up and traced it lightly, and more tears fell.

He was shaking, he realized, and then noticed that she was too. Much more of this and they would both end up on the floor. He walked her backwards again, pulling her down with him on the sofa. He wrapped his arms tightly around her, hiding her face in his neck on the unscarred side.

"What, ah, when did this happen?" Her tone was quiet and there was no hint of her tears in it.

"In A-bad, when we were all blown up." He realized that his voice sounded a whole lot shakier than hers and cleared his throat. "I didn't realize at the time that I was hit in the face, just in my legs. Didn't know that the blood on my face was from an injury. It wasn't until the medics got me back to the field hospital that we knew the bomb had torn away so much skin."

In his mind, he was back in the dirt and confusion. It seemed like it was still happening when he visited the memory like this, crisp and clear and just as scary. He shuddered with the force of it. He wanted to scream, the terror of seeing a friend die very real in his mind all over again.

And he felt something pull him back. Serena was there, gently rubbing his chest. Something was wet on his face and he thought that he should dry her tears. Except her face was still buried in his neck and he realized that he was the one crying.

"I'm here, sweetheart, I'm here."

Her soft croon in his ear made more tears come, surprising since he'd never cried. He applied that same stoic distancing of himself that he always used with those he considered his subjects to Anderson and the others.

She was rocking him gently in her arms and he was bawling like a baby.

*****

Serena didn't think she'd ever experienced that phrase described as time standing still, but right now, she knew exactly what it meant. Dane's shudders were lessening, his tears dried up and some of the tightness finally beginning to leave his body. She wanted to look at him again, trace those scars, not in horror about how they looked, but in horror about what he'd experienced. Her heart ached for him, and she realized in that split second that even if he never shared more than what he had today, she'd given her heart over to him a long time ago.

Finally, all became quiet. His arms loosened around her, and he was motionless. She pushed back against his hold and he let her go. He wasn't looking at her as she moved back. He was looking any place but at her.

"Dane, it's okay." She put a hand to his scarred cheek and forced him to focus on her.

The pain she saw in his eyes was almost overwhelming. Her eyes brimmed again, wanting to take that pain away and knowing that she couldn't. And knowing, even more importantly, that he had to face it too if he was going to come out whole on the other side.

With feather light fingers, she traced the line of scar again, the puckered skin rough and foreign, pressing lightly as if to erase it from his features. His eyes never left hers. The pain remained, but there were questions as well. And a suspicious wariness.

She never let go of his gaze, smiling tentatively as she continued her gently tracing. She knew her sadness for him shown in her own eyes. There was no need to say anything. She could see his understanding build, a relaxation of the tension as he realized she accepted him and cared about him, scars and all.

Time again stood still. She opened her mouth to speak but choked on the words. She knew she should say something, something to let him know that she loved him, loved much more than the condition of his body or even the fear he had faced and how it had changed him.

She started again, her voice wobbly with complex emotions too countless to name. "Dane, it's okay. I'm sorry that you had to go through something so awful, both what you saw and what you felt. The injuries both outside and in."

He brought up a hand with just a trace of a tremble to cup her cheek, running a thumb across her lips even as he still watched her eyes. His were changing now, turning into that lighter blue that meant the terror was receding. A corner of his mouth rose. His face was the same but so different without the beard, and she grinned back at him suddenly, delighted that she could actually now see his full smile.

He left whatever he was feeling unspoken between them. Serena knew it might take time for him to be willing to tell her all about it, but some major wall had come down between them with his scars exposed to her.

Dane's mouth descended gently on hers, and other barriers dissolve as well. There was a wave of emotion from him in the kiss, and she put all of the love she felt for him in her response.

Exploring her mouth with his tongue, she felt his tentativeness. Then he moved to trace her ear and kiss the pulse that beat on the side of her neck. She let her own mouth roam, and her tongue replaced her fingers on the scar. He stilled, sucking in air and tightening his arms around her. She kissed her way from ear to chin and back again. He shuddered and pulled back.

Standing and still silent, he pulled her to her feet and down the hall to her bedroom. He turned her into his arms and set his mouth on hers in a deeper kiss as his hands reached for the bottom of her shirt, lifting it up slowly. She stepped back to give him access, and his hands went immediately to make short work of her bra clasp. His shirt followed hers, and soon they were pressed skin to skin in another soul-stealing kiss.

His hand reached to find the button fastening her skirt, and she stepped back with a laugh and pushed the stretchy material down her legs to step out of it. His expression was so solemn that her laugh of anticipation ended on a sob. She reached out for the light on the nightstand, ready to click it off as they always did.

And he stopped her hand.

Confused and questioning, she brought her eyes to his and waited, linked hands outstretched. His hands finally dropped to his jeans, slowly working the button free and getting ready to lower the zipper.

She realized he was giving her the most incredible brave gift. Himself, just as he was, in the light.

*****

He couldn't say a word if his life depended on it and Dane shuddered at the depth of feelings sweeping through him. Serena, his lovely and beautiful Serena, was smiling her perfect smile, and her hands were stroking the jeans down his buttocks to the floor. He stepped out of sandals and denim, kicking them aside with more force than needed.

He was rigid already, but another stronger tension also filled him. He was afraid of what Serena would see in this light, the other scars he had hidden up until this point. On his thighs he'd lost skin and muscle, and it was only through some miracles of modern medicine, multiple surgeries, and months of painful rehab that he was able to move normally again. The scars were hideous puckers of tightly drawn skin and caves where the structure below should have been.

It was ugly. He was ugly. He couldn't separate himself from it.

And yet, here was his brave and noble woman smiling at him. Her hands ran down his body again, and she pulled the briefs down before examining the gruesome ridges, not saying a word. When she looked back up at him, her smile was tremulous, and her tearful gaze was full of understanding and acceptance and something else.

Love? Could it be love? He didn't want to hope.

She pushed him back on the bed and stripping off her panties, joined him. Her body on top of his was heaven, and her mouth moved from gentle to eager in a few beats of their hearts. He didn't think he deserved this, the bliss of her moving on him in his disfigurement.

And then he couldn't think at all.

*****

Serena let her body slide down Dane's, reveling in the hard planes and valleys fitting so perfectly with the curves and softness of hers. She kissed his jaw, tracing a line down the scar that marred his otherwise perfect face. She kissed his eyes, still so serious but dancing with bright blue lights of desire now. Gratefulness and something else showed there, something to analyze later. Now, she wanted to concentrate on bringing him all of the loving feelings racing to the surface inside her.

Her mouth traveled down his neck to his chest, playing in the light hair surrounding his nipples, lingering to suck there until his low moan distracted her. Moving lower, she nuzzled the indent of his belly button and blew on the curls that guarded below. His proud length twitched and got harder as her hand wrapped around.

She needed to let him know that it was all okay, the way he looked, what he had tried to hide from her. Her mouth moved to a hip, trailing open-mouthed kisses over skin she had never been allowed to explore before. She reached his inner thigh and pulled back, tracing the hard ridges of scars with gentle fingers and then with her lips. She heard him hiss as he put a hand on her hair in a gentle caress of his own.

Acceptance, she realized, was perhaps the most important component in any relationship. In their case, scars were just the outside evidence. Scars inside were harder to see. Accepting this part, then, was easy.

Lingering on the puckers of tissue, she let him know with her actions what her words might never get through to him. She hurt for him, for the pain he had to endure and the marks he would always carry, but she rejoiced in the fact that he was here with her now.

Finally, the temptation became too intense, and she moved again, tracing a path back up to the juncture of leg and hip. She cupped him and gently licked her way from base to tip. He cursed, and she smiled. His hands tightened in her hair. She could feel the tension rising in him with each stroke, each caress, each gentle squeeze and pull of pressure.

He shifted so fast that she didn't have time to react. He pulled her up his body in one move and rolled them, his weight landing on top of her even as his mouth claimed hers in a searing kiss. All she could think was a screaming yes inside her brain, a need to let him feel the passion he built in her.

He entered her in one swift motion and their groans collided as they both started to move. Hands locked. Eyes locked. They moved faster and harder until it was impossible for Serena to tell where she ended and he began.

And as Serena cried out, she felt Dane convulse inside her. They never blinked, eyes still staring into each other's souls.

Neither one of them wanted to break the gaze or move apart, so they stared at each other and held on. Their breathing slowed and pulses dropped but still they didn't shift.

Finally, when Serena thought that there never would be a moment more perfect than the one they had just shared, Dane spoke.

"Serena, I love you."

Chapter 33

He was so sure of it, of them, of her. Dane realized that as he had looked into Serena's hazel eyes, drowsy and light with spent passion, and knew that he could spend the rest of his life very happily just like this. And it had popped out of his mouth, his heart speaking for him before his head could intercede to stop it.

And he was damn glad that it had.

Serena's eyes got huge and round. He really ought to move, but if their bodies were no longer joined, he wasn't sure he could stand it right now. He wanted to be with her, inside her, for as long as she would have him.

"I love you too, Dane." Her quiet words and the smile that kept growing on her face surprised him. Then his joy took over and his face cracked into a big smile as well.

She laughed, and so did he. He slipped out of her on that laugh and gathered her up against him, rolling them to tuck her into his shoulder and pull tight arms around her.

His woman. His woman who loved him. Imagine that.

Time passed silently as he considered this amazing miracle. She had probably fallen asleep. Turning to look at her, he saw that she was staring up at him. And she wasn't staring at his scar, which was saying something since she was tucked right underneath it. She was looking into his eyes. He could see the love. But there was something else. Fear?

"Mine," he growled and nuzzled her hair, kissing her forehead and her eyes. She was solemn and that made him fearful in turn. He tried to tease another smile out of her. But she looked away and pushed at him gently, moving back.

The distance killed him. It hurt to be away from her, even by inches.

"What is it?" He had to know. He reached out to thread fingers through her hair, now tousled and tangled by their lovemaking. He thought about the precious gift of acceptance that she'd given him. Maybe she wasn't ready for loving him and it had just slipped out on the heat of the moment. Except they'd said it after the heat of the moment, when they were both quiet and sated.

Serena sat up and turned away from him, pushing her hair out of her face and setting her shoulders. She pulled up the sheet to cover her breasts, and when he tried to push it back down, she clutched it harder. Then she faced him.

"I have a confession to make."

She looked so somber as she said it.

"Actually, a couple of them."

He went still. What could she possibly have done that would make her look so serious, particularly after what they'd just shared and what they'd said to each other?

Fear stabbed at his gut, worse than anything from the war zone. The potential for loss suddenly felt a whole bigger than anything he'd ever faced.

*****

It was hard, so hard, when they'd just shared the most earthshaking moments of her life. But she wanted to come clean so that it wasn't hanging between them every second. Then at least on her side, things could move forward.

Serena played with the edge of the sheet, folding it into a fan, then pulling it flat, only to fold it again. Keeping her hands busy let her mind process what she wanted to say. When Dane put a hand on her shoulder to bring her gaze to his, she thought she was ready. She was, until she looked into his concerned eyes and realized that she was a coward inside.

"Serena, sweetheart, what is it? I hate it when you look so sad and solemn." He moved to take her in his arms again, to bring her back to the security of the bed and their shared passion, but she resisted.

"There are some things you should know, Dane." She kept her voice quiet, out of both fear of what she had to say, and disappointment in herself for having to say it in the first place.

Movement made it easier to talk, she'd found. Right now, it hurt her heart to stand and walk a few steps away from the bed where he lay, watching and waiting. He moved to get up too but a wave of her hand stopped him. He grabbed for a blanket at the foot of the bed and pulled it up, hiding himself from her.

It made her heart ache even harder. She knew the symbolism probably wasn't intentional, but he was stepping back from her, even as she had moved away from him. Their closeness might have been a mirage. The words might not be enough.

She started again. "Remember the morning after the meteors?"

He smiled a small smile, heat in his expression, and nodded.

"Well, when you were making breakfast, after I took my shower, I was in the cabin by myself."

God, this was hard. She should just blurt it out and get it over with but she couldn't, seeing as she'd been snooping.

"I remember a beautiful woman who brought me to life that night, under the shooting stars. Brought me to life many times that night, in fact."

He was trying to tease her back into a better humor, and she longed to crawl back into the safety of his arms.

"I, ah, I had some time while you were cooking, and I looked around a little bit." She noticed the sudden tension in him, a stillness that would be read as casual relaxation by others, except she knew him so well. Already he wasn't happy with what he was hearing.

"And?" His terse delivery of the single word made her bite her lip.

"And, I saw that the portfolio you keep, the big black sleeve, was open, unzipped and propped against the table."

He'd risen on the pillows now, propping himself on an elbow and watching her carefully.

"I, ah, I thought that the plans for the house were inside, and I was curious about them. I wanted to see what you planned to do with the interior, like we talked about. You know…" The last words trailed off as she saw his eyes go dark, the fury that was gathering a bad sign for forgiveness.

He dropped back on their pillows and closed his eyes.

"You looked inside the folio, didn't you?" He wasn't so much asking her as making a statement. His tone was resigned.

She felt tears threaten as he turned away from her, eyes open and dark staring up at the ceiling.

At least he wasn't leaving her bed.

"I did," she stammered, stepping forward with a hand outstretched.

He ignored her, continuing to examine the ceiling as if it had contained the secrets of the universe.

"I wanted to tell you, wanted to ask you about the pictures." There, she'd said it. "I'm sorry I snooped, Dane. I really am. I should have just asked you before I looked. I don't have any excuses."

She waited, but still he didn't look at her. Tense energy was coming off him in waves that drowned her.

"The ones of the children, of the animals, were incredible." She hesitated again. "The ones from the war were – shocking. They took my breath away. Were those from, well, from the bomb that day?"

Time stood still yet again. She waited at the side of the bed, wrapped in a sheet that carried the scent of their shared passion. He lay on the bed, eyes closed again, a deep frown marking the features that he so recently bared to her. The scar on his jaw was a bleak reminder, growing tighter with the grim set of his mouth.

She wanted to say something to break this ugly silence, but she didn't know what else she could tell him. That she was sorry he'd faced such tragedy? That she understood his reluctance to share his horrific experiences?

That she loved him and she wanted to understand all of him, the good and the bad?

Her tears were very near the surface as she waited, unable to move or breathe.

*****

She'd seen them, those pictures that he kept to remind himself of what he'd done. The ones he rarely needed to look at because he could remember it all so vividly in his mind. He'd been looking for a shot he remembered from Africa, one that held colors he wanted to match in the house, ones that made him peaceful.

And he'd left the portfolio open without a thought, so used to being alone.

Serena had looked at the harsh devil that was war, seeing some of the worst evil at the heart of it. People bloodied and scared, or screaming in searing anger and hurt, people who just realized that their lives would never be the same, if they even lived. She'd looked at what he saw, the pictures he now had burned into his brain as much by the revulsion he felt for himself as by the experience.

Continuing to shoot those photos even as his friends lay severely injured around him. Continuing to shoot even as his close friends lay dying, shooting even as he should have been offering them support and care in their final moments.

He might never get over his self-loathing. He kept his eyes closed, the indescribable pain of it unbelievable so quickly on the heels of the declarations of love he and Serena had shared. He doubted she would understand.

He realized she was speaking again, her voice quiet, as if she was afraid to interrupt him in his musings. "Were they from the day you were injured?"

He sighed, a disgusted sound that came from what was left of his soul. He needed to tell her, though he was afraid repulsion might make her kick him out of her bed for good.

Funny what you think about when the seconds slow like this. He understood now why he'd been reluctant to use that key, because it symbolized so much. There was so much promise in her action of giving it to him.

And still, he hesitated. If he told her everything, would she understand with the same gentle acceptance that she gave him for his marred looks?

He inhaled sharply. He wasn't angry with Serena, but with himself. Maybe at some unconscious level, he'd wanted her to look at the photos and ask questions. Maybe he wanted her to bring the answers out of him.

But now that he was presented with the perfect opportunity to tell her the rest of the story, to lay himself bare in front of her, was he man enough to do it?

Chapter 34

Serena felt the tears surge now, convinced she had driven him away. He hadn't answered her questions about the war photos. He hadn't moved from his place in her bed either, but she could see the coiled tension in him, feel the anger that was held so tenuously in check. He was a man with secrets, and he wanted to hold on to them.

Her love was now an ache. She'd blown it. If he couldn't forgive her, she had only herself to blame.

Suppressing the panic rising in her, Serena stepped back and fumbled on the floor for the clothes she'd stripped off so happily not long before. With her back to him, she tried to turn the top right side out and nearly cried out with the frustration of making her hands obey. She was shaking, and if she didn't get out of the room soon, she would start to cry in earnest. She didn't want Dane to see that.

"It was that day, that day that changed so many things for me."

Dane's voice was quiet from the bed, and she stopped, one foot raised, trying to pull on her skirt.

"It was hell, that day."

She turned slowly to look at him. He was still lying in the middle of the bed, eyes closed. His tension was palpable, heart-rending and profound on his features.

He hadn't moved towards her and he wasn't looking at her, but at least he was talking.

Forgetting about her clothes, she perched tentatively on the edge of the bed.

"I have to keep the photos." He sighed deeply on a pant, like he was catching his breath to go on. "Even if some pictures are ingrained so deeply in my mind that I don't need to see them anymore to remember."

His eyes opened then, staring into hers, his full of pain and loss and such destroying sadness. She wasn't even aware that she had put a hand out to him until he clasped it hard in his and pulled her to him. He didn't tuck her against him, but rolled on his side to face her.

"It was hell, there is no other way to describe it. One minute, everything is normal. The world is spinning right on its axis and you and your buddies are laughing, talking about what you'll do when you get leave or when you go home for good. Or what the bets are on dinner, that was always a treat." His face was grim, but he didn't flinch back from her when she set a hand on his cheek in a soft caress.

"And then there's a roaring percussive sound unlike any other. You're numb and unable to move. You can't feel, can't breathe, can't even see because of the dust and debris flying everywhere. The ringing in your ears makes it impossible to hear a thing." He hesitated, somewhere in the past reliving that day.

Her hand tightened on his.

"Then it all comes flooding back – the noise, the fear, the pain. People are screaming, and then you realize one of them is you. Your friends are either lying in blood or attacking in revenge. You want to move, but the pain makes you stop and take inventory to see if you can. You still can't hear anything clearly."

He hesitated, his face grim. "The smell, the smell might be the worst. Blood has its own scent, like iron backed with sharp edges of acid. And you smell your own fear and the fear of everyone around you, because yelling or not, angry or not, everyone is afraid."

He fell silent again, his eyes not seeing her. She wanted to take his pain away but she knew that wasn't possible. She could only let him know that she was there and she loved him. She squeezed his hand and caressed his cheek.

Finally, he blinked and his gaze fell on hers again. She stroked soothing fingers on his clenched hands, letting him know with her touch that she was aching for him. She wanted to ask so many questions, but she was afraid to break the silence. If she started talking, he might stop.

His eyes traveled over her face. Unclenching his fingers and shaking just a bit, he pushed her hair back behind her ears. He traced her lips. Serena dropped her cheek into his cupped hand to let him feel the weight of her love.

She hoped he understood the simple gesture.

The silence stretched out, and she finally knew she had to say something. "Why do you keep the pictures?"

He seemed to waver, unsure of either her question or his response to it. When he spoke again, his voice was gruff. "Sometimes, you think it must have been unreal, that it didn't happen, that your memory is playing tricks on you. I keep them to remind myself that my memories are real."

*****

He shouldn't be telling her this. She didn't deserve to be touched by the filth that clogged up his mind. But she'd seen the pictures, and there was no way to shield her.

And you're not really telling her everything, a small voice said in his head. Because he kept the pictures not only to remind himself, but because he'd shot them. He wasn't willing to volunteer that information.

If she asked him straight out, it would impossible for him to lie to her.

She surprised him, though. "I loved the shots of the children. Their faces were so, I don't know, so open and welcoming to the soldiers. Like they were kids anywhere in the world and they just wanted some attention. And the wildlife photos were incredible. I could see the lions racing, feel the elephants charging. It's like they were there, right in the cabin. I could almost hear them, smell the savanna."

She was playing with his fingers, gently caressing and squeezing each one, just like her words were squeezing his heart.

"Whoever took those photos has amazing talent. They are breathtaking." And she looked up at him again.

Damn, she wasn't going to ask him. Maybe he should be glad about that, but suddenly he wanted her to ask, wanted to be forced to tell her, so that she could see that some of what he'd done, at least, had been good.

She was waiting, the question on her face but unsaid between them. He watched her warily. He wanted to blurt the words out.

"You took all of those pictures, didn't you?" Her question was gentle, not demanding.

She knew the answer already. It was written all over his face.

He sighed, feeling something crack open inside his heart. "Yes, I took them. All of the them." He didn't have the courage to tell her the rest of it.

Serena watched him with so much compassion in her expression that his heart lurched. She loved him unconditionally, letting him tell his story.

He owed her more of an explanation. This was hard, because at some point, they would cross a chasm where his old world and this new one were going to meet. And at some point, she'd know about the rest of the story.

*****

"I can't imagine how hard it must have been, to be taking pictures while you're injured, while your friends are hurt around you. Weren't you afraid, shaking?"

Serena was tucked against Dane's side on the bed, and she watched his face as she asked her questions. She wanted to understand this part of him, this new revelation.

"Training takes over, I suppose. Years of being in difficult situations and holding your body still for that perfect shot. Training is a blessing, because you act on muscle memory, without thinking. Without feeling."

She still didn't quite understand what he had been doing there. Serena was sure there was a reason he was shooting pictures instead of a rifle in the middle of a war zone, but he seemed to be hesitating about telling her more details.

Now her curiosity was getting the better of her.

"I don't understand." She really wanted to, but she was going to have to be more direct, that was clear. "Why were you shooting photos in the first place?"

Dane withdrew as far as she let him. She kept her arms around him, giving him no opportunity to put distance between them. She wanted him to feel safe here, safe to tell her what happened.

"I am, or I was anyway, a photojournalist. I was embedded with the platoon. I was chronicling the war effort, the peaceful side of it and the bloody one. Only it hadn't been that violently bloody before, not to the men and women in our platoon. We were keeping the peace in that sector for the most part."

She tried to imagine what it must have been like for him, embedded but the outsider, watching things through the viewfinder of a camera. Keeping himself apart from people and things, much as he'd tried to do with her. Present but distant.

"I bet you were able to tell some wonderful stories about what you saw."

She knew he must have. She would spend some time searching out those stories on the laptop some other time. Right now, she wanted him to tell her more about it.

With each new admission, each part of himself he was revealing, she felt the distance that he had put between them lessen. There was some way to go yet, but he had his arms wrapped around her and he was talking. The painful loneliness was still in his eyes, but she was hoping she could make that disappear too.

Chapter 35

"It's good that you got your mystery solved. And what a horrible story, for him I mean. Now I can understand why he ran away that day in the store."

Roxy chopped the carrots effortlessly. Serena, perched on a stool, envied her that ease with a kitchen knife. Every piece was the same size, and she was fast. This peaceful place, the quiet kitchen with its huge grills and ovens, soothed her.

"One of the things he told me is that since that day, he's had a hard time with sudden loud noises. The sound of a bus backfiring in New York sent him running, or rather hobbling because he was still in rehab, for a couple of miles before he was able to stop himself. That day in the store, the can dropping set him off because it sounded like a gunshot. He's been using a nail gun on the house, and at the end of the day, he said that his adrenaline is so pumped up he has a hard time sleeping."

He'd told her so much, about his past, about his work up to that day. About what it was like to live in the aftermath.

As much as she'd learned over the years from the vets she'd worked with, she'd never experienced what they'd told her through the unrelenting filter of love. And the love she felt for Dane made what he had suffered all that much more poignant.

"God, what we do to our service people in the name of war! What we put them through! Why, I bet if the people who voted for the idiots who approved that could see..." Roxy came to an abrupt stop when Serena lifted a hand. She sighed. "Off my soapbox now, sorry."

"It's okay. That's my reaction too. But you see, that's what Dane was doing. He was trying to tell the story, the real story, of what the daily lives for those soldiers was like. Often it was sheer boredom, patrols day after day filled with tension but just that, tension. No action."

She stopped then, drawn back into the explanations he provided of the other side of war, the angry side. "And then there's the brutal side, the part that never makes the nightly news or sound bites because it's so tragic. He was telling that side too." She gave Roxy a small smile that held great sadness as well.

"What's he going to do next? Does he have another story he's working on?"

"He said that he's retired," she put the last word in air quotes, "from that line of work. He said his inspiration dried up along with the pools of the blood of his friends, as he put it, and that he'd never pick up a camera or lay words on paper about something again." Serena sighed. "He was adamant."

She played with a pepper on the counter in front of her, keeping her hands busy. "It explains one mystery at least, why I could never find him in the military databases. He wouldn't be listed because he wasn't in any branch. He was an outsider."

Roxy frowned. "But then why did that foundation make such a big deal about helping him in the vet programs?" She looked at Serena. "What did Dane have to say about that?"

Serena held herself still. She hadn't mentioned that to him yet, the one remaining thing she felt guilty about.

"I haven't told him about it." The pepper wouldn't spin like a top, much as she tried it. Kind of like not being able to get her relationship with Dane spinning evenly yet either.

"Are you going to?" Roxy had given up all pretense of chopping now as she watched Serena and the unfortunate pepper.

"Yes, I will. It doesn't matter anymore anyway. After I told them that Dane refused to enter the program, they pulled the promise of any remaining funding. At least they didn't require Balance to return what they'd provided so far."

"Oh sweetie, that means that the agency's at risk again, isn't it?" Roxy came around the counter and gave Serena a hard hug. "Maybe we need to organize a fundraiser..."

Serena laughed, but it held little humor. "That and about a dozen other things to get some money flowing in again. Believe me, I have plenty churning in my mind right now." She paused. "Besides, something is still weird in the Dane story." She stopped speaking abruptly, getting off the stool to pace the kitchen.

Roxy watched and waited, curiosity written all over her face.

"I tried to find Dane's stories, looked all over on the internet, and I can't, find them I mean. There's no photojournalist or writer out there named Dane Ashland."

*****

Serena examined the vegetables in front of her with something akin to loathing. She wished she was as creative as Roxy in turning this mound of ingredients into a treat that was as beautiful to the eye as it would be to the taste buds. Sighing, she realized that she'd settle for something passably edible, good-looking or not.

She heard the key in the front door and smiled. Dane was using the key. That alone made her feel warm all over.

"In here!" She heard him drop something in the entry and come up behind her, wrapping his arms around her and kissing the back of her neck.

She giggled. She couldn't help it, it tickled. She felt almost giddy with the excitement he always brought to her.

Spinning her around, he dropped a kiss on her mouth, first teasing and then demanding. It stole the air from both of them until their breathing was fast and their eyes were bright on each other.

Then he grinned at her, peering over her shoulder at the beginnings of dinner on the cutting board. "Making something from scratch? I'm impressed!"

He even sounded impressed, though there was a trace of mischief in his eyes too. Damn, he could still bring her a new facet of himself every day. The teasing and playful Dane was a new addition, after that night of true confessions. There was so much new information to process.

It reminded her to ask him about the lack of stories with his byline on the internet. She was proud that he'd been doing such important work and she'd wanted to read something he wrote.

Before she could ask him, though, he dropped another kiss on her mouth, then moved her to the side and took over the knife and the unforgiving vegetables. His movements were quick and sure, so unlike the slow mangled mess she'd been making.

"Did I tell you recently how much I love you," he said, taking a side step to kiss her again before returning to the cutting board, "and how grateful I am for whatever reason you had in your head to come visit me that first time at the house?" He smiled as he worked, waiting for her reply.

This was her chance. She could come clean on that other little confession, the reason she'd begun to see him. Then everything would be said, right?

When she didn't reply, Dane put down the knife to face her with puzzled wariness. "What is it, Serena?"

Clearly, her non-response to his declaration was enough to concern him.

"I, ah, have another little confession to make." She stared at him, wondering if he'd be as upset about this as he would be about her prying. She hoped not.

He waited, leaning back now, arms crossed on his chest. His expression was guarded, but his eyes were still bright blue, a good sign.

"I had a very good reason to come see you that first time, in fact, the first few times." She moved away from him, taking a seat at the kitchen table because her knees were shaking. "But after the first couple of times, everything changed, you know?"

She looked at him hopefully. He remained by the counter, aloof now. He never was one to pepper her with questions. He just watched and waited. His training and his profession, the distance he maintained while getting close through the camera, was evident.

She folded and unfolded a paper napkin, and started again, at the beginning this time. "Balance lost a lot of its funding. First, the feds reduced the budget for vets programs, and then the state followed. The agency was running out of dollars, and we could only continue with reduced programs. Eventually, some of the programs would have to be cut entirely. And there are so many people in need."

She swallowed and looked at him. He face was a blank, impossible to read.

"I found a new nonprofit in Sacramento that was willing to give us what we needed to keep the vets programs going. But they had one condition." She stopped again. Crap, this was so hard.

"That condition, the only condition, was that we helped you get into treatment, into counseling or whatever you needed. Specifically you." She paused again but kept her eyes on the shredded paper in front of her. She couldn't stand it.

Emotion had her voice dropping low. "The first time I saw you, I felt something, something I hadn't expected. You didn't want our help, but I had to come back and try again. I was, I don't know, pulled towards you. Like gravity." She shifted on her feet, uneasy. "So I decided that helping you with the house was a way to get close to you, get to know you better, earn your trust so that you'd give counseling a chance."

He was wordless and she couldn't bring herself to look up. "But the joke was on me, because each day I spent with you, I was drawn to you even more. And then I had a choice to make. I could either push you to become a client and never date you, or I could keep you for myself, meaning that Balance would probably lose the money."

She finally folded her hands in front of her, having turned the napkin into molecules of paper that shown like dust on the table. Daring to look up at him, she found his stare dark and unreadable.

"I love you, Dane, and I'm really glad that the foundation put me in your path. I'm sorry I made the decision about becoming involved without telling you the full ramifications. That night, the night of the meteors, I realized that I had fallen for you, and fallen deep. And selfishly, then there was no going back."

It had all been too much. He wasn't saying anything because he was angry. She'd never given him a choice. Her eyes dropped back to the pieces of paper napkin piled like the debris of their relationship in front of her.

She was so intent on her own brooding that she jumped when his arms came around her. He dropped a kiss on her head, then turned her chair around and dropped to a knee in front of her with a grimace. Some movements evidently still weren't that easy for him. His eyes were serious on hers. His hands were gentle, prying hers open and releasing the last flakes of paper to flutter to the floor. Then he got up, pulling her with him.

"I'm glad that you were so persistent," he said quietly, wrapping her into a tight embrace. "I'm glad that you thought that hammering away at me by swinging a hammer would work. And I'm glad, very glad, that you made the choice for us instead of for your work." He stepped away and grinned then. "I'm selfish that way too."

Chapter 36

The past wasn't as scary when it was out in the light. But the lingering darkness remained in his shadows.

Serena asked to read some of his work, and he declined, saying he hadn't kept anything when he decided to start over. He was sure she'd try to find him on the internet, and there would be continuing questions when she still didn't find anything at all. Maybe, though, he could come up with a good reason for that.

Or maybe he needed to tell her why she couldn't find him. He examined that idea, rolling it around in his brain even as his hands finished twisting the wiring in the wall in front of him. Then she'd read about that day, though, and he wasn't willing to risk their new feelings for each other with that.

At least not yet.

Dane had often wondered why she'd wandered into his clearing that hot summer day, and now he knew. She'd risked sharing that with him. He could see himself safely telling her that he worked under a pen name. His family had never appreciated his career choice, and he could never redeem himself in his father's eyes no matter how many awards or accolades he received.

Even if he didn't practice those gifts anymore, even if he could never redeem himself for that last story from the war, they were still a vital part of him.

He was so intent on his thoughts that he wasn't processing his surroundings. And he started when Powers stood, quiet and waiting, next to him. He jumped a few fast steps back before he caught himself.

Cursing himself and his brother, Dane nearly shouted, "Can't you remember it's a bad idea to startle someone who's been shell-shocked?"

To his credit, Powers looked guilty. "I'm sorry, bro, really I am. I called out but I didn't get a response. I saw your truck out front so I knew you were here some place. I wanted to see how you're doing." He stuck out a hand and waited.

Dane shook the anger off and realized that his brother did in fact look very contrite. And he had been off in his own head. You could probably have toppled a wall on him and he wouldn't have noticed it falling until the first brick hit.

Sticking out his own hand, he gripped Powers in a death hold before surprising them both and grabbing him in a hug.

Yes, being in love was definitely making him soft. He smiled inside, thinking about how happy it would make Serena to hear that he was losing some hard edges.

Stepping back, Dane eyed his brother with rueful grin. "I'm sorry too. I was a thousand miles away. You surprised me."

Powers smiled in turn, and hesitating a beat, he threw an arm around Dane's shoulders and started to walk them out of the dusty interior.

"No problem, man, I'm just happy to see that you seem to be better." Then he stopped, as if waiting for another outburst. When Dane didn't say anything, he turned to his younger brother, peering at his clean shaved skin closely.

"My god, what has happened to you?"

Dane felt his face heat, something that rarely happened to him. He wasn't ready to share the reasons why, not ready to risk admitting that he was in love. His brother would want to know all of the details.

Evidence of the changes, though, was obvious in his appearance. With the beard gone, Dane knew he appeared a lot more open than he had before.

"It was just time, time for some changes and time for me to move on."

Powers watched him carefully, the hint of a hopeful smile on his face.

"So you're better, things are really better?"

Dane drew a deep breath and let it out slowly. "Better, yes."

And he had Serena to thank for it.

"So tell me how things are going in your part of the world. Has Ashland Construction taken over Sacramento yet?"

Dane listened to long explanations about the projects Powers had been able to win, the work they were doing, the crews they had down in the valley right now. He asked questions about the projects, listening closely enough to quiz Powers on some of the details. In many ways, it was like they had been a few years ago, during the quiet times when they'd made their rocky peace after Mom had died.

And before Powers had given Dane so much grief over his choice to follow his muse into the world of extreme photojournalism.

"We've working in the community at a different level too," Powers shared.

"What have you been doing, in the community I mean?" Dane fiddled with some wires sticking out of a wall, not looking at Powers but making it clear he was listening. He had to remember to cap these off soon…

"I formed a foundation this summer to provide financial support to programs in the local community. You know, important stuff where people are losing out because the government coffers are dry. Kids programs, adults who need help, vets. That sort of thing." He seemed to be very proud of it and glad that Dane expressed an interest.

Powers continued. "I named it Vision Quest. I think we're even funding a nonprofit up here in Flynn's Crossing. Or at least we were. Something got screwed up and we had to stop."

He stopped speaking abruptly, his eyes suddenly wide on Dane's face. Powers turned away quickly, but not before Dane saw a confused frown cloud his face.

That name didn't ring a bell. The situation, though, was too similar. Dane knew he was looking at his brother strangely, suspicion wafting across his mind.

Fiddling with wires and running fingers over wall studs, awkward uneasiness radiated from Powers. He didn't want to go further in this discussion. Was this the same foundation that pulled funding from Balance?

There was no such thing as coincidences like this.

Another abrupt change in direction brought Powers to the windows framing the canyon views. Dane moved next to him, and the two stood side by side staring out. Dane knew Powers would blink first.

"So you never got any counseling, did you? But you were able to snap out of it anyway?" He never could leave well enough alone.

Dane didn't want to react as Powers expected. His brother could stew over this for a while. He frowned and gave Powers an intentionally puzzled look. "No, I never did. How did you know that?"

Powers back peddled. "Didn't know anything, just made an assumption."

Yes, no such thing as coincidences.

Chapter 37

The beginning of fall in the foothills always brought on a lot of activity. Fruit trees were heavy with crops that needed picking. Farm stands with tables piled high with produce took up residence at every corner on the meandering country roads. Grapes ready for harvest perfumed the air. It wasn't unusual to see small trucks laden with the square white boxes holding bunches of the fruit, bound for pressing, heading up and down the roads. The shorter days and lowering sun added intensity to the pace.

Dane appreciated these snapshots in time. These were the kinds of activities that gave meaning to the agricultural side of this community. And the grapes, apples, artisan cheeses, and other goods brought visitors to wineries, ranches and shops. Things bustled with hectic energy at this time of year, and then the many families who hunted the farms to cut their own Christmas trees took over. It wasn't until after the holidays in the new year that everything returned to its usual slow pace.

He was a little jittery about today. It was the blessing of the harvest and first crush party at a new winery, and Serena had convinced him to come with her. Her girl tribe, as she called them, would be there.

He would be inspected. It made him nervous, because these women were important to Serena. Their opinions mattered.

He had faced down the horrors of war and survived, only to be set quaking by the hoped-for approval of the friends of his love. He had to laugh at himself.

And then there was the whole Powers mystery. Something wasn't ringing true, that suspicious buzz in the back of his mind the same kind he always got on the trail of an important story. Serena said that a new foundation offered Balance a donation on the condition that they help him specifically. She never mentioned the name of the foundation and he never thought to ask. But they'd withdrawn all future funding when Serena reported that he would not become a client.

Powers said he had started a foundation this summer to help the local community, including vets. He'd mentioned a program in Flynn's Crossing where they pulled their funding. And he'd known that Dane got better without any treatment before Dane had said so.

The niggling feeling that somehow it was all connected kept growing.

*****

She stood at the edge of the crowd, an eye on the driveway leading up to the winery parking area. She was eager for Dane to get there, eager to show him off. And a bit anxious too. She hoped that her friends would behave themselves. And that he would like them, and they would like him. They'd teased her on the drive up, finally relenting when they saw how worried that made her.

She heard Tess and DK come up behind her, Tess's praises ringing out. "Your sculpture looks truly amazing, DK. It was gorgeous when it was in your studio, but here, in the courtyard, well, you've just outdone yourself."

Serena turned to see DK's grin, so large that it seemed her face might split. Tess was smiling too, awe in her expression.

"Now if I could just finish it. It started out as a contract, but I fell in love with the piece too." They stopped next to Serena and all three women turned to stare down the driveway.

"So today we get to meet Mr. Mystery Vet." Tess gave her arm a squeeze to lighten the teasing mood.

"Please don't slip up and call him that to his face, okay?" That was the problem with playing name games. You had to worry that one would stick and come out accidently at the worst possible time.

"I won't, don't worry. You are nervous. What's wrong? Afraid we won't measure up?" Tess and the others were curious, since Serena had been mysterious herself on what she'd learned about Dane. She hadn't shared his latest revelations, wanting him to have the opportunity to tell his story his way.

"I'm afraid he'll decide that this is too big a step. He asked what kind of event this was and I told him. He raised one eyebrow. Then I told him that the dress code was business or business casual, and the other eyebrow went up. He didn't say anything about it after that."

She was nervous, afraid that he'd be a no-show. She had hoped that they'd come far enough for this.

DK got called away by their hosts and Tess remained by her side, talking to her about the people in the courtyard. The gossip did little to distract her. It was almost time for things to start.

Her heart was falling, second-guessing herself for even asking him. It was too soon. He wasn't ready. They might have been ready to love each other, but it evidently was still a private thing.

Then she saw the familiar dark blue truck come slowly up the gravel drive. He was following the posted speeds but she wanted him to hurry. All of the indecision and uncertainty left her as he pulled into a parking space down the drive. Her feet were glued to the gravel. Stepping out of the truck, he worked himself into a jacket and finally shut the door and started towards them.

"Ah well," Tess commented next to her. Serena knew her friend was smiling at her but she was too busy appreciating Dane to care.

He was dressed in a light gray suit that brought out the bits of gray in his black hair. As he got closer, she could see the collarless light blue shirt that she knew would be the perfect match for his eyes. Those for the time being were hiding behind sunglasses.

She grinned.

"Yup," she said, "mine."

*****

The introductions had gone smoothly. Dane charmed each woman in turn. Tess was her usual calm and soothing self, Gabby bubbled, and Roxy immediately started teasing him, saying he was the first man who had ever inspired Serena to try to cook a meal.

She was right, but still.

That left DK, who was busy gathering congratulations, standing next to the owners of the winery. There was no time for her to come over before the activities started and her introduction would have to wait. A priest blessed the crop, the workers, the owners and the winery. He blessed the art that DK had created, along with blessing her too. The county agricultural commissioner, the elected supervisor from the county board, and the owners gave short speeches of welcome.

And through it all, Dane kept a hand in hers or an arm around her. He'd shed the sunglasses and he looked relaxed and happy. She was so glad.

He liked her friends, he whispered in her ear. Kissing it, he added, "They take good care of you."

She was positive the frisson of heat down her spine at his mere breath raised the warm temperature of the afternoon by quite a few degrees.

Soon, the five of them were having a fast and intense conversation standing in a tight circle off to the side. Dane fit right in, trading barbs with Roxy while he answered Gabby's questions and engaged Tess with his own inquiries about her business.

They were waiting for DK to have time to visit. She was still talking with a small crowd. A tall blond-haired man seemed to be arguing a point with her and she flung a hand out and pointed at the fields. He huffed out a laugh. She turned and headed for them, grabbing a glass of wine from a passing waiter as she paced over. The tense disgusted expression on her face spoke volumes about the discussion she just left.

"Some people think that any art must be an exact replica of the idea it was meant to translate. Like taking a picture. That idiot complained because my representation of the grapes on the vine was not depicted 'accurately', as he put it. I told him he could just go look for himself and see if he could come up with something better." DK took a fast sip, breathed deep, and took another slower one to appreciate the flavor.

"Okay, sorry, I hate art critics is all." She eased out of her funk and looked around the group, eyes finally settling on Dane. He held out his hand to introduce himself.

She stared and didn't move. Dane frowned. Serena glanced quickly between the two of them.

Their entire group was now staring at DK in various stages of confusion or concern. The shock on DK's face was out of place.

Dane's face morphed into a blank look. Serena noticed his eyes getting dark and distant. His hand dropped.

DK finally opened her mouth. "Oh my god, Dane Matthews."

Serena blinked in confusion.

And Dane turned and walked away.

*****

"What do you mean you know him?" Serena hissed at DK as they watched Dane pause twenty feet away and look out over the vineyards.

"I saw him in New York at an opening, a photography exhibit. He was one of the artists. I never got to talk to him, but his bio on the wall was impressive. This must have been, what, five or six years ago? He'd already been covering wars and famines and disasters as well as the standard feel good stories. He's a legend for the causes he undertakes to document, sometimes at risk of his professional career or his life. I didn't recognize him from the picture that you gave me. That beard covered up too much of his face."

"But why did he walk away?" Gabby's worry was prominent in her expression.

"Maybe he doesn't want to be recognized," Roxy suggested. "Why did he drop off the face of the earth in the first place, do you know? It couldn't just be because of his injuries."

DK was already shaking her head. "His last story, the one about the bomb that blew up his friends. That's why. He got a lot of criticism for that story, specifically for the pictures. Some people said he made blood money off the grief of others. The lieutenant who died was the subject of one very horrible shot. The shot was good, the subject bad. It must have been like the one you showed us, Serena. While his wife gave permission for Dane to use it, the lieutenant's parents were irate. They sued him, said that Dane was getting rich off their son's heroic death. The case got thrown out of court, but not before there were a lot more angry words all around. It was very ugly."

"And then he just disappeared." Tess didn't need to ask the question. They all understood now.

"You said that he was trying to get the story out about how the war really was," Roxy said. "You were never able to find any of his bylines. And now we know why."

Dane shrugged out of his jacket and picked up his pace again, a straight line taking him to his truck. Serena called out to him but he kept walking. She sprinted after him, doing the best she could in the spiky heels and narrow dress.

"Dane, hold on. Let's talk about this. Please." She cursed the heels but couldn't take them off. She'd never get across the gravel barefoot. The sound of her voice slowed him down some, but he kept moving.

He reached the truck and yanked open the driver's door, sunglasses slammed back on his face with so much force she was surprised he didn't break them. She had twenty feet to go. He seemed to be having trouble getting the key into the ignition.

Ten feet.

The engine roared to life and she heard the gearbox scream in protest at its rough treatment. Serena yanked open the passenger side truck door and jumped in as Dane spun the tires and kicked up rocks, peeling through a quick u-turn down the driveway.

Chapter 38

The truck bounced along the driveway at more than the suggested speed until they reached the black top of the main road. Tires squealed as they bit into asphalt. They came close to taking some of the bends in the rural road on two wheels.

Dane didn't say anything. He was still too stunned and a little sick that his name, his work name, popped out that way. He didn't recognize DK, but she obviously knew him.

He hadn't said anything since DK's outburst. Even if he wanted, he wouldn't have been able to because his throat felt swollen shut to the point of strangling him. Serena too was silent beside him. He wasn't sure why he hadn't locked the truck door when he'd jumped in, but he hadn't. He did feel some sense of relief that she'd chosen to get in and leave with him rather than letting him leave alone or telling him to go to hell.

He'd wanted to explain it to her in his own schedule, and then give her a chance to read some of the controversy about him with comfortable space to ask questions.

Or maybe he would have printed off the original story and given her a chance to read that, then explained the rest of it.

It was hard to know exactly what he would have done because now it was out of his hands. He could still tell his side of the story. But Serena would now know what name to query and when she googled him, she'd have enough reading material to last a weekend or longer.

In the past, he had been tired of answering everyone's questions and hearing everyone's opinions, even if the vets and active duty he was in rehab with were mostly appreciative of the work he'd been trying to do. He finally went back to using his birth last name, Ashland, because too many people connected the dots that the name Dane Matthews provided.

Serena was too quiet, and his occasional glance in her direction let him know she was staring out the side window, her face turned away from him. He slowed their speed to a more reasonable pace. When he thought about it, he remembered to breathe.

He was driving back to her place, he realized. He would drop her off if she didn't leap out of the truck when it was still moving down her street. Then he'd go back to the house, maybe work a little.

Maybe just sit at the edge of the canyon and wish for a hole to open up in the earth and swallow him.

He pulled up in her short driveway, relieved to see that she must have gotten a ride to the event. Her SUV was still there. She didn't get out immediately.

He waited, and he could feel her eyes on him.

"I'd like you to come in." Her voice was quiet but it shared little about her mood.

"Serena, I don't think it's..." he started.

Her 'please' cut across whatever he thought to say next. It wasn't a command and she wasn't begging, but it still speared him.

He folded and opened his door.

*****

His face in profile was impassive. He was waiting as she had asked in the living room. He wasn't doing anything, staring at the wall of bookshelves in front of him as if memorizing each title.

She looked back at her laptop screen. She'd read his final story, the one he said took it all out of him. She could understand why. It was poignant, roughly emotional, and full of so much heartfelt grief that she was surprised he had anything left inside at all. The pictures were wrenching, gruesome in their reality.

She also read the criticisms from the soldier's parents, countered by the wife's impassioned commitment to getting it published. The list of awards and accolades that it earned him was extensive, even though it appeared he never accepted any of them.

It explained so much. He didn't want to be Dane Matthews anymore. She understood that. But the Dane Ashland she knew was still a talented and caring man.

She got up from the chair and stretched to give herself time to think of what to say. He didn't turn to watch her. He hadn't said a word since he'd come into the house, seating himself on the sofa. He was wary, giving her the impression of a coiled spring ready to let loose. She thought that if any loud noise sounded right now, he'd be crabbing across the floor and out the door in a second.

She knew she needed to keep the sympathy she felt for him out of the conversation. He wouldn't accept it. He didn't want it, preferring, it seemed, to set himself apart as a villain or a martyr.

From what she'd read, he was regarded as a greedy bastard in some circles and a hero in others. His military friends stood by him, saying that he'd been trying to tell the story of the war, their real war. His critics said he was only in it for the shock value and the money and fame that brought. They'd easily forgotten that it was his friend who died minutes after that critical picture was taken.

No words broke their silence. Birds twittered outside in the late afternoon sun. Somewhere a car honked. She could see a few dust motes drifting through the spear of sun coming in a crack in the window blinds.

And still, he didn't say anything. Other men might defend themselves with excuses, justifications and rationales. Or they'd try to explain their point of view, taking out their own hostility at what happened by blaming everyone else and pointing fingers at fate.

Dane just sat there as if he waiting for her verdict.

It pained her to see him like this. He had done such a good and noble thing, putting himself in the line of verbal fire from everyone while trying to do something honorable. He'd taken a picture of Anderson's final moments of life and told a heart-moving story of both the man and the bigger picture of war. It was an amazing story, and the pictures illustrated everything he had poured into it.

It had nearly killed him physically as well as emotionally.

Slowly she moved to the sofa, seating herself next to him, close enough to feel the heat of his thigh. He didn't move, either towards her or away. She clasped her hands in her lap, mainly because she wanted to grab him and hug him to her, telling him she understood. But she knew that he wouldn't accept that from her right now.

"It must have been horrible, to lose your friend, do him such as great honor, and then be crucified for it." She let the words sink in before she looked at him. His expression was hidden, a blank, the eye she could see in profile dark to almost black. A small twitch caught the edge of that eyelid. Otherwise, he was completely still.

"I can't understand some people, you know?" She shook her head. "You helped millions understand what the war was like, and Anderson, he was a hero and you made that clear too. Why did his parents hate you so much?"

He didn't give any indication that he heard her. His stare was empty.

"Please, Dane, help me to understand. You didn't even fight them in court and they lost anyway. Clearly, you were in the right. Why have you isolated yourself so much?"

His face changed with that. He snapped his head around to face her, and the self-disgust he felt was evident in the sick twist of his features. He stood up so quickly that she fell sideways. And he stood looking down at her for what seemed like hours.

"I was isolated already, by everyone and everything that happened. Being embedded with the unit was both a blessing and a curse. I broke my cardinal rule – never become personally involved with the subjects. I made friends there, good friends, the kind that you know you'll be bonded with forever. Anderson and the others, they were those kinds of friends."

He paced, front door to kitchen and back again. He pulled a hand through his hair, frustration in every movement.

"When they needed me," he barked out, "when they needed me to comfort them or reassure them or just be there for them, what was I doing? I was taking pictures. I couldn't spend a second to say a word to them, make it easier for them somehow. Listen to their last words or requests. No, I was taking their pictures." He spit out the words like rifle fire.

Serena had no idea what to say to that. She understood his anguish. He had wanted to comfort his friends, but he had a job to do, and when the shock of the moment was upon them, he reverted to the one thing that could keep him sane in the craziness, his work.

His pacing hadn't slowed. "Not only did I take their pictures, but I published them, along with a story. And that story won me all sorts of awards in journalism and photography. I made money off it too, did you know that? Lots of money." His laugh was harsh and self-recriminating. "That's all so many people saw, the money."

"But the people who were important, they understood. Anderson's wife, she came out in the press and supported you. Other spouses did too. And the soldiers who survived, they all called you a hero for telling it like it was, not sugar coating it as the popular press was doing at the time."

She didn't completely understand why he was being so hard on himself. Sure, he hurt from the critical comments he received, but he'd gotten so much support too.

He stopped in front of her. "Don't you see? I did profit from it. My fame, the legend they call it, just grew even bigger. I didn't want that. I'd be happy with no legend at all if we were all still bored to tears in some dust pit, all of those soldiers around me."

"The money. Is that how you were able to afford the land and the house?" She hated to ask, but it needed saying.

He gave another harsh bark of laughter, except nothing was remotely funny. "That's exactly it, that kind of thinking. Is that what you think of me?" His gaze was disappointed and hurt on hers, hands clenching at his sides.

She held his eyes and rose to stand in front of him. "No, that's not the Dane that I know and love. The Dane that I know and love is kind and gentle and would help another out of any bind he could. So what did you do with the money?"

He wavered then, indecision on his face. The anger and self-loathing lingered.

"I set up trust funds for each of the kids of the soldiers who were killed and those who were injured. They don't know where it came from. It's anonymous. There was a lot of money. The spouses got something too, again anonymous. It's blood money, their blood, and they deserved to get some benefit from it."

"Did you keep any of this for yourself?

Running a hand over his face, he said quietly, "No."

"And you paid for your house and land from…?"

He stopped facing away from her, his voice far away. "From the proceeds of the sales of my previous work. Photography brings a sizable paycheck when it's considered art." His voice got hard and sarcasm bit out the last word.

"Then why do you still feel guilty?"

He turned back around then, fast and furious. "Don't you see? I should have been comforting them. I should have been caring for them. I should have been easing their way or whatever, or at least trying to help them stop their bleeding. Instead I was taking pictures!" Those last words he spat out slowly, syllable by syllable.

Serena felt herself get very calm. She walked back over to the laptop and flipped through some screens before she found what she was looking for. Holding up a finger when he would have started in again, she read the words in an article that came out months after the bomb and his story's ugly aftermath.

"'Today the Army announced the successful deployment of new body armor and weaponized tanks and other vehicles for the troops in Afghanistan. Recent stories have shown in graphic detail why the escalating fighting in regions previously considered settled is even more dangerous than was once thought. Officials in the Pentagon cite the work of photojournalist Dane Matthews in raising the outcry for more protection for troops in these dangerous areas.'" She stopped and looked at him. "It seems that what you did was good, all things considered. Do you want me to read you more?"

*****

He heard what she read. She still didn't get it, did she? Despite all the pretty words, he'd had friends die, right in front of him, and he hadn't even taken the time to say goodbye.

She was talking again, not reading this time, but moving slowly towards him. "I think that what you did, what you were able to capture in pictures and words, did a whole lot more for them and for thousands of other soldiers like them. You got people worried about their safety. You got people, important people who could make decisions about their protection, interested and enraged and involved. You changed lives." She stopped in front of him.

He wanted to believe her. He'd had two years to think about this, and his thinking always led back to his own remorse. He wished he'd been able to do more.

And he'd wished he'd been able to comfort them and say goodbye, directly instead of through the camera's lens. Especially Anderson.

She reached up a hand to touch his face. He wanted to drop his cheek into that softness and let it sooth him. She gave a small sad smile and traced the vicious scar, then put a hand behind his head and pulled him down to her. She matched her lips to his, seam to seam, and gently worked his apart until her tongue could find his.

Acceptance was in her kiss, in the hands she ran over him, in the way her body molded to his.

Tears stung his eyes. Dane wanted to believe that there was hope for them, that he could move past this ugliness. He would never be able to pick up a camera again because nothing would ever redeem him from those last shots. All he saw was their faces. All he heard was their screams. But he had a woman who loved him despite his flaws and his past.

Without another word, he broke their kiss, and Serena took his hand. He led the way to her bedroom. He found his hands were shaking, and he could feel her answering trembles.

The clothes were complicated, more buttons and zippers than usual in these dressier outfits. Taking a quick moment to appreciate the picture she made in her sleeveless dress, Dane found the side zipper and lowered it slowly, running his fingers over her soft skin following its path. Serena sighed and it raised his pulse higher. She stepped out of the dress and shoes as one, and stood before him in lace bra and panties, his angel of redemption.

He wanted to rush now, yank off his dress shirt and slacks, lie down beside her and gratefully pleasure her until she cried out. But she was taking the same slow journey he had. Her fingertips brushed his chest as she fumbled with buttons that were suddenly too small, and he pushed her hands away to tear the shirt off, sending those buttons everywhere. She giggled, nerves in the sound.

Then he stripped off his slacks, briefs, socks and shoes as one and stood before her, scars and all, proud of his nakedness for the first time in years. She reached down between them even as her eyes stayed on his, and the intense glow of love on her face gave his future so much promise.

Dane couldn't wait any longer. He walked Serena back against the bed and followed her down. His hand unhooked the bra impatiently and shoved both it and her panties out of the way. Her arms locked around his neck and pulled him in for a hot kiss, tongues dancing. He felt like he would explode with the energy she gave him, and the intensity of everything he felt kicked up another notch.

He wanted to see her face as he took her up and over, and he leaned back on an elbow to brush hair out of her eyes. She gave him a saucy smile and traced his lips with a fingertip. His hand traveled down her body until he reached her core, and the sound of her sudden gasp made him smile. There were no more secrets between them. She redeemed him in so many ways, and now he could only think of thanking her with his commitment of body, mind and soul.

Fingers moved to pleasure her, gentle strokes that grew stronger as her hips moved. When she shifted restlessly and tried to make him hurry, he paused and spent long minutes teasing her lips and tasting her deeply. When she wrapped a leg around him to pull him closer, he held himself apart and his fingers dipped in to bring her to a new plateau. Her hand moved between them to stroke him, and he waited until she was close, so close, before he shifted and positioned himself right at the edge of her heat.

And when she would have lifted and sheathed him, he paused, poised above her, and cupped her face with a tender hand. Looking deep in her eyes, he let his soul do the talking. "Serena, I love you with all my life, and I'll devote the rest of it to making you as happy as your acceptance has made me."

Chapter 39

Serena was tired in the best way possible. Yesterday had been a rollercoaster of emotions. First, finding out who Dane really was. Then sharing his grief and pain at the faults he perceived in himself. And finally, the long night of passion, heights of tenderness inscribed with such deep feelings that she almost cried just thinking about them today.

She'd been reluctant to leave their bed this morning. Dane pulled her back twice, the first time when she opened her eyes to find him watching her, hard and ready, and he had eased inside her before she even had a chance to run her fingers through his hair. His desire for her matched hers for him, and the quiet words of love they couldn't seem to stop saying still cocooned her in warmth.

Much later, she intended to shower, and he came in as she'd waited for the water to heat, coffee cups steaming. He moved his naked body against hers, and the shower turned into another sensuous layer that ended with them in bed again, albeit wet and a bit wilder this time. She smiled as she remembered his groans of pleasure as she'd run her lips over the length of him.

Stretching, she turned to the computer screen. She hated to leave him on a Saturday, but she needed to prepare something to give the board of directors next week. With Dane's permission, she would be telling the board why Vision Quest discontinued their funding. He agreed that they should know, and he'd even offered to come to the board meeting with her to explain his side of things. He didn't want her to come under any criticism for their relationship.

It wasn't anyone's fault that they'd fallen in love.

It seemed like hours passed, but the clock moved painfully slow. Shifting categories in the budget, checking assumptions, and recalculating what was needed in some programs didn't bring any different results. There wasn't another way to make the numbers work. Serena sighed. There was enough left in the budget for about four more months of the vets programs and then they would have to start turning people away and cutting back.

Some of the counselors would work pro bono for a time to carry them over. Some, like Eduardo, had pensions from their own military service or other sources of income from private practices to sustain them. But those were temporary solutions. They needed to create public awareness to both garner support from the elected officials who voted on the funding streams and to gather some public donations and foundational support.

If only they could tell the stories of some of these people they helped, similar to what Dane did before. She wanted to ask him to help but he had been clear on the fact that he would not be picking up a camera again. He'd actually let her sit beside him as he engaged in the ritual of cleaning the camera bodies and lenses, but he didn't plan to use them.

But maybe he knew someone else who could do what he used to do, tell the story of Balance and the work that it accomplished through the lens of a camera and carefully selected words. She set her forehead on the cool of her desk. She would ask him later today. Maybe he had an answer to her dilemma.

*****

Dane smiled at the receptionist behind the glass enclosure and waited as she buzzed him through the locked door to the offices. Serena had brought him here the first time a month ago, introducing him to the staff as her boyfriend. He smiled at the memory. Since then, he'd dropped by when she didn't expect him, just to see the smile of happy surprise light up her face.

The offices were quieter on Saturday, with only a couple of counselors handling the weekend groups and individual sessions. He knew his way around now and moved down the hall of small counseling rooms to Serena's office in the back corner. He could see the lights on from here, and he chuckled as he thought about the smile he would receive with his present of savory croissants for lunch.

Easing open the door, he expected his love to be hard at work pounding the keyboard. His smile grew tender when he saw Serena with her head down on the desk, snoring gently. They hadn't had much sleep last night, too busy pleasing each other and talking without barriers or secrets between them.

He loved her, and she loved him. It all seemed so simple now. Never in his dreams had he expected this, a few short months ago. At times this summer, he doubted he wanted to go on. Now he had everything to live for. He had Serena to live for.

And himself too, once again.

He hated to disturb her when she was sleeping so deeply, but he also knew that she would be mortified if any of the staff found her like this. Their teasing would be good-natured and based on their fondness for their leader. Still, it would be better for her to be at home, curled up with him, both of them snoozing.

He tucked a long strand of hair behind her ear and she stirred. Wonderful aromas from the bag of fresh croissants he set on her desk tickled her nose with a twitch as she started to come awake. He couldn't resist the desire to kiss her ear and she smiled even before her eyes were completely open.

"Hello my love," he whispered in her ear. Her eyes locked on to the bag in front of her nose, then she sat back to look up at him. Her smile set his heart beating faster again. He realized that if they had a hundred years together, his heart would always beat faster when she looked at him with such love in her eyes.

"Hello yourself. I must have dozed off. I can't imagine why." A saucy wink accompanied her last words before she pulled him down for a hard kiss. "And you brought food – yum!"

"Are you, ah, getting much done?" Crumbs fell everywhere as he followed her lead, grabbing a croissant out of the bag and biting into the flaky crust.

"I've been through the numbers forwards and backwards. I think I've already squeezed out every last penny. There isn't anything left to move around. Unless I can find some donors or a couple of grant opportunities come up, we'll need to cut back on our vets programs in about four months." She picked at the edge of the croissant, her face sad.

She shifted towards him. "I know you don't want to pick up a camera again," lifting her hand to stop him as he started to speak. "I'm not asking you to. I know how deeply the last venture hurt you and I would never want you to feel that kind of pain again."

He wanted to help her. But if he was back in the public eye, the risk of hurt and criticism would return as well. He was still too brittle to contemplate it.

Serena was talking again. "Do you know of anyone else who could come up with a piece that tells the story of our vets and the help that they get? You know, the kind of thing that you used to do. Someone who's almost as good as you, because we all know you were the best."

She smiled at him and he knew that she was okay with his refusal. Still, she also let him know that she had high expectations of whomever he suggested. "And they'd have to be willing to donate their time and expenses too."

She didn't want much, did she? "Let me think on that." He shifted uncomfortably in his chair. But that reminded him of a question he'd been meaning to ask her since his brother paid his last visit.

"Did you think about going back to that foundation, the one that had the condition on their donation? What was their name again?" He tried to make the inquiry casual.

"Vision Quest? No, I don't think they would be willing to reconsider. Their executive director, a Ms. Simpson, was clear about that. At least they didn't ask for any money back, which some funders would do. But no, I don't think we'd be able to approach them again." Serena continued to shuffle some papers around her desk, putting things into neat stacks as she waited for the computer to power down.

Even though he'd had his suspicions, Dane felt stunned. Vision Quest. He swore his brother had named that same organization. Did Powers have a hand in all of this? Damn if his brother hadn't meddled again.

"So what are we going to do today?" Serena's yawn was huge behind her hand as she looked at him. He shook himself into the present and gave her a quick smile.

"I think you, my love, need some sleep. I didn't let you get much rest last night." He put some lechery in his smile and had to laugh when she giggled and batted her lashes at him. "Don't tempt me, woman! I have an errand to do today, an important one. How about you go home and get some sleep, and I'll call you later. Maybe we could camp out tonight and watch the stars."

She grinned as she bit back another yawn. "That sounds lovely. Are you absolutely sure you don't want to join me in that nap?"

He was tempted, so tempted, but he needed to confirm his assumptions. He and his brother were going to have some words yet again.

Chapter 40

"Dane, what are you doing here?"

His brother's voice held surprise and shock. Dane would have smiled at this, but he'd worked himself up into a good buzz of pissed off on his way down the hill. Instead, he stared right into the security camera as if he could see Powers through the one-way feed. And he let himself look as pissed off as he felt.

His brother's condo building was what Dane expected, elite and sophisticated, set in midtown Sacramento at a prestigious address. He shocked his brother by coming here.

The buzzer remained silent. Maybe Powers wasn't going to let him in. He probably hadn't made any friends since he'd come to town, too busy working and interfering in the life of his one and only brother to socialize. Maybe he'd never had to use the thing before and was trying to figure out how. The thought should have brought him some humor, but he was still too mad.

Dane still hadn't said anything, and he sensed Powers waiting silently too, staring at him through the security system. He waited, and the buzzer finally sounded.

When he'd given Dane his home address in Sacramento, Powers probably never expected that he'd visit. The fact that he was here was going to be a big deal. Dane was counting on that.

The elevator to the top floor penthouse was quick, the short hall to the suite's front door plush. Dane was still deciding how he wanted to play this, direct or not. He stood at the door, staring at it but not seeing it. His anger was fading. His brother did have his best interests at heart, he knew, even if Powers didn't know how to express that without making all sorts of messes.

He lounged to one side and knocked, keeping his expression neutral. Powers must have been waiting with his hand on the doorknob because the door was thrown open immediately.

"Hey man, this is a surprise, a big surprise, but a happy one." He stuck out a hand, and Dane took it slowly. It was a very civil handshake, more like one between two business associates then brothers.

"Come in, come in! Let me clear away some of this debris." Powers moved back to the living room, running a hand through his close-cropped hair in a motion Dane knew well. His brother was nervous, surprisingly. He shuffled stacks of papers on the glass and chrome coffee table, and Dane took note of the Ashland Construction logo and another he couldn't identify.

Turning slowly to look out the wraparound windows, Dane realized that his brother had selected his own prime location to settle. The condo was spacious with a killer view. He doubted that Powers got to spend much time here relaxing, as he took in the piles of paperwork, rolls of blueprints and scale models of buildings covering every inch of flat space. There was a chair pulled up next to the coffee table and a cup of something in front of it. Powers had been hard at it on the weekend, still the workaholic that their father had trained him to be.

"So to what do I owe the honor of this visit? I'm pleased that you made the drive down the hill."

Powers probably didn't realize how pompous he sounded. Dane felt that he should soften his opinion of his brother. The guy didn't know how much he sounded like their dad right now. It was sad.

Dane moved around the room, coming to stand in front of the floor to ceiling windows, and looked towards the mountains. Somewhere up there, he realized, Serena was waiting for him to come home so that they could get on with their life together.

"Oh, checking up on you. You know, coming to stick my nose in your business." He turned around. Powers was standing halfway to the small kitchen.

"Coffee? I just made a fresh pot and it's strong." Ever the good host as well.

"Sure." He walked over to the only other place to sit in the chaotic room, a low-slung leather sofa. Dropping to its seat, he glanced over the papers strewn on the coffee table. Mostly plans, contracts, estimates. All the stuff that a busy construction mogul would need to be reviewing on a weekend.

And then his eyes found it again, that new logo. Bingo. Letterhead that clearly read Vision Quest.

Powers returned with a steaming mug. "Still drinking it black, right?"

"Only if it's decent coffee. Otherwise I'll add anything I can find to make it taste passable."

"So, a visit from you. This is terrific. Clearly you're feeling a whole lot better to be venturing out this far. I'm really happy to see that, bro. Really happy to see that you're doing so much better."

Powers fidgeted uncomfortably, perching on the edge of his chair, and his next words provided Dane with evidence of just how much he wanted to try to get things on a different footing.

"Would you like to look at some of the projects we have underway? The company's doing great in this region, you should know that. Things are moving fast and we have a ton of work. I know you said you'd never work in the family business, but in case you've changed your mind..." Powers trailed off, watching him.

Dane realized that he still hadn't given any reasons why he was there. He had his reasons, but they weren't something he was going to ask about directly.

"No, still no interest in construction unless it's what I'm doing on my house." Powers looked disappointed and he could feel for his brother. There didn't appear to be anyone in the next generation who was interested in the family business anymore except Powers.

The silence that followed was awkward. But Dane was used to letting things rest in silences. Sometimes that's how you found out the most information, he'd discovered in his years of interviewing.

Restless Powers, though, couldn't leave a void unfilled. He moved papers out of the way on the table, stacking things hastily as he went.

Dane saw an opening he could use. "Working on the weekend again? I thought you were trying to give that habit up years ago. Too many companies to keep track of?"

The shuffling stopped as Powers grinned a bit sheepishly. "Yeah, there's a lot to do. And that foundation I mentioned? I didn't realize how many decisions needed to be made there. The executive director I hired is great, don't get me wrong. But a lot of things need board level approval, and as chair of the board, I've been sorting through that as well."

"That's right, you mentioned the foundation. What did you end up calling it again?"

"Vision Quest. Want to look at it? I've got some of the information right here." He turned back to the stacks and began sorting.

Even though he'd strongly suspected the foundations would be one and the same, confirmation jolted Dane. How many lives had this disrupted? How many people stressed over potential losses because of these manipulations, the ones that Powers couldn't avoid? His anger became more profound.

After a few minutes, Dane's lack of response registered and Powers stopped and raised his eyes.

"Couldn't stay out of my business even now, eh?" Dane kept his face as neutral as possible, but he knew it wasn't welcoming and bordered on grim. And he knew that the scar made his expression a whole lot darker. For once, he'd use that to his advantage.

"I don't know what you mean." Powers sat back and his face became neutral as well, though Dane knew better.

"I mean, giving money to a nonprofit on the condition that they get me into treatment, that's what I mean. Money with strings attached." He felt his anger come to the surface once more and rose to walk a room length away. "Why were you messing in my business?"

Powers stood too, putting his hands on his hips. His mad was rising too. "Look," he all but shouted. "You needed help. You weren't going to get it sitting out on your mountaintop by yourself. I was just trying to get it to you in whatever way I could." He moved to the opposite corner.

So many times, Dane realized, they had stood like this, on different sides of an issue, faced off against each other. Powers felt the need to direct things when he thought that's what a situation called for. He was every inch as controlling as their father had been. And, Dane realized, he probably didn't know that this is why people pushed away from him.

Love must be making him more understanding, he thought. Serena's loving acceptance of him made it easier for him to do the same with those around him. Particularly, perhaps, his brother.

"So I should be pissed as all hell that you meddled again. You made a promise to that program to fund them, and then you withdrew that promise." He moved closer to the center of the living room again.

"There were conditions on that funding, helping you. They never got you into any treatment, you said so yourself. It's like a contract. They didn't fulfill their side of the deal, so they don't get any more money."

Powers was defensive and a pulse on his temple was visibly throbbing. Dane watched it with some fascination.

"But people counted on that money. It's not like a construction contract where you can turn off the equipment and wait for better weather or the right supplies. People are trying to rebuild their lives and that funding was letting Balance help them do just that."

Two more steps and he was at the table again.

"Listen, they can submit another proposal and we'll look at it with all of the others we've been receiving. There are many organizations out there, a lot who are helping people. I just wanted to jumpstart something for you."

Powers had run out of steam and Dane watched his hands unclench at his sides. He drew an audible deep breath that echoed the mental breath Dane took.

"I'm sorry I was meddling. I was worried about you after everything that happened. I know I reacted first and asked questions later, after you were blown up. I wasn't exactly the most supportive brother."

Powers now moved towards the table. They were still standing on opposite sides, but at least only the width of the glass was between them.

There were so many ways this could go, Dane realized. He could stay mad at Powers and dig a deeper rift between them. He could walk out the door and hope that they went another couple of years before they saw each other again.

But all things being equal, he had to be grateful for the meddling. That had brought him his love, Serena, who brought him out of his funk with a hammer and an open heart. And for that reason alone, he could forgive him.

Dane walked around the table to where Powers stood, watchful and tensed. He stuck out his hand. Pulling in a deep breath, he answered in the only way he now knew how.

"Thanks, Powers, for the best thing you could have ever brought into my life."

Chapter 41

Serena felt the light touch of nerves as she prepared for the board meeting. Some of the members might hold her more responsible than others for the loss of the Vision Quest funding. Others, she knew, would be supportive. She did feel responsible.

But not enough to give up Dane and their shared love.

He had been very mysterious these last couple of days. He'd also been oddly energized. She couldn't think of another way to describe it, little waves of excitement coming off him. She asked him about it, but he only smiled and said he was simply happy with where they were in life.

Right now, though, she had to concentrate on the board meeting. Many of the members had already arrived, and in a few minutes, the meeting would be called to order. Dane said he would meet her here to explain his side if needed. She could have used the support right now, but she understood that coming in together probably wouldn't put the best appearance on things.

Settling the binder on her left arm so she was free to shake hands with the board, she opened the door to the conference room. She was surprised to see Dane sitting against the back wall, behind the seat she usually used during these meetings. She had no time to greet him as the members approached with various degrees of warmth or depths of coldness in their hellos.

Before she had a chance to do more than shoot a smile at Dane, the board president rapped for attention and the meeting was called to order. The drone of voting on old business didn't take very long, and then the president came to the budget discussion on the agenda.

"Serena, we all appreciate how hard you've worked to keep the doors open for all of the programs at Balance," the board president began. "But it appears we need to make some difficult decisions to save what we can right now. It's too bad that Vision Quest withdrew their support. Is there anything more you can tell us about that?"

This was the moment she hoped would never happen. The board knew about the condition that had been placed on the donation. And they knew it had been withdrawn. But they didn't know who Dane was.

"Yes, Ms. Williamson," piped in one of the old vets. His military service dated back decades and he never seemed to understand why anyone wanted to talk to solve their problems. Serena never understood why he wanted to be on the board in the first place. "All you had to do was get him to come in and talk, am I right? Why couldn't you just do that?"

"I heard that you've been spending a lot of time visiting with a certain vet, and I'm wondering about the ethical issues with that. Is that really, I don't know, professional?" This from a younger woman who was the board know-it-all.

"And I heard," added another man, "that there's more to this guy than what we would led to believe in that funding agreement. Is that legal? Don't they have to disclose things?"

This was worse than Serena expected. They clearly felt like blaming her. Did she have any defense? Once she'd become involved with Dane, she didn't encourage him to become a client. She folded her hands on the binder and opened her mouth to speak.

"If I may?" Dane had risen from his seat behind her to place a hand on her shoulder. "My name is Dane Matthews Ashland, and I'm the reason that Balance lost that funding."

She could only look up at him in amazement. They hadn't planned for him to present anything. She looked around the table to see varying expressions on the faces of those around it. All eyes locked on to the scar on his face. Some were stunned and looked away quickly, and some were set and grim. I-told-you-so was shared in a couple of glances.

The board president looked from Dane to Serena and back again, then said, "Mr. Ashland, welcome, I think. This sounds like it will be an interesting story. Please, go right ahead."

*****

He'd practiced what he had intended to say a number of times, what approach might be best, how things could be explained in a way that made sense and allowed the board to accept the realities of the situation. But he had good news too, and he wanted to share it.

"I want you all to know how much it's meant to me to have Balance and its staff reach out to me." He moved to stand at an open spot at the table to tower over them. "A lot of terrible things happened to me in Afghanistan. It's where I got this," he pointed to the scar, "and a whole lot of deeper injuries, the kind to my soul that are the hardest to heal."

He had their complete attention now, most sitting forward and leaning towards him. He smiled inwardly. He always did know how to spin the story in the best possible way.

"But you see, none of this is Ms. Williamson's fault. She tried to get me to come in for treatment, tried to help me see its value. I wasn't ready to talk about what happened, at least not then. And really, I may never be willing to share all of my feelings about what happened the day a bomb blew up and killed close friends of mine," a couple of distressed gasps came up from his audience, "and almost killed me."

Now they were openly staring, even the naysayers.

Serena was watching too, not sure what to make of his performance. He gave her an encouraging smile and moved back to where he had been seated, rummaging behind the chair. He pulled up a large black case.

He heard Serena gasp now, and looked up to see that she had her hands to her face. She recognized the portfolio. He smiled again, putting all of his love for her into the locked gaze.

"Ladies and gentleman, I am sorry that Balance lost its funding from Vision Quest because of me, even though I didn't know anything about it at the time. It wouldn't have changed the outcome anyway." He clicked open the clasps and the top of the case folded back.

"So I have a couple of proposals for you to hear. And then I'd like to tell you a love story."

Epilogue

The last two months had flown by. With the holidays looming and money running out, Balance had entered a level of frenzy that surprised even those who were used to the ebbs and flows for an organization like theirs. But today, they celebrated a new major donor, actually – a group of them.

Serena couldn't believe the impact that a half hour of programming brought. Two months ago, Dane proposed to the board that they hire him – pro bono – to develop an informational package about Balance and its programs. It featured personal interest pieces about clients who agreed to tell their stories. Stuart and Sarge loved their clips and made sure to tell every Brew Bank customer where to find them on YouTube.

Dane told the story of the agency through the stories of the many it had served. He highlighted programs, explained how people could get involved, and noted how important it was to donate now, in light of all of the government funding cuts. Some elected officials, clearly seeing an opportunity to highlight the ravages of budget cuts, jumped on board to become big supporters of funding reviews at the state and federal levels.

It was all Dane, how he built the message and told the stories through his pictures and words. He called the presentation 'Redemption', and only he and Serena knew the real reason why they'd selected that title.

He smiled down at her as the crowd waiting to offer congratulations eased for a minute. "So, does this finally take care of all of your money concerns for the time being?" He knew it did, but he liked to see her face light up when she got to say it again.

"Yes, you know it does." She elbowed him in the ribs and then asked the same unanswered question, not for the first time. "What made you change your mind? You were so sure you'd never pick up a camera again."

He still hesitated to tell her. His brother had stayed scarce since they'd seen each other, not answering Dane's voicemails and not appearing at the various events Balance held for community awareness. While he hoped that they could reconcile again, he didn't want Serena to hold anything against Powers.

"I found out something, something about Vision Quest."

She seemed to sense his reluctance. This was more than he'd said before. She pulled his arm until they were in a deserted counseling room, and then closed the door.

"What is it? Remember, we promised no secrets between us ever again."

That promise had come with the promise of the engagement ring on her finger, the one he'd placed there at the board meeting in front of a group of unlikely witnesses. After promising to work on Balance's behalf, he'd explained how Serena's love inspired him. Even the hardest hearts at the table that night were sighing with the love story.

When Dane completed it by dropping down on bended knee in front of Serena, the crowd, as they say, went wild. The fact that she launched herself at him with a resounding yes made for a perfect ending to a perfect day.

He sighed regretfully. She always did get everything out of him eventually anyway.

"Vision Quest was founded by my brother, Powers. He was meddling, thinking that he could force me into getting some kind of help. He put the funding in place and set the condition. And he was the one who ultimately made the decision to pull it when you didn't reel me in." He tried to keep his tone light.

"That Saturday before the board meeting, the day you told me when the money would run out, I asked you for the name of the foundation. I found out that Powers was the head of it. So I knew he was involved somehow."

Serena frowned. "Is that why I haven't met him yet? Are you two not speaking?"

He stroked a hand down her face. He never got tired of watching the expressions chase across it, and he'd even captured it many times now. Still, he would always hold it inside his heart as well.

"He must love you very much." Serena's eyes were serious.

Surprised, Dane moved to look out the window and thought about it. Yes, he guessed that was part of it. It was probably the only way that Powers knew how to express it. His brother meddled, trying to eliminate the negatives in the lives of those he cared about. Another whole new insight to explore.

"Yes, I guess he does. And I guess I'd better go easy on him in the future."

Serena smiled. "Yes you should, because if he hadn't meddled, I wouldn't have pushed, and if I hadn't pushed, you wouldn't be holding me in your arms right now."

He turned and grinned. "In my arms, huh? Then I guess I'd better come over there and redeem myself right now."

THE END

From *FLASHES OF FIRE*

If you enjoyed *Pictures of Redemption*, be sure to pick up the next book in the Flynn's Crossing series, **Flashes of Fire.**

And here's an excerpt:

"Patrick, settle down and eat your dinner. Your father will drive you to practice as soon as you're done, and you're already late, so hurry up!"

"Ma, I don't want to…"

"Quiet! You'll do as you're told! Elisabeth, that science project won't build itself! Mary Margaret, the piano is waiting – at least 45 minutes now, mind, or you won't be ready for your lesson with Miss Christine. Michael, have you finished your confirmation assignment for Father Esposa?"

The chorus of voices continued throughout dinner, Ma and Dad directing and demanding, her siblings complaining because they didn't want to do what they were told. She could sit among the confusion and be completely overlooked. Her brothers and sisters were always busy doing something, practice for sports or music, their catechism lessons, studying for school. If she stayed quiet, Ma would pass right by her since she didn't seem to take to anything. It helped to be the middle child too, and with an older sister and brother and a set younger, there were few expectations put on her.

They thought she was shy and afraid of the world, so she was regarded with something akin to pity when she wasn't being teased by her brothers. Her sisters liked to boss her around, even the younger one, but they were all protective too.

She played with the stew in her bowl. If she turned the chunks of beef just so, she could create a pattern with the potatoes and carrots, making a nice design.

"Diane! Diane Kathryn! Stop playing with your food and eat it. There are children starving in Africa who would appreciate that fine stew. And don't forget to study your spelling tonight! You got a C on your last quiz, and you need to do better than that."

She cringed to hear her full name, which meant she was in trouble again. Shoveling in a spoonful of dinner, she sighed. She hated spelling, math too. She was completely lost in science class and was sure she only passed because her teachers felt sorry for her. They knew that her brothers and sisters got the brains in the family.

School was a painful chore, except when she got to art class. She loved art! From the time she could hold a crayon, she knew inside that this is what she was meant to do. She could draw well even before she could recite the alphabet. Give her clay or paints, and she was in heaven, producing fanciful things that her teachers loved.

But her parents, they were another story. They didn't believe that art was a real skill, something that could earn her a living when she grew up. And that was their focus, hoping that each of their children would go to college and be successful in some field that didn't involve manual labor. To them, playing with clay and drawing had no future.

"Diane Kathryn! That's it, you obviously aren't hungry. Up to your room. I will come up in one hour and we will see if you're ready for that spelling test tomorrow. And stop chewing on your nails."

Her mother was staring at her, expecting compliance. Then her mother's expression softened. "You want to go to college, have a good job, don't you? Just like your brothers and sisters? You need to study, my girl, so that you can have a profession when you get older."

She didn't want to go to college, but she would do as she was told. She'd end up going wherever everyone else wanted her to go, and she'd muddle through as she always did. A career, a profession? She had no clue what that would possibly be. The only thing she was any good at or interested in was art, and her parents had already been clear that they didn't consider that a way to make a decent living.

Diane picked up her bowl and took it to the sink, rinsing it out before placing it in the stack. It wasn't her turn to wash up tonight, but she liked doing that sometimes. The bubbles could make some pretty colors if the lights hit them just right.

She took a moment to look at her nails, chewed to the quick when she was nervous. Hanging her head, she shuffled to the doorway that led to the front hall and the stairs. Conversation resumed behind her, her father prompting her brother to get a move on it and her mother now intent on her other brother's religious studies.

No one noticed her as she paused and looked back at them. She was, again, forgotten and invisible.

About the Author

I love to hear from readers, so feel free to contact me through my website, www.yvonnekohano.com, or directly on Facebook as Yvonne Kohano, on Twitter @yvonnekohano, and at yvonne@yvonnekohano.com. Please leave an honest review of this novel at Amazon, Goodreads, or your favorite book discovery site of choice.

A HOLT Medallion Award of Merit recipient in Romantic Suspense, Yvonne enjoys channeling her characters' voices and passions as they overcome real world problems and discover love. Her Flynn's Crossing contemporary romantic suspense series is set in a fictional northern California foothills town not unlike the one where she used to live. Of course, the beauty and wonders of the Sierra Nevada Mountains and the surrounding counties play costarring roles in her work.

The first six books in the Flynn's Crossing series follow the developing love interests of the girl tribe, a group of successful women who work through real world conflicts and challenges to find acceptance and love - with some suspenseful happenings thrown in! In the next six books, single guys in the wolf pack find their true loves, but not without their own issues to conquer. Periodically, Yvonne will be adding seasonal novellas to the series, featuring the first person voice of a character from one of her previous books experiencing an event that we can all relate to.